a Change in Tide

NORTHERN LIGHTS COLLECTION

FREYA BARKER

To Stephanie,
There's a
purpose
for everything!

xox
Freya B.

1

2

A Change In Tide
a novel
Copyright © 2017 Freya Barker

ISBN: 9781988733043

Cover Design:
RE&D - Margreet Asselbergs

Editing:
Karen Hrdlicka

DEDICATION

This book is dedicated to my brother and sister-in-law, whose capacity to redesign their lives in pursuit of new dreams has in no small measure inspired the spirit of this story.

Their beautiful lakeside property served as muse for its setting.

Their creative adaptability is always an example to me.

TABLE OF CONTENTS

ONE

Mia

Seriously?

I go inside for five minutes and this is what is waiting for me?

When I discovered a single guy was moving in, and I saw some of the luxurious renovations done to the home, including a two-level deck, I was afraid something like this might happen.

His cottage—although it can hardly be qualified as such anymore—is clear across the small inlet from me on Spence Lake. Frank and Harriet, the former owners, decided to sell and move closer to their grandchildren. I'd been pretty upset to see them go. They'd been on the lake for over twenty-five years and had been a great source of information, since I bought my place a few years ago.

The only activity our little private bay ever saw was the splashing and giggles when their grandkids came to visit, but in the few days since the new guy moved in, all I've heard is the revving of that blasted speedboat of his. The same boat I just saw his lady friend diving out of, squealing. Definitely not what I'd consider the sweet sound of kids at play. And here I thought that with the disappearance of the construction crews, I'd be able to start enjoying my peaceful solitude again. Apparently not.

In stark contrast to the large home across the water, I just have a one bedroom log cabin, with a kayak and an old canoe pulled up on my ancient dock. I love my little corner of the world, with my dog, wilderness at my back, beautiful views in front of me, and still close enough to civilization. Hell, the local grocery store even delivers to the top of my drive. It's perfect.

My favourite spot is my screened-in porch, I can smell the pines, feel the breeze off the lake, and hear the sound of the occasional loon or cormorant visiting, yet not get eaten alive by the bugs. I have a little desk set up, where I'll sometimes eat my dinner, or play crosswords, along with an old, beaten-up leather love seat, where I've spent many an afternoon nap and currently Griffin is doing the same.

A large splash of water draws a sleepy woof from Grif, and I look over to the dock on the other side. My new neighbour has apparently joined his guest in the water. If I didn't know any better, I'd think he was murdering her by the way she's screaming and carrying on.

I determinedly tear my eyes away and focus on my sandwich, and my new book, while the dog settles back to sleep. I've been looking forward to this one and it appeared on my Kindle this morning. Every morning is a little like Christmas when I start up my Kindle, considering all the books I tend to pre-order.

Life has certainly improved since I had my wireless router installed. Hooked up to the world at large makes living in relative seclusion a lot easier. It's also much simpler to stay in touch with the few folks I care about. I dislike talking on the phone with a passion, and the only one I speak to regularly is Steffie. For some reason, I get tongue-tied and awkward, and much prefer letting my fingers do the talking.

A giggle catches my attention and this time I get an eyeful. I'm positive I saw the blonde woman go in the water with a bathing suit on, but she's naked as a jay when she climbs up the ladder on the side of the dock. Her body; a picture of perfection with long tan legs, delicately rounded hips, and a set of substantial, gravity defying breasts, I want to bet nature had no part in creating. The giggle apparently is courtesy of the man behind her, who seems to be biting her butt? Holy Mary, Mother of God! A hot blush shoots up my chest when my neighbour pulls himself from the water. I knew he was big, I could see that, but I had no idea exactly how big—everywhere!

Instinctively, I scoot back a little in an attempt to hide, although, I'm quite sure they can't see me anyway. Not that I think they'd particularly care, since I'm watching him pull her to where he's kneeling on the dock. The bulk of his back, still wet, ripples in the sun. Even from here, I can see the muscles of his ass clench as he hoists one of the woman's legs over his shoulder. Oh my...

Her hands hold on to his dark head, which is dipped low between her legs, and I watch as she drops her head back and moans loud enough for the sound to carry. I'm mesmerized. I know I should probably go inside, but I can't stop watching. I can't remember the last time...heck, what am I saying? I'm pretty sure I've never experienced anything like the thorough treatment the woman is receiving.

I place my hand on my chest and feel my heart beating hard, before it slides down, almost of its own accord, to find the swell of my breast. My nipples are hard and straining against the material of my old tank top. The moment I pull down my top, and expose my breast, a breeze whispers over the tight nub, sending a charge straight through my center.

I watch as he carefully lays her down and stretches himself over her body, his hard white ass standing out in stark contrast. I can almost feel the invasion of my own body when I watch his hips surge forward, his tight ass clenching as he enters her. My breath hitches when my hand closes over my exposed breast and plucks, almost distractedly, at my nipple. I see him raising up on his arms, the full width of his shoulders impressive as he holds himself up over her body and powers into her with increasing force.

The entire scene feels illicit—taboo—and unbelievably erotic.

In the privacy of my enclosed deck, watching my neighbour fuck his guest, my body craves like it's never craved before, aching for release. My other hand slips under the waistband of my flannel PJs, skims through the damp patch of curls and easily finds the slick evidence of my arousal. As the woman starts to keen over the audible grunts from her lover, my fingers rub furiously over the throbbing heat between my legs. I feel the vaguely familiar tension coil and build, until the sight of his furiously bucking hips and the sound of his loud groan of completion, tips me over the edge.

I don't mean to make a sound, but I must have. In seconds he is on his feet, pulling up his companion and urging her to the house, before he turns around. With his hands on his hips and his legs slightly spread, he stands shamelessly exposed as he glares in my direction.

I duck even further back into the shadow of my porch. Surely he can't see me?

Holding my breath, I wait until he finally turns and follows her into his house. I rush inside mine, the hot flush of embarrassment burning my face and the dog close on my heels.

I'm a voyeur.

Jared

Fuck me. You'd think I'd have learned by now.

I wince when I hear Lori's girly voice call out from the bathroom over the sound of the running shower.

"Are you gonna join me?"

Fuck no.

With Jordy arriving next week, it seemed like a good idea to have one last hurrah before my transition to a responsible adult. Of course, at thirty-nine, most people have long grown into one, but my life thus far has allowed me to indulge selfishly. I am—or I used to be—a feared and revered NHL defenseman. With a heavy traveling schedule and substantial fan adoration, especially from females, I was happy to play the field. Many, many fields actually. But when Jordy dropped that bombshell on me six months ago, I knew my player days needed to come to an end.

Easier said than done, when recognition and reputation made it hard to walk into any establishment, without two or three women putting their hands on me. That's how I met Lori, two nights ago in a restaurant in town. Blonde, stacked, and with a sweet demeanour and obvious crush, I'd easily talked myself into one last indulgence before I'd have to hang up my jockstrap.

One night turned into two, and now she's in my house, making herself as comfortable as she can. Not going to happen. I may be ready to settle down some, but those plans do not include Lori. I was ready to send her home yesterday, but when she surprised me with a nice dinner she'd prepared, while I was taking a nap, I couldn't rightly toss her out. Then this morning, she'd been all excited about going out on the boat, and I figured it's probably the least I could do before I make her leave.

Of course, then she jumps in the lake and pulls her top off, taunting me with those tits. They feel fake as shit, but they look fucking phenomenal. Especially bobbing on the water. Not sure whether it's the knowledge of this being the last opportunity, or the buzz of my pain meds combined with the steady stream of alcohol, but I dive in after her. Before I know it I'm fucking her on the dock, my ass out for anyone to see. Way to keep a low profile, dickhead.

The reality of it doesn't hit until I hear a faint yelp coming from the log cabin on the other side. I've seen the woman who lives there exactly twice. One night at dusk when she was hoisting her kayak back on the dock, and once when she was weeding the sad-looking vegetable patch she's apparently trying to grow on the side of her house. Each time she was wearing those ugly, flannel, men's lounge pants and a shapeless men's T-shirt from the looks of it. I have no idea whether she's twenty or sixty, but my educated guess is somewhere in between. Her dog has been more visible. A friendly creature who came by one early morning, while I was sitting on the dock, apparently to check me out. He allowed me to give him a scratch behind the ears before he turned and loped off on the narrow trail along the water, back to his mistress.

I ended up pulling out of Lori in a hurry and rushing her inside before turning toward her place. I caught a slight movement behind the screen of her porch, but it may well have been my imagination. Last thing I need is someone snapping pictures and selling them to the highest bidder. Granted, the pay may not be as much as it was a year ago, before my knee blew out, but I bet someone would still pay a pretty penny to see my white ass bumping uglies in broad daylight.

With Lori in the master bath, I slip into the second bathroom for a quick rinse, before I give her the heave ho. When I lift the toilet seat for a quick wiz before I hop in the shower, I notice the sticky evidence of stupidity on my cock. *Son-of-a-fucking-bitch!*

This is what happens when I drink too much.

In ten minutes, I'm as clean as I'm going to get, my Johnson raw from my furious scrubbing. Not that it would do any good, the semi-sober part of my brain realizes, but the slightly painful scrape of the loofah over the tender skin seemed an appropriate punishment, considering. Better write myself a note to get checked out ASAP.

Lori is already in the kitchen, pulling shit out of the fridge. I have to put a stop to this now.

"Listen," I start, to which she turns to face me.

"Oh hey," she chirps with a little smile.

"I didn't use a condom," I blurt out, eager to get this shit over with.

"Oh, I know," she says, apparently unfazed. "No worries, I'm covered."

Yeah, I've heard stories like that. Not about to let it go with that.

"How exactly are you covered?"

"Depo," she says by way of clarification, but it really doesn't help me. I have no clue what the fuck she's talking about. "The injection? I get it every three months."

Right, I've heard of those.

"Okay." I nod, more than a little relieved. "But what about…"

She won't let me finish and cheerfully jumps in. "STD's? Not to worry, I get checked every time I go in for my shot." When she sees my eyebrows shoot up at the frequency of her health checks, she shrugs her shoulders. "Got my shot just last month and the handful of guys before you were gloved, so we're good."

16

Handful of guys? Okay, so she's a player. I feel part relieved and part worried, because a sweet girl like her should maybe be a bit more discriminating. I catch myself being the biggest hypocrite on the face of the earth. I never thought I'd measure with a double standard. Especially given that, although in recent years my gallivanting has slowed down dramatically, in my younger days I'd think nothing of five different partners in a week, let alone a month.

Still, she should be a bit more concerned.

"Good to know, but you don't know if I'm clean, right?" I watch as her face pales a little. "I was clean at last check and I've been safe...until now. Look, you're a nice girl, Lori. I just want you to be careful, okay?"

"Okay," she says sweetly. "Does this mean you're ready for me to go now?"

Stumped and more than a little. I don't think I've ever met a woman this casual and easy. Just like me, except—female.

"I think so," I tell her with just a hint of regret.

Fifteen minutes and a friendly, angst-free hug later, I give one last wave to the retreating taillights of her car going up the hill, when I hear my phone ring inside.

"Hey," I manage breathlessly by the time I find it.

"Oh no," Jordy says on the other side. "What did I interrupt?"

"Nothing," I'm quick to answer. "I was just outside and left my phone on the kitchen counter. What's up?"

17

"Just saw my OB/GYN this morning. The baby is right on target and my medical files were transferred to the clinic in Bracebridge."

"That's great, honey. So I've scheduled the movers to be there next Tuesday at nine in the morning, that still good for you?"

"Should be, I've packed up seven boxes with small shit already and will get the rest packed up over the weekend."

I take a deep breath and run my hand through my hair. The woman is so stubborn. Every time I've offered to drive back and help her pack up, and each time she's shut me down, claiming she needs to do this 'on her own.'

"I can hear your exasperated sighs, you know?" she says, a smile in her voice. "Don't even start with me, Jared. I'm fine. I have a few friends helping out and I'll be good to go. It's important to me to do this without having your sweet, caring, and very controlling self looming over me. Please?"

I love her to distraction and perhaps over the years I've been a bit overbearing and overprotective. Knowing that she'll be here soon, where I can properly look after her, helps me give in. "Fine. Just call me before you leave." I walk out of the sliding doors and onto the deck, breathing in the late afternoon air. "It'll be good to have you here," I add a little gentler.

"Thanks, Jared." Her voice has softened as well. "Love you lots."

"Love you too, Pipsqueak."

I swipe my finger across the screen to end the call and slip the phone in my pocket. I take in the lake and the sparse cottages and cabins dotting the shore, before my eyes land on the cabin next door. The kayak is missing from the dock, and I automatically scan the span of water, spotting her only a few hundred feet out, slowly paddling into shore. All I can make out from here is the stiff set of narrow shoulders and an occasional curl twisting from under the brim of her hat. I can't see her face, but from the tilt of her head, and the stilted movement of her paddle strokes, I'm guessing she sees me and knows I'm watching.

Intriguing—and far too tempting.

I turn on my heels abruptly, forcing my thoughts on my little sister's impending arrival—and away from the strange woman who'd all but sounded like she got off, watching me this afternoon.

TWO

Mia

A cool morning breeze blows onto shore when I pull the door shut behind me, locking Griffin inside. I'm tempted to rush back in the safety of my cabin, just like every other Tuesday. The weekly trek into town for my standing appointment with Rueben Moulin, a highly recommended therapist in town, is an ongoing struggle. At the same time, it's a trip that forces me out of my self-induced isolation, and Lord knows I need that, otherwise I'd never see the light of day again. And I don't want that. I've been there and it's a scary place to be.

So for the past couple of years, every Tuesday except holidays, I've battled the panic clawing at my insides at the prospect of getting in my seldom-used car and driving for fifteen minutes to the medical offices on the other side of Bracebridge. I always bring grocery bags, in hopes that I'll feel bolstered enough by my session with Rueben to hit the grocery store afterward, instead of ordering for delivery.

It's a funny beast, agoraphobia. The fear and anxiety itself becomes the cause for fear and anxiety. And round and round you go. That's why I know I can't allow myself to skip a single appointment. Especially not since I've weaned off the meds I took for years, turning me into a virtual zombie. That was almost worse than the panic attacks, the way those pills would make me feel disconnected from the world around me—from myself.

With my empty grocery bags tucked under my arm, and my ball cap low over my eyes, I walk over to the make-shift garage. More like a shed, but just big enough to house my lawnmower and my ten-year-old RAV. Every time I get in and turn the key in the ignition, I keep my fingers crossed it'll start. I've been lucky so far. The engine coughs once but thankfully catches, and I ease the car out. A bit of a tight fit, but one I've mastered. I get out to close the shed behind me, and when I turn back to my car, I see a flash of bright red in my peripheral vision. I turn my head to see a sporty little car come racing down his driveway.

I've avoided looking in the direction of the house across the inlet these last couple of days. Every time my eyes go there, I mentally slap myself, remembering the mortifying moments when he appeared to be staring right at me. I even took my kayak to the other side of the lake the last few days, after I spotted him watching me that same night. This time I look, only to find him step out of his front door as the car comes to a stop. I watch as he pulls open the driver's side door and leans down, obviously saying something to the driver. When he steps back, a very pregnant brunette steps out of the car and wraps herself around him.

I didn't know it was possible to be disappointed in someone without actually knowing them, but I feel it clearly. Less than a week ago, this guy was drilling a blonde on his dock, for the whole world to see, and now he's got his hands on a different woman. One who is very pregnant and obviously comes with a shitload of luggage, judging from the moving truck pulling in behind her red car.

Not my business.

I shake my head before climbing behind the wheel and spin my tires on the gravel as I drive up the hill.

"You seem tense today," Rueben points out when I walk into his office, twenty minutes later.

"As opposed to any other day?" I throw back sarcastically, making him chuckle.

"Okay, let me rephrase that; You seem tens-*er* today."

I sit in the comfy club chair I've been plotting to smuggle out of here one day, and remove my ball cap, running my hand through my curls. It's about time for another trim. Something else I'll need to gear myself up for.

"My new neighbour moved in."

"Oh? And did you go introduce yourself?" Rueben hones right in on the discussion we had just a week ago, when he gave me that assignment as homework. I had balked, as I usually do, and he'd pressed, as he's prone to do. I'd had every intention of following through with my eventual promise that I'd go knock on my new neighbour's door. In fact, I'd been working up the courage when I'd seen him speed off with his guest in his damn noisemaker that afternoon. Since I couldn't get the image of what happened on the dock, just an hour after that, I'd

23

steered clear. Any hopes of developing a friendly connection with the man were efficiently crushed.

My troubled thoughts must be legible on my face, because Rueben starts chuckling. "Must've been some introduction," he says.

"Of sorts." I try to play it off, but he won't let me get away with it.

"Mia…"

"Can we just leave it at that?" I plead, already knowing it's not going to get me anywhere.

"Mia." This time a little sterner and I look up at his friendly age-lined face, his eyes calm and accepting. *Oh, what the hell.*

"He's noisy, he's obnoxious, and he did his girlfriend right on the dock, in broad daylight."

"Did?" Rueben echoes.

"Fucked. As in fucked her bare-ass naked on the dock. In the middle of the damn afternoon. Who does that?"

"Anyone smart enough to grab that opportunity?" Rueben catches me off guard and I bark out a laugh. He's seventy if he's a day, but you could never tell from the twinkle in his eyes as he smiles broadly at me. "Are you sure you weren't envious instead of irritated?" he teases. I can feel the hot flush on my face reaching my hair roots.

He studies me like I'm a bug pinned to the wall and I drop my gaze to the floor, grateful now for my outgrown hair, which obediently obscures my face.

"Too close to home?"

"Yes," I snap. "Way too close to home; they were going at it just a few hundred yards from my house!"

"You know that's not what I mean," he says patiently, irritating the snot out of me.

"He's a douche anyway," I defer. "Just as I was leaving this morning, he was welcoming another woman. This one a brunette and very pregnant. She looked like she was moving in. The man is reprehensible," I finish on a huff.

Rueben pauses with his fingers steepled against his chin. Something he tends to do when he's *thinking.*

"Do you think it's possible you're jumping to conclusions? That you're judging a situation not based on what you know but on what you choose to see?" He leans forward with his elbows on his knees, his hands clasped between. "One of the reasons I keep pushing you to interact more with the world around you is because that world keeps changing. You get comfortable in your routines, in the handful of relationships you maintain, but my dear, even if you prefer standing still in time, in isolation, nothing else does. You're a young woman still, and although you've come a long way, life is still rushing on without you."

It hurts—the truth does. I can't even remember the person I was thirteen years ago. Can't imagine getting on that crowded subway train and… But that was me at some point. Back when I was still a married woman, with a career I treasured, and friends I loved. I was happy then. All those things are lost to me now, slowly disappearing one by one until there was just me. Disconnected and invisible.

"I know," I whisper without looking up, and I feel Rueben's hand lightly touch mine.

"Transitions of any kind are bound to cause a disturbance. Your objective is to keep an open mind, to push yourself to step out of your comfort zone, and trust yourself enough to know you are able to deal with whatever comes your way."

I leave his office a little later, with the promise not to close myself off from getting to know the new guy, and to stop at the grocery store on the way out of town. I manage to get as far as the crowded deli counter at the Metro before I feel the panic taking over. A tingling starts in my extremities and spreads over my body, setting every nerve on end. I can actually feel every hair on my head. Immediately followed by my breathing turning shallow and my heart beating erratically in my chest. The skin on my face draws tight and my chest feels like it's being squeezed. I hang onto my cart as black dots blur my vision.

I work hard to visualize gliding my paddle through the water, my safe place, and struggle to breathe in through my nose.

"You okay, ma'am?"

I nod curtly at the young girl behind the counter, but can't make eye contact or form words.

"Should I call someone?" she asks. Very sweet but it cuts me right where it hurts, and I can't stop the moan from leaving my mouth.

There's no one to call.

Jared

Holy shit.

I'd forgotten how damn messy Jordy can be. A few hours after she got here and already the place looks like a bomb exploded.

In all fairness, she is still in the middle of unpacking, but I shiver when I find her underwear on my kitchen counter.

"Jordy, Jesus," I complain, holding up a lacy bit of confection, which has no place next to the toaster where I just recently made myself breakfast. My brat sister just snickers as she snatches the bra from my hands.

"Chill—I missed that one in the drawer and stuffed it in with the last of the kitchenware." Waving the offensive piece of lingerie over her shoulder in a taunt, she disappears to her 'wing.'

Really, it's just a small hallway with a second master, a smaller bedroom for the nursery, and a second full bathroom. I have a similar layout on the other side, and the living, dining and kitchen are all at the front of the house. All open concept with large windows to the lake.

I have to admit, part of me is a bit concerned about our new arrangement. I like things tidy and in their place, something that served me well being on the road so much, but Jordy? Man, she's something else. Add a new baby into the mix in a month, and I foresee chaos.

Carrying a box into my sister's room, I catch her leaning on the dresser with a pained look.

"Are you okay?"

She swivels around and tries to smile, but I don't miss the tears she's blinking away. Shit. "I'm good. Just a little tired," she says with a wobbly voice. I drop the box on the bed and walk up, wrapping my arms around her. She immediately slips hers around my waist and tucks her face into my shoulder. I can feel the baby moving between us. My nephew.

"He's an asshole," I mumble into her hair and feel her chuckle in response.

"He so is," she says. "I just can't believe the one-eighty he did when he was faced with this pregnancy. He...he accused me of trying to trick him. I didn't. I swear..." Her cries are muffled by my shirt.

"Shhh. No need to tell me that, I know, honey. I know. This shit happens." It sure does, I think, remembering the stupid risk I took just days ago. "And for the record," I add. "If I see his face, I'm gonna rearrange it for him."

Jordy snorts against my shoulder before pulling away. She giggles when she sees the mess she left behind on my shirt. "Oops," she says, but this time the smile on her face reaches her eyes. "I'm afraid I messed you up good," she teases. "Good preparation for when this little man decides to regurgitate breast milk all over you." She proudly pats her stomach.

28

I roll my eyes, fighting the automatic gag reflex, and lean down to kiss her forehead. "He doesn't scare me off that easily," I lie through my teeth. The truth is, I'm terrified, but I'll be damned if I let my little sister do this alone.

"Thank you," she whispers, her hand stroking my cheek.

"My pleasure, honey," I assure her, ruffling her hair before I turn to head to my room.

I need to change my shirt.

The loud whine of an engine trying, but not managing to catch, reaches me as I walk out on the deck. A small, white SUV is sitting at the top of my neighbour's drive. It's the same car I saw her leaving in this morning. I only hesitate for a second, before I step off the deck and follow the overgrown trail around the inlet to her side. She keeps cranking that damn engine, and I can smell the gasoline from the bottom of the hill. By the time I jog up to the top, the stench is thick.

She startles when I knock on the window, indicating she should roll it down. I lean and take in her pale, pasty face, her eyes red-rimmed. Just my luck, two crying women in one day. Pretty, though, and younger than I thought. Green eyes, narrow nose, and full lips, her obvious crying bout doesn't hide her appeal.

"You're flooding the engine," I explain, but she looks at me confused, like I'm speaking a different language or something. "The engine?" I point at the hood, while speaking slowly, as if that's going to help her understand. "It's flooded. You need to turn it off and let it rest."

The fingers that were clenching the keys in the ignition slowly let go.

"Oh," she says. So she does understand.

"You may wanna come out before the fumes make you sick." If anything, that seems to make her turn even paler.

"M-my groceries," she stammers, her eyes big and frightened looking as she points to the back of the SUV.

"I'll get them." I round the back, open the tailgate and look at about a week's worth of groceries piled up, along with a giant bag of dog food.

I try not to think about the fact this woman may well have seen me with Lori. The whole situation is awkward enough.

By the time I've got the dog food over my shoulder and the other bags clutched in my fists, the woman is out of the car, pulling a baseball cap over her hair. She pulls the bill down low over her eyes, before leaning back in the car to pull out a few more bags.

"I can give it a try for you in half an hour. See if it'll start up." She nods without saying anything and starts walking, so I try again, falling into step beside her. "By the way, now's as good a time for introductions as any, I guess. I'm Jared. I moved in next door last week?" I don't miss the quick sideways glance or the soft grunt.

"I saw," she says, before her free hand shoots up to cover her mouth. "I mean I noticed the trucks. Mia." She abruptly stops and sticks out her hand, except I have my hands full. More awkward. Fuck me, this chick is odd. "Mia Thompson," she says, dropping her hand and her face now beet red. I start moving again and she follows suit. No doubt now as to who was watching last week.

"Nice to meet you, Mia. Great place you have here," I look at her cabin as we walk up. It's nice. A bit of a rugged look for a woman, but a sweet place nonetheless.

She stops at the steps to her door and turns. "Thanks," she says, and I just notice how soft her voice is. I almost have to lean down to hear her. "You can just leave those here. I'll grab them." She indicates the bags in my hands.

I guess that means no invite inside, but I can't resist asking, "Are you okay?" Her eyes shoot up from under her cap and take me in for a second before she answers.

"I'm good. Thanks."

Just like that I'm dismissed. I figure I've done my bit to get to know my neighbour, the ball's in her court now. If she needs me to help her with the damn car, she knows where to find me. I put the bags on the bottom step and back away.

"Let me know if you need a hand."

"I think I'll manage, but thanks," she answers with the hint of a smile, but without looking at me again. Taking my cue, I walk back to my place.

Forty-five minutes later, I hear an engine and look across to see her drive her Toyota into the shed.

She managed.

THREE

Mia

"Hey, girl. How's the Great White North?"

I smile at the sound of my best—and just about only—friend, Steffie.

Our history goes back to the first year of university. We were assigned roommates in residency, and immediately clicked. The fact we were both studying midwifery helped, and shortly after graduating, we opened a small clinic in the Beaches area of Toronto. We'd stuck together through the years, stood up for each other at our respective weddings, and when Steffie had her own kids, I'd been her midwife.

She'd also covered for me when I started staying home, more and more, and supported me through my divorce. She was the one who'd stuck it out with me when everyone else in my life had slowly, but surely, allowed me to withdraw. Not Steffie—she never let me get too far.

"Beautiful—as usual. It's about time you came to check it again for yourself," I tease her. She's been here a few times in the past years, but the clinic, her family with teenagers, and a busy husband tie her firmly to the city.

"You're evil," she groans. "You have no idea how much I need a break from this rat race."

"Then come," I soften my voice. "Just get in that disgustingly, expensive vehicle of yours and drive yourself up here. Even just for one night." I try to laugh off the almost pleading tone my voice had taken on, but Steffie is not my best friend for nothing.

"What happened, honey?" she immediately asks.

"Nothing happened. I'm just...I miss you." I stop myself from telling her I've been overwhelmed with loneliness since *he* moved in and brought our quiet little inlet to life. Unlike with Frank and Harriet, who generally lead as quiet a life as I do, their house is now filled with activity, music, and even laughter bouncing across the water.

In the past week, since Jared helped me with my groceries, I'd purposely kept to my house, even though my vegetable patch badly needs weeding and the little bit of grass I have should see a mower. It had shaken me to the core. *He* had shaken me to the core. I'm not sure what I was expecting, but it certainly wasn't the friendly, bright, smiling, and painfully handsome guy. It'd been impossible not to think of all his now covered...attributes, I'd been given an eyeful of on the dock. And he smelled good. Even over the fumes of the engine, I could smell the scent of clean man.

Griffin had taken to trotting around the inlet, when I let him out in the morning, to greet Jared; who apparently is an early riser as well and likes to drink his coffee on the deck.

"I miss you too, honey." Steffie drags me from my thoughts. "Let me talk to Doug, and I'll see if I can swing it sometime this weekend."

I blink hard to fight back the unexpected tears. I haven't even told her about the massive panic attack I had at the grocery store on Tuesday. One that resulted in the manager bringing me into his office, while he had one of his employees collect my groceries for me and load them in my car. He didn't call an ambulance when I asked him not to, but when I felt ready to go home, he insisted I call him to let him know I got there safe. So kind. So very kind, and at the same time, unbelievably embarrassing.

Of course then the damn car stalled just as I reached the top of the hill, and I almost disappeared in my second panic attack of the day. Except Jared knocked on the window, and without knowing it, pulled me back from the brink by being kind as well. My ogre of a neighbour, whom I'd developed an almost instant dislike to, was nothing but friendly. And I'd been an asshole to him.

I think of Rueben's painfully true assessment earlier this week. I can't continue to pretend I'm an island, to stand by on the sidelines while everyone and everything rushes past. If anything, this week was proof that sometimes you just need to grab onto the hand someone holds out. There's nothing wrong with that.

"I'd like that," I simply say to Steffie, but with it, tell her much more than the just words. Steffie knows it, too.

"I'll do my very best," she says softly before hanging up.

Wiping the silent tears from my eyes, I turn to the dog, who is napping on the love seat.

"How about it, big guy? Want to come out for a bit?"

Griffin doesn't need telling twice, he's up off the couch and standing by the front door before I can get out of my chair. He's a good dog. I got him right before I moved here and he's as loyal as they come. He's never taken off on me. Not even when in the first weeks of spring, a black bear had wandered onto the property. Griff stood on the steps at the front door, growling incessantly and eventually the bear took off.

I open the door for him and he leaps out, completely missing the two steps, while I grab my gardening tools. Time to get off my ass.

-

I'm wrestling with my old-fashioned push mower on the far side of the cabin, when I hear Griff barking from the driveway.

The sun is low in the sky and I'm starting to get hungry, realizing I've skipped lunch. On the plus side, my vegetable patch is completely weed free, and I've pulled off a couple of zucchini I'm going to use for a zucchini lasagne.

Giving up on the angled slope I've been trying to mow for the last forty-five minutes, I push the mower in the direction of the shed, only to find a familiar Lexus SUV blocking my path.

"Steffie!" Abandoning the mower, I rush to where my dog is laying on his back, getting a two-handed belly rub from my friend. "What are you doing here?"

She stands up and brushes off her pants, that now sport a decent collection of Griff's fur, before wrapping me in a hug.

"Delivered a baby at noon, called Doug to get his ass home, so I could pack and drive up to see my bestie," she mumbles in my hair.

I hug her a little harder while fighting those damn tears for the second time today. "He came?" I hear her snort before she takes a step back and looks at me with a glint in her eyes.

"He knows what's good for him, or he won't be *coming* any time soon," she deadpans. "God, Mia—every time I forget how absolutely, disgustingly perfect this place is," she says, spreading her arms wide as she turns to the lake and breathes in deeply. "Christ I needed this."

I hide my smile, I know she's only partially telling the truth. She may have needed this, but she's here because she knows I needed her.

She sits at the kitchen table, drinking wine from the massive bottle she unearthed from her overnight bag, while I put together my zucchini lasagne. Her constant flow of chatter about the clinic, patients, Doug, and most of all her kids, soothes my soul like a balm. She doesn't care that I don't say much, she never has.

"So I told Doug we had to find a cottage near here, before the kids won't want to go anywhere but the mall anymore."

"You know you're always welcome here, right?"

"I know," she says, smiling at me. "But I also know that you get fidgety when my whole family is here longer than one night."

I'm a little embarrassed to admit she's right. I do get fidgety. I love having them around, but after a full day, I feel like the walls are closing in on me. Doug is a quiet guy, in perfect contrast to Steffie, who's a bundle of energy. The kids take after their mother and can't sit still to save their lives. And yet I love having them.

"Anyway," she changes topics. "Tell me about that hottie neighbour of yours, flexing his muscles over there."

I can't help it, my head instantly swivels around to see Jared pulling himself out of the lake, water sluicing off his broad back. The impressively sculpted muscles I hadn't really noticed before—maybe because I was busy looking at his tight ass—span the width and length of his back, and I can't help wonder what they would feel like under my hands. A giggle snaps me out of my scrutiny.

"Careful," Steffie warns, teasing. "You're gonna burn him with your eyes."

I harrumph and turn back to shove the two trays into the oven, ignoring her.

"What's he like?" she asks, walking up behind me to refill my glass. With my wine in hand, I lead the way onto the screened-in porch and curl up on one side of the couch. Steffie does the same on the other side.

Then I tell her everything.

Jared

"Are you okay with chicken?"

Jordy's stomach has been queasy all day. I suggested she call her new doctor in Bracebridge, but she just laughed at me. I admit, I freaked a little when she came back from her first visit there earlier in the week, to tell me she was apparently already two centimeters dilated. I don't want to know anything about my sister's vagina, thank you very much, but the knowledge that bump in her belly was actually going to result in a baby, and apparently soon—that got me good and nervous.

Jordy's all cool and collected, going about her business like she's not about to drop my nephew, and I just want to drop her off at the hospital so *they* can worry about her. Apparently that's not done, although for the life of me I can't figure out why they'd make you wait until labour is already well under way.

No—strapped safely to a hospital bed, where she can't do stupid shit like climb on a stool to dust the tops of the kitchen cabinets, is absolutely the way to go.

Now she's nauseous.

"I'll try the chicken," she calls from her bedroom. I almost had to arm-wrestle her into taking a damn nap.

I grab some chicken from the fridge, season it only lightly, for Jordy's sake, and take it out to the BBQ, where

I already have some veggies roasting. Glancing over at the log cabin, I notice that the car I saw pull in earlier is still there. I didn't see who was driving it, but have wondered. In fact, I've caught myself checking, from time to time, to see if I could catch a glimpse, but no luck so far. This time I see her dog lying on the dock and instead of the kayak, the canoe is missing. Before I obsessively start scanning the lake, I shake my head sharply and turn my back. *Idiot*.

"It actually smells good," Jordy says when she joins me on the deck, a few minutes later, a beer and a bottle of water in her hands. The beer she hands to me.

"Did you sleep?"

She's turned to the water so I'm looking at the back of her head when I ask, but I can still tell she's rolling her eyes before she answers. "Yes, brother dear—I slept. I actually feel a bit better." She steps up beside me and slides an arm around my waist, giving me a sideways hug. "Thanks for forcing me." I look down in her upturned face and try very hard not to display the smugness I feel.

"Welcome, Pipsqueak," I tell her, bending my head to kiss her forehead. "For future reference, it's easier to just listen."

Immediately she pulls away from me and socks me in the arm. "Men are pigs," she proclaims, before stalking off to one of the deck chairs.

"Ahoy the shore!" I hear a woman's voice call over the water.

"Ahoy the boat!" my silly sister yells back.

I turn around to see Jordy waving frantically at the canoe, carrying Mia and her visitor; a blonde woman, who is equally excitedly waving back at my sister. Not quite sure if it's that or the fact Mia's visitor is a woman that has me smiling broadly.

"Why are you smiling like an idiot?"

I look at Jordy, who is squinting her eyes at me, then turns her head slightly to look at the approaching canoe, before turning back to me. "I knew you were interested," she says, suddenly looking smug.

"She's strange," I counter.

"You're still interested," Jordy fires back. "And the fact that the car in her driveway, which you've been glaring at for the past couple of hours, actually belongs to a woman who makes you smile."

I chuckle. My sister is like a terrier; give her the smallest bit of information and she'll yank at it until she pulls the entire truth from you. "She intrigues me," I admit, to which Jordy waves her hands dismissively.

"Just a fancy way of saying what I've been saying for the past week. You're curious about her."

"I am. I mean, a good-looking woman, living alone, and virtually off the grid, with just her dog for a companion, it makes a person wonder."

My sister looks like she's fighting a smile. "Does it make you wonder enough to consider that blonde woman in the boat with her might be her lover?"

She's teasing, I know she's teasing, but she's also got a point. My head immediately swivels around to watch Mia and her…visitor, climbing from the canoe and subjected to an enthusiastic canine greeting. I never even considered the possibility she might be gay.

41

I didn't realize I said the last out loud until another solid punch lands on my shoulder. "Ouch!" I turn to my sibling to see her with her arms crossed, resting on top of her substantial belly and squinting at me once again.

"I'm teasing, you idiot. How would I know if she's gay? I'm just saying it to make you feel better about her not instantly falling for your charms."

"I never had a chance to show her my *charms*," I return.

"Ugh—like I said, men are pigs."

After throwing me a disgusted look, Jordy disappears into the house and I have chicken, that is crisping a little too much, to tend to.

It's after we've eaten—she manages to get down half the chicken breast and some vegetables, and we've watched some sappy movie which had Jordy in tears—she doubles over as she gets up.

"What's up?" I ask, putting my hand on her back. "Junior kicking?" She told me these last few weeks the baby's seemed restless, especially at night.

"Braxton-Hicks," she says, making no sense.

"What?"

"Braxton-Hicks contractions. It's normal," she adds, seeing my panic at the word *contractions.*

"Sure?"

"Absolutely." She seems very sure, but I still urge her to go lie down and to leave her door open, just in case.

I do the same with mine, but still I don't sleep a whole lot that night.

FOUR

Mia

"Sure you're gonna be alright?" Steffie asks, rolling down her car window.

We had a great time last night, going out with the canoe, with Steffie already half in the bag. Thank God, I managed to get her into a life jacket, because the way she'd been flailing around in the boat; she almost tipped us over a few times. Of course she embarrassed the shit out of me when she started hollering and waving like an idiot at the couple on the dock as we were paddling back home. The woman had returned her wave, but he'd just stood watching. Unsettling.

By the time we rolled into bed, it had been after one and we were all caught upon each other's lives. Still, it took me a while to get to sleep, a gnawing emptiness in my chest as I thought about the life I'd left behind. I'd loved my job. My calling really. Midwifery was truly a labour of love, both in giving and receiving. Who wouldn't feel privileged, being witness to the miracle of life on a daily basis. Humbling and fulfilling in a way nothing else makes you feel.

"I'll be fine." I smile at Steffie, grabbing the hand she sticks out of the window to give it a squeeze. "Thank you," I tell her sincerely. "I didn't realize how much I needed this. Love you."

She pulls me closer and sticks her head out of the window, kissing me smack on the lips. "Love you too, sweetie," she says, tearing up. "Any time you need me to come drive you crazy for a bit, let me know. In the meantime, stay in touch this time? Let me know you're doing okay? I know you can manage on your own," she quickly adds when she sees me getting ready to throw up my defenses. "That's not the point—that's not even in question—the point is you don't have to. I'm always just a phone call away."

Now she has me swallowing down the lump in my throat, and I quickly lean down to give her a final hug through the car window.

"I know," I concede, rapping my knuckles on the roof before stepping back. "Drive careful and let me know when you get there."

"Will do," she calls out through the open window as she backs up the car. "And you, don't do anything I wouldn't do!"

"Then what's left?" I yell after her, snickering as I hear her laughter disappear around the bend.

Gone.

I stand in the drive until I no longer hear her car, just the familiar sounds of the water and woods, before I turn back to the cottage.

It's still early. The sun is up, but still partially hidden behind the tree line on the other side of the inlet. The lake is quiet. No boats out this early, just an occasional splash of a cormorant diving for fish just outside the shore and the odd guttural grunts as they call to mates across the lake. It had taken me a while to recognize the difference between a loon and a cormorant, but their calls are distinctive. The piglike grunts of the cormorant are much less appealing than the haunting call of the loon.

Before I walk in the door, I throw a last glance at the house across the bay, half wishing he'd be having his morning coffee on the deck, but it looks quiet. They must still be asleep. I quickly shake my head and resolutely step inside.

The rest of the morning, and into the afternoon, I spend on my computer.

I scroll through my emails, most of which are immediately redirected to trash. A wide variety of ads, from a new brand of dog treats to the latest fad in skin care. All the result of some innocuous surfing I did when I first got set up with Wi-Fi. Creepy, really, to know that somewhere, someone is keeping track of your online movements through a cleverly constructed maze of algorithms. Enter a search or hit a certain website, and the information dooms you to years of related promotional crap, filling your inbox daily. I'm actively deleting when one email pops up. A Toronto client I've done work for before.

Years ago, I started toying around with Photoshop when we needed some artwork for the clinic's website. It was more of a hobby than anything else, and I enjoyed doing up the occasional ad or flyer. It had been something that kept me somewhat occupied after I left the clinic. Something I could do from the safety of my home that would keep my mind engaged. After I moved up here, it became a way of creating a little income to sustain my meagre needs. Since I was able to buy the cottage outright, from the proceeds of the sale of my half of the clinic, and my divorce left me with a decent-sized chunk of change after the sale of our marital home and division of properties, I only needed a little for my day-to-day expenses. The rest of the money is tucked away safely. A little nest egg, which I rarely need to tap.

The client, a small publishing house, wants a revamp of their logo, and therefore all of their print materials as well. Business cards, letterheads, website art and social media promo. I'm smiling huge; this means work for next few weeks and probably a big enough paycheck to last me a while. Without any hesitation, I email them back, letting them know I'm willing and able to start right away. For the next little while, the world around me disappears as I create three new logo mock ups and email them to the client for review.

When Griffin starts whining, I close my laptop, and stretch my body, before getting up and letting him outside. I watch him bound off into the trees, when my stomach starts growling. Closing the door, I head straight for the kitchen. I haven't had a bite to eat since breakfast. I'm shocked to see it's already closing in on four o'clock; much later than I thought it was.

One of the benefits of living alone is that time is yours and yours alone. Although, truth be told, it's probably as much of a curse as it is a blessing. It's easy to forget, or frankly care about, mundane things like getting dressed or showering when it's just you. Especially when you're busy, meals tend to get skipped. I'm not in the mood for a big meal, so it'll be cheese, crackers, and an apple.

When I take my plate out to the porch, my late lunch or early dinner immediately seems inadequate, when the smell of BBQ hits my nostrils. Sure enough, my neighbour is out on his deck again, manning the grill, and sending mouth-watering aromas my way. At least, I think it's the smell of grilling meat that has me near drooling, not the shameless and, for the record, shirtless man wielding an impressive set of tongs. My mother always said that there's no harm in looking as long as you don't touch. So I look, while quietly munching on my apple.

By the time he is joined by the very pregnant brunette, my plate is empty and my belly full. Maybe that's why I feel slightly nauseous when I see him wrap an arm around her and kiss the top of her head. *Ugh, I bet she smells nice.* A little disgusted with myself, I get up and head inside, dropping my plate on the counter, and walking straight into the bathroom for a much-needed shower.

I feel a lot better once I've got on a pair of clean cutoffs and tank top. I grab a flannel, men's shirt to ward off the slight chill coming in from the lake, before making my way outside to the dock.

"Stay, Griff," I tell my pooch, his tongue is hanging from his mouth in his eagerness to come out on the water. I'll sometimes let him come when I take the canoe, but I'm taking the kayak tonight. He whimpers pathetically as I push off and start paddling, trying hard not to look over, but still noticing the obnoxious speedboat missing from the neighbour's dock.

Jared

"Are you done?"

Jordy hovers over me, her hand outstretched to grab my plate as I'm still chewing on my last bite of steak. She's been jumpy all damn day long, almost bouncing off the walls. To my surprise, she corralled that energy into an uncharacteristic need to clean. That is usually my MO, walking around behind her picking up the mess she leaves behind. All day she's been like this, restless and short-tempered.

With my mouth still full, I drop my knife and fork on my plate and allow her to snatch it away. I'm not about to risk any kind of confrontation with her, not after the emotional sermon I received earlier today when I left crumbs on the cutting board on the counter. She even burst into tears when a kitchen towel, she'd just hung up, slipped off its hook and landed on the floor. I swear to God, I hope this shit doesn't carry through once that baby is born. OCD as I am, this is too much, even for me. Violence may ensue.

"How about a quick loop around the lake?" I suggest, listening to her bang and slam her way around the kitchen. I'm hoping perhaps the fresh air and water will snap her out of whatever crawled up her butt. The noises stop suddenly, and for a blissful moment it's quiet, before a distinct sniffling can be heard. *Fuck me*, here we go again.

Almost dragging my ass, I push back my seat and move to the kitchen where, as expected, my sister is crying like someone shot her puppy. She's draped on the counter, her head down on her arms and her back and shoulders heaving with loud sobs. Knowing better than to say anything, I pull her up, wrap her in my arms, and rest my chin on top of her head.

"What's wrong, Pipsqueak?" I try to sound comforting, but I can't quite hide my exasperation. It only makes her cry harder.

"I—I…I don't know!" she wails against my chest, and I'm mentally preparing myself for another shirt change.

"Come on," I urge her, setting her away a little as I grab a kitchen towel and run it under the cold tap. With my hand under her chin, I use the towel to mop up the mess on her face. "Let's get some fresh air. I'm thinking maybe you've been cooped up too much. We'll swing around the lake and when we get back, I'll build a fire and we can make s'mores for dessert," I try with some success. At the mention of s'mores, her face lights up.

A clean shirt later, I help her into the back of the boat. Not an easy feat, since she's pretty much top-heavy with her massive belly. I make sure not to remark on it, though. I joked about it a few days back and she took it hard—judging by the dent in the drywall beside the fireplace, left by the jar candle she narrowly missed my head with. Checking my words is not something I have a lot of experience with, so this tiptoeing act is getting on my nerves.

Jordy settles quietly on the bench behind the pilot seat, and I tuck a blanket around her legs. It's still early in the season and the chill can set in quickly once the sun starts going down.

"Thank you," she mutters behind me when I start the engine and steer away from the dock. "I'm sorry I'm being such a brat."

I can hear a wobble in her voice and before she can start with fresh waterworks, I quickly joke, "Just so you know, this is my last dry shirt, Pipsqueak."

"Asshole," she fires back, but this time I can hear the smile in her voice. Crisis averted.

We tour around the lake, low throttle, commenting on some of the more elaborate homes and cottages, and are just passing the mouth of a small river.

"Jared…" I hear my sister whisper behind me and I turn around. She's pointing at the shore, where a large moose cow and her newborn calf are standing in the underbrush. I shut off the engine and let the boat coast, as we silently watch the majestic animal take a few steps into the water and lower her large head to drink. Her little one, more interested in its mother than the water, is nuzzling her side, eventually dipping its head and latching on to feed.

I turn to smile at Jordy, but my smile disappears instantly when I see her face contorted in pain. The moose and baby forgotten, I rush over and drop on my knees in front of her.

"Hey…what's happening?" I say softly, brushing her hair from her forehead to find it slick with sweat. I'm trying to be calm, even though I'm fucking worried.

"Contractions," she manages to bite out between clenched teeth.

Okay, now I'm not calm anymore.

"The baby?" My voice is pitched about two octaves higher than normal as my throat slowly closes on me. I guess it was a stupid thing to say, because I suddenly find myself staring into Jordy's very angry eyes, shooting daggers.

"Yesss," she hisses, with a hefty dose of venom. "The fucking baby."

Scrambling to my feet, I head back to my seat to start the engine. My heart sinks when I push the button and nothing happens. Not a click, not a sound, not even an engine gurgle. Not a thing. I try again, with the same results.

"What's wrong?" Jordy asks, a worried look on her face.

"Not sure. Let me check," I say, moving by her to get to the large outboard engine, even though I don't really know what the fuck I'm supposed to be looking for. I'm a hockey player, not a mechanic. I like playing with motorized toys but I don't have a fucking clue how they work.

"Shit!" I hear Jordy yell behind me and I swing around.

"What?"

"I think my water broke…" She looks at me with a trembling smile before casting her eyes down. When I follow her gaze I notice the puddle on the seat underneath her. Now would probably be the time to panic.

I turn back to the engine and start randomly fiddling with fuel lines and other loose bits, without any idea what I'm doing. With one last ineffective knock on the engine housing, I rush to the pilot seat to try the engine again. Nothing.

When I hear Jordy softly moan, I cast a quick glance at her before letting my eyes wander to the shore, in hopes we're not too far from a house or cottage I can swim to, but this side of the lake is mostly crown property. Land that is owned by the government and generally preserved in its natural state. Meaning we're shit out of luck, and in more ways than one. I notice we're moving. And not just a little; with the breeze picking up and in the current flowing from the river, we're slowly drifting away from the shore.

Anchor. I dive past a whimpering Jordy and grab the small anchor. I narrowly have the presence of mind to make sure the rope is firmly attached to the cleat before I toss the hardware over the side. I let out a sigh of relief when I can feel the anchor snag on something.

Straightening up, I spot the familiar sight of a kayak heading in this direction. Without thinking, I start waving my arms and yelling for help.

Like the idiot I am.

FIVE

Mia

What on earth?

I almost turn right around when I spot my neighbour's boat, but just as quickly realize things seem off. Something in the way Jared moves around the boat that appears to be aimlessly drifting. I slowly continue paddling closer, watching him drop an anchor over the side, only picking up my pace when he spots me and starts yelling and waving frantically. Something is most definitely wrong.

"It's Jordy," he says, when I'm close enough to the boat so he can lean over the side to grab the rope from the kayak's bow. I know instinctively he's talking about the pregnant brunette. "Her water broke." Concern is evident on his face.

I don't think, this is familiar territory for me, and I grab his proffered hand without discussion, letting him pull me onboard. Not an easy feat, to transfer mid-water from a damn kayak onto a boat, but I manage. Or rather, he does when he shifts his hold so he has me under my armpits and simply heaves me over the side. I don't even have time to steady myself when he's already shoving me toward the bench in the stern.

"How many weeks?" I ask, as I sink down on the floor in front of her. She looks like she's in the middle of a decent contraction and is focused inward, rocking her body back and forth. "Jared?" I look over my shoulder to prompt him.

"Oh, thirty-six weeks? Maybe more?" he mutters uncertainly as he ties my kayak to a cleat.

I tamp down the rush of anger. The asshole doesn't even know how far along his wife is. *Figures*. Focusing on the woman again, I notice her breathing is deepening, telling me she's coming through this contraction.

"Sweetie?" I try to get her eyes on mine and when they lift, I see the surprise in them. "Hi." I smile easily, as if we're not bobbing around in the middle of a lake. "I need you to lie back on the seat, okay? I just want to make sure your baby's head is properly engaged." I gently manoeuvre her while I talk, lifting her legs up on the seat. I take note of her lack of communication, it worries me a little because it might indicate she's hitting transition.

"What the hell are you doing?" Jared's angry voice comes from behind me when I start easing the woman's shorts and panties down her hips.

"Checking to see her progression, what the hell do you think I'm doing?" I snap back, before adding, "Why don't you get the damn engine started."

"It won't start," he says, a little defeated.

"Try again," I suggest when I measure her, and my fingertip encounters the silky feel of the baby's head during the next contraction. "She's fully effaced and about eight centimeters dilated. We need to get to shore."

54

"I don't even know what the fuck that means," he mumbles as he steps around me and heads to the front.

"I'm a midwife," I quickly explain, as I pull up her shorts to cover her, realizing he couldn't know. "This baby will be here imminently and I'd much prefer we find a way to get her on land before she delivers." Guttural grunts from the woman make it clear time is running out and I turn to look at Jared. "Try again," I say softly, urging with my eyes.

When he pushes the start button nothing happens, and he slams his fist on the boat's wheel in frustration.

"Maybe if you put the throttle in the starting position?" I suggest, spotting the gearshift forward instead of upright.

"Fucking hell!" he exclaims, immediately pulling the lever in neutral and hitting the start button again. This time the engine immediately turns over and before I know it, he's engaging the throttle.

"Wait!" I yell out. "Your anchor."

A stream of colourful language flows from his mouth as he slips the engine back in neutral and steps over me to get to the anchor rope. He's lucky he didn't get it wrapped around the engine blades. Rookie. Before I can say anything, the boat lurches in the water and I'm trying hard to hold Jordy and myself steady as Jared races us to shore.

I whisper to her, reminding her to breathe, in hopes she holds off on pushing until we're somewhere more appropriate than the small bench in the stern of the boat. Relief courses through me when the boat docks. I instruct Jared to lift her out of the boat, trotting after him as he rushes her inside, his legs eating up the distance with his long strides.

"The couch," I direct him when she starts grunting in his arms. "Call an ambulance, then grab me a shower curtain or garbage bags, some clean linens. In that order." I know nothing about this woman, her medical history or her pregnancy, and I don't want to risk anything. Jared comes back, an arm full of sheets and towels, and a bunch of garbage bags fisted in his hand.

"Help me lift her up." The poor girl is barely aware of her surroundings at this point, completely at nature's mercy as her body does what it needs to do. In no time, we have the couch and the floor in front of it covered with garbage bags, a few towels and clean sheets. I'm removing Jordy's clothes and cover her with the remaining sheet. Jared looks a little green around the gills. "Did you call for an ambulance?" I ask, as I quickly take off my flannel shirt and walk over to the kitchen sink to wash my hands.

"On their way."

I look up at the gruff tone of his voice and watch as he leans over to kiss her forehead. Whatever is going on with that other woman, he loves this one. It's obvious.

"How are you doing, sweetie?" I ask the woman when I see her eyes are more alert. "Feeling any pressure?"

"Yes," she whispers, the first time I hear her speak. "I have to push."

I gently smile at her. "Then push. Your body knows what to do, trust it."

It takes her a while to find a position that works for her, until I suggest she sit on her haunches in front of the couch, with her arms hooked over Jared's knees, who is sitting behind her. This way, there are no restrictions as her body makes room for the baby. Almost automatically, Jared's hands curve protectively over her belly, and other than her grunts when the next contraction takes her body in its hold, there is just the peaceful quiet of the lake. Even Griffin, who at some point toddled over from the other side of the little bay, sensing something was up, is curled outside the sliding doors on the deck.

Just as I hear the sirens of the ambulance coming over the hill, with one last surge, Jordy's little baby boy slides warmly into my waiting hands.

Jared

"Here, help hold her and the baby up. Cup your hands under his bottom."

I've never felt so out of my element. This situation became surreal the moment Jordy told me she was having contractions. That one word created a panic that paralyzed every last one of my functioning brain cells. I don't even want to think what might have happened if our quirky neighbour hadn't shown up.

A midwife. What are the fucking odds?

So different from the skittish, awkwardly timid woman I encountered last week, this version of her exuded a confidence that was instantly settling. I'm not normally one to take orders lightly, but I found myself craving her directions. Giving me a sense of purpose and peace.

Sitting here with my near naked sister hanging between my knees, my arms keeping her and this purplish, slippery, wrinkled little thing secure, was completely beyond my comfort zone. Yet, I wouldn't have wanted to miss this for the world.

"I'm just going to open the door for the EMTs, okay?"

I notice the tear streaks on Mia's face as she pushes up from the floor to get the door, and only then realize my own face is wet. She returns right away, with two bulky men and a stretcher following her in. I have to keep from growling as one of them crouches down in front of my still half-naked sister, who is muttering in what can only be delirium, at the baby pressed to her chest.

"You okay?" Mia asks me carefully, once my sister and her baby are strapped down to the stretcher. I haven't said a word yet and my voice sounds odd when I answer.

"Yeah. I…that was…thanks," I lamely finish, clearly not yet in control of my faculties.

"Do you think you can drive?"

Her words are enough to shake off any lingering jitters, and make me stand up straight, slightly jutting out my chest in defiance.

"Of course I can," I snap defensively, instantly feeling like an ass.

"Good," she responds, trying but failing to hide a smirk. "Because I'm going to ride in the ambulance with her. She still has to deliver the placenta." She chuckles softly when an involuntary shudder washes over my body.

"Right," I mutter, looking around for my keys.

-

By the time I've parked my car, they've already wheeled Jordy into the emergency entrance. A friendly nurse directs me to the room where they've taken her. It's not until she congratulates me, that I realize she seems to think I'm the father. I'm slowly clueing in she's likely not the only one.

When I step inside, Mia pulls me to the side. A doctor is examining my sister, and the large EMT I'd wanted to slug earlier is standing on the opposite side of the bed, talking softly with the doctor. I can't see the baby.

"Where is he?" I ask Mia urgently.

"Relax," she soothes, even though she herself looks like she's about to come apart at the seams. She looks just like when I found her in her stalled car. Eyes red-rimmed, her skin almost translucent, and the muscles around her mouth twitching erratically. "He's in the nursery being checked over by the pediatrician. They should have him back soon. Mom is doing fine," she assures me with a shaky smile.

"She's my sister," I hiss, needing to set the record straight. I can tell by the blatant shock on her face, she had come to the same conclusion as the nurse earlier.

"Oh."

Suddenly she darts from the room, leaving me to stare at a slowly closing door, wondering what the fuck brought that around. I don't get too much time to think, when the doctor calls my name.

"Dad?"

I turn to him, getting a little annoyed that everyone is jumping to conclusions. Not surprisingly he flinches when I snap, "I'm not the father!" The silence that follows is thick as every pair of eyes turns to me. My sister, bless her heart, finally pipes up in a soft voice from the bed.

"Jared's my brother," she explains, smiling as she looks at me. "He's taking care of me."

Before anyone can respond, the door opens and a bassinet is wheeled into the room with my loudly protesting nephew. Because the doctor is still busy with whatever he's doing to my sister, the nurse waves me to a chair in the corner and comes at me with that screaming bundle. Holy fuck, this kid has lungs. I throw what likely is a look of alarm at my sister, whose face is beaming.

"Go on," she says. "You might as well get used to it."

Resigned, I turn to the grinning nurse who puts the kid, who's wrapped tighter than a burrito, in my arms before walking out the door, the EMT close behind her.

My eyes drop down to the loud little bundle in my arms. I don't *do* babies. I've never done babies, but I swear the moment I curl him against my body, he stops screaming. His little squinty eyes open and the moment they hit mine, the world disappears.

"Hey, little bruiser…" I stroke my fingertip over his downy cheek.

"His name is Oliver, not bruiser." I flick my gaze up to Jordy, who is thankfully completely covered up again.

"Oliver?" I repeat, my eyebrows raised. "Ollie?"

"No. Smartass. Ole," she says, repeating slower, "*Oh-luh*. Like dad."

"Pipsqueak," I chastise her. "You can't do that to a kid who's got more wrinkles than an elephant's scrotum."

"Jared!" My sister is predictably insulted, but the doctor can't hold back a chuckle, so he's next in line for a dirty look.

I'm teasing her, of course. Just a way to cover up the emotions bubbling up when she gives the little worm our father's name.

Jordy and I lost our parents in a car accident a month after Jordy graduated college. It had been a hard blow for both of us, but for Jordy, who was just about to start her life, the loss was devastating. I'm actually not surprised, giving her son our father's name was a way to keep his memory alive. Plus, my dad was a great, compassionate man. The boy could do worse than to be named after him.

I wink at her and see her mouth twitch. She knows I'm just kidding.

"The wrinkles will smooth out with a few days," the doctor quickly covers his faux pas as he scuttles toward the door. "We'll keep you overnight, and I'll check in with you tomorrow morning to see how your night was, before we send you home." Before either of us can respond, he's out the door.

Just a minute later, the same nurse comes back in and reaches out to take Ole from my hold. I have to admit, I'm a little reluctant to let him go, but the next moment, I'm ready to bail.

"Get ready, Mom, your little one needs to nurse," she says to my sister with a smile. I'm at the door in a flash. I've already seen enough of my sister to scar me for life.

"Where are you going?" Jordy pipes up, when she spots me heading for the hills.

"Just gonna see if I can find a coffee somewhere." Lame excuse and my sister knows it, but the nurse unwittingly comes to my rescue.

"There's a Timmie's in the lobby. It should still be open."

I mumble my thanks and pull open the door to make my exit, but not before my sister fires off a parting shot.

"You know you'll be seeing a lot more of this at home, right?"

I wave my hand over my shoulder, without looking back, and let the door slam shut behind me. She's right. Of course. But for now, I'm happy to escape.

Besides, it gives me an excuse to see where Mia took off to. I haven't seen her since she beelined it out of the room.

I'm not sure, but I could've sworn she was crying when she did.

SIX

Mia

Breathe.

I have to breathe.

The lights, the sounds, bodies around me, it's building into a crescendo that threatens to scatter my carefully controlled fragments. Someone touches me—says something—it makes me jump. I force my feet to keep moving. All I see is the lobby doors, it's like staring down on a hurricane; blinding chaos everywhere around except in the eye of the storm, where all is calm. The doors. If I can only get outside.

The swoosh of automatic doors opening is followed by the touch of a breeze on my face. I still don't stop, not even when I hear the screeching of brakes and a loud car horn. Not until the lights and the noise dim in my peripheral vision and I can pull fresh air into my lungs. Sanctuary.

I have no real concept of time passing, but know it has when my body feels cold. I left my flannel shirt on a chair in Jared's living room and am only wearing shorts and a tank. When my teeth start chattering, I know I have to move. My joints groan when I get up from where I'm curled up against the trunk of a large tree. I

63

absentmindedly brush at twigs and needles that are sticking to my body, as I move toward the lights shining through the brush.

Apparently I didn't get too far. The copse of trees I step out of is directly opposite the hospital's circular drive, outside the entrance. My head is quiet again, my heart rate back to normal, but my body is chilled to the core. The nights up north can still be deceptively chilly this time of year. Still, I don't particularly want to head back into the hospital, where I know I'll be warm. Instead, I take a seat on a bench in front of the doors, pull up my legs and wrap my arms around them, while I come up with a plan.

I want to go home, but since I came in the ambulance, I don't have transportation. The only person I know enough to call is Rueben, but I'm not so sure if that's appropriate. If I had my wallet I could call a cab, but I don't.

I've just about decided my only option is to go back inside, and find Jared to see if he can help, when the doors slide open and the subject of my thoughts walks out, looking around like he's searching. Then his eyes land on me.

"There you are. I was wondering where you'd taken off to."

I try for a smile as he walks over and sits down beside me, a questioning look on his face.

"I'm kind of stuck here," I admit. "I have no way to get home."

"Right. Of course," he says, slapping his palm to his forehead. "Let me run inside and let Jordy know I'm driving you home." He gets up and moves toward the doors before he suddenly stops, turns, and walks back. "You're freezing," he points out, holding out his hand. "I've got a blanket in the trunk of my car. You can wait in there. I won't be long."

I don't say anything, just put my hand in his and let him pull me to my feet.

True to his word, it doesn't take long for him to get back to the car, and I'm pretty toasty, wrapped in a fleece blanket in the passenger seat. He gets in behind the wheel and immediately turns the engine on, eyeing me as he does so.

"Are you okay?"

"Hmmm," I hum, without really saying anything. "How is your sister?" I've had some time to digest that little tidbit of information that stuck, even in the midst of my panic attack. Rueben's words coming back to haunt me. I *did* jump to conclusions—the wrong ones—and even though I never really spoke on my misconception, I still feel the urge to be apologetic. The fact the pretty brunette is his sister really messes with my preferred view of him; as a philandering, spoiled, rich boy. It certainly did the job suppressing my somewhat unhealthy fascination with him.

I study his features and notice this close up, that his hair is not all dark, but actually has a good amount of gray streaking. He's also not as young as I thought he was, with prominent grooves around his mouth and forehead, and fine lines fanning out from his eyes; proof he laughs well, and often.

"She's nursing," he sighs, with a hint of revulsion. It tickles an unfamiliar giggle from my belly. I've seen that expression on his face, a few times over the past few hours, and had attributed it to the guy being a douchebag. Now I realize that he likely was uncomfortable having quite so much of his sister exposed. "You're laughing at me," he snaps, which only has me giggling harder. I can't help it, this entire evening has been a little too much to wrap my head around all at once, and I'm coming a bit unravelled.

Jared starts up the car and starts driving, while I desperately try to get myself under control. To my horror, all I manage is to morph my hysterical snickering to a different kind of emotional release.

"Are you okay?" He asks the same question he did before, but this time I answer.

"N-no..."

"*Christ...*" I hear him hiss under his breath.

I turn my face to the side window, where the rugged Ontario landscape whips by unseen. I vaguely register the sound of the glove box opening, before a wad of tissues is pressed in my hands.

"Thanks," I mumble, mortified.

The drive is silent, except for the occasional pathetic snivel that escapes me, and I'm relieved beyond belief when he turns onto my drive. The sight of my cottage at the bottom of the hill instantly settles me. An excited bark draws my eyes to Jared's side of the inlet, where poor Griffin has noticed the car. Protective as he is, he immediately gets up from where he apparently was still curled up outside his house, and still barking, comes tearing around the little bay.

"Heyyy…good boy, Griffy," I coo when he jumps up on me the moment I get out of the car, giving him a good rub. No sooner than Jared gets out of the car and Griffin beelines it to him. Traitor. I can hear him mumble praise to my dog as well.

This is a little awkward. Should I thank him? Apologize for my emotional behaviour? Run and hide inside the cottage? I'm still contemplating my options when I'm suddenly wrapped up in a set of strong arms. I almost disappear against his bulk, with my face pressed between his distinct pecs. Okaaaay…didn't see that one coming, but I'll roll with it.

"Thank you," I hear his voice thick with emotion in my hair. "Without you, I…*fuck*…I don't even want to think about that."

"It was nothing." My voice is muffled against his chest.

"It was not nothing," he says firmly, setting me back by the shoulders. I'm eye to eye with his chest and have to tilt my head way back to see his face. "It was everything," he emphasizes. "I don't know you—your struggles—but I'm not blind. This *cost* you, so don't minimize what it means to me."

"Oh-okay," I stammer when he gives me a sharp nod, before releasing me and making his way back over to the car, where he turns and gestures in the direction of the cottage.

"Get inside, Mia, before you get cold again."

Like an automaton, I nod my head and do as he says. With the door open, Griffin comes barrelling in, undoubtedly looking for food. I turn for one last look as

Jared raises a hand before he gets in his car, turns it around, and disappears over the hill.

I feed my dog, drink a glass of water, and without even turning on the lights, I shuffle to my bedroom where I collapse face first on the bed. My brain just can't handle any processing tonight, and blissfully sleep takes me.

Jared

What a goddamn night.

I'm giving myself a headache, squinting as I eye the sides of the road for errant wildlife. It's not uncommon for anything from fox to moose to step out into the road in these parts. I'm coming down from an adrenaline rush, the proportions of which I don't think I've ever experienced before. Not even on the ice during a Stanley Cup playoff game.

The letdown happened in Mia's driveway, and I'll be damned if I didn't almost burst into tears right there. *Christ.* Almost made a fool of myself, but I meant every word I said, though. She'd seemed shell-shocked herself, sitting on that bench outside the hospital, big liquid eyes in a ghostly white face. She was shivering against the cold, and looked like she'd just crawled out of a haystack with all sorts of outdoor detritus stuck in her hair and to her clothes.

She didn't say much other than to voice her wish to go home, but then proceeded to have what looked like a mini melt-down in the car. Probably coming down from the rush herself. Funny, she'd never shown any edge while helping Jordy. She'd been cool and collected through the whole ordeal, which had a distinct calming effect on me, too.

Movement from the corner of my eye has me slam the brakes, narrowly missing a nice-sized buck darting across the road. Fuck, that was close. I shift in my seat and lean a little closer over the steering wheel. Better keep my eyes on the road and my mind off my neighbour.

My phone starts vibrating in my pocket, just before the telltale ring of an incoming call hits my hands free. I hit the receive button on the steering wheel.

"Talk to me."

"It's me. Where are you?" Jordy's tired voice fills the car.

"Halfway back to the hospital. Why? What's wrong?"

"Nothing's wrong. I'm about to crash. Ole's fed and sleeping, and I'm about to doze off myself." I wince at the reference to the baby nursing, but shove it down. Best get used to that. "I was thinking you should just go home and get some sleep," she continues, chuckling softly. "May be the last chance you get for a decent night's sleep for the next while."

I pull over to the side, turning the car into a dirt drive to get off the road.

"You don't want me to sit with you?"

"Nah," she says dismissively. "Baby needs feeding every three hours. You wouldn't get a lick of sleep and I have the nurses helping out tonight. It's on you starting tomorrow, so I suggest you grab sleep while you can."

"You sure?"

"Positive. Go home, Jared. And thank you for everything. Love you."

Before I have a chance to respond, she's already ended the call. I run my hand over my head, noticing it's probably time for a haircut. Cranking up the radio, I lower my window, and pull back onto the road in the direction I came from. Home it is.

-

A quick glance over to Mia's cottage, when I roll down my own drive, shows the lights are all off. She must've gone straight to bed. My own body is shutting down at a rapid pace, and I feel like an old man when I drag myself from the car. My knee is aching more than usual. Another indication retiring after last year's injury was probably the right decision.

I push open the front door—which I'd failed to lock earlier—noting once again how different things are here compared to the city life I'm used to. I'd never leave my condo without engaging the alarm and locking up tight. But then hardly anyone seems to know me here. No screaming fans or annoying stalkers. Life up North is much more laid back. Relaxed and peaceful. Although, as the reality of having a baby in the house is starting to settle in, we may be done with the peace for a bit. My nephew is loud.

By the time I roll into bed, I can barely keep my eyes open. My mind is not done yet, though. With my body relaxed, it seems to conjure up the events of the day. It had not been what I'd envisioned. I figured I'd have lots of time to drive Jordy to the hospital and hand her over to people who knew what the hell they were doing. I planned to make myself scarce with a paper and Timmie's, and wait for someone to come tell me when the baby arrived. I wasn't prepared to be taken by surprise, to be this hands on and *right there* when it all went down. It's messy. It's tough. And it's a fuck of a lot more intense than I ever imagined. But it also gave me a deeper respect for women. Jordy's strength and tenacity. Mia's calm, her confidence and faith that Jordy would be able to pull it off.

I've had my share of pain, and I'd like to think I'm pretty tough as a defensive enforcer, but I tell you, even with years of practice and training; I still wouldn't have been able to roll with the punches like these women did.

When I finally drift off, a smile on my face, my last thought is how blessed I am I got to share this experience.

SEVEN

Mia

"What do you mean, you delivered a baby?"

I smile as I listen to Steffie's incredulous voice.

It's been a few days, and other than a big gift basket with treats for me and the dog—which made me smile—that was delivered yesterday with a thank you card, I hadn't seen much of my neighbours. The card was signed Jared, Jordy, and Ole, which I thought was really cute. They must have Scandinavian heritage, although I always thought of tall and blond, not tall and dark. At least Jared is tall.

Ole's delivery had an impact on me. One I hadn't quite been prepared for. It was a vivid reminder of how much I'd always loved my profession. A profession I didn't realize I was missing so much. It's such a powerful experience, not just the birth of a child, but the birthing process itself. And stealing an occasional snuggle with a newborn baby is the cherry on top.

I never got to snuggle with Jordy's little one and I was craving it.

I'd been watching. I'd seen Jared's car leave early the morning after and saw them come home in the early afternoon. Part of me wanted to go over and check up on Jordy and her little one, but instead I stayed hidden inside and buried myself in my new design project.

I hadn't seen them at all yesterday, but this morning, while I was having my coffee on the porch, I watched Jared saunter outside in swimming shorts. I was mesmerized when he dropped his towel and stretched, before diving into the frigid lake. I found myself following his progress as he swam with his strong arms slicing the water. Realizing I was once again bordering on voyeurism, I resolutely got up and went inside.

When I couldn't concentrate on work because my mind kept wandering to the other side of the bay, I decided to call Steffie.

"My neighbour? The cute brunette? They were out on the water when she went into labour. I just happened by in my canoe." I chuckle and I tell her how Jared had been so flustered, he'd forgotten how to start the engine when I found them.

"You miss it," Steffie says when I finish my story, skipping over the panic attack that followed. It's more a statement than an inquiry, and yet I feel compelled to answer.

"More than I thought," I whisper, afraid to voice it out loud. "I miss the magic. I miss my sense of purpose; letting the moms feed off my calm and confidence, allowing them to start trusting the process. I miss the feeling of being there for someone when they need me. Being needed. And God, Steffie, I so miss my babies. He was so beautiful. Thirty-eight weeks and already so strong, so eager to make his presence known," I ramble as emotions take over.

"Honey…" she commiserates, but I'm not done.

"I walked away from that, Steffie. My heart was in it and I walked away from it. It tore me apart when I couldn't do it anymore. Now that I've tasted it again, I can't stop thinking about it."

"Mia…" she tries again. "You took yourself out of the game when you realized your emotional struggles were affecting your job. To me that's telling of the person you are. You don't want to give less than your all, and that's commendable. I always expected you to come back, honey. Not once did I think you wouldn't one day be back delivering babies."

"It's been years!" I exclaim. "A decade. And I'm not better. I had another attack at the hospital. Was in such a state, I didn't know where I was going."

"I'm not saying for you to jump into anything," Steffie soothes. "All I'm suggesting is that perhaps you should stop thinking your life is over, and start considering there's plenty left to live. It's not so bad to want something badly that is just out of reach. It just makes you work harder to get there."

We don't talk long after that. Steffie gets a call and needs to head out, and I'm left feeling adrift, with just the smallest niggle of hope in my heart.

Her words follow me around the entire rest of the day.

-

I'm out in my vegetable patch, pulling off a cucumber to go with the fresh strawberries and lettuce I already picked. A few spring onions, some chicken, pine nuts and that raspberry balsamic vinaigrette, and I have a meal. I love summer. Love how, when you pick your crops carefully, you can eat homegrown the entire season. Saves money, too. Sure it takes a little time, but there is nothing more gratifying than just walking outside and picking what you need. I happen to think gardening is soothing, although it wasn't always that way. I never really even considered going through the trouble of growing anything myself, when it took much less time and effort to hit the produce section at the grocery store. But I've changed. A lot, and not all in ways I like, but this change I like. Getting in touch with my 'earthier' self has been a good experience, and I enjoy discovering new things I'm good at. Even if it's just growing veggies.

I'm lost in thought when I round the side of the cottage, almost bumping into Jared's bulk, bent over giving the dog a pat.

"Careful," he rumbles in a low voice when he straightens up, grabbing my upper arms to steady me.

"Hey," I manage, once I catch my breath. I look down accusingly at Griffin, who never bothered alerting me or barking. He's usually very protective of me. I didn't even notice him leaving me in the vegetable patch. Traitor. "Everything alright?" A glance at his face makes it clear someone hasn't been sleeping a lot. I bite down a grin.

"Actually—no," he says, running his hand through his longish hair. I'm immediately alert.

"Jordy okay? The baby?" My eyes slide over his shoulder to his house across the water.

"He won't nurse. She can't get him to latch on and she's been crying half the day. Don't know what the fuck to do anymore. I called the hospital and they gave me a number of some kind of breastfeeding place? Stupid sounding name...*Leche* something?"

"La Leche League?" I offer.

"Yes. Anyway, I tried calling, got the answering machine and decided to ask you instead." He looks a little, no, correct that, a *lot* uncomfortable.

"Sure," I say, looking at the vegetables in my basket. "Let me just put these...wait, have you had dinner yet?" I ask him, and he shakes his head in response.

"No. Haven't even had a chance to think about it," he confesses apologetically.

"Hold this," I say, shoving the basket in his hands before running inside to grab the chicken I roasted this afternoon. It was meant to last me a couple of days, but now I'm glad I did the whole chicken. It should be enough to feed all of us.

"Thanks," Jared says when I fall into step beside him on the trail around the bay. He's still carrying the basket of vegetables, after refusing to hand it back when I came outside with the chicken. I'm not sure if it's the sight of the burly man with a basket hooked over his arm, or the promise of a delicious armful of newborn baby to snuggle with, that has me smiling all the way to his front door.

Jared

I can't deal with tears. Not when everywhere I turn, someone's crying. Fuck, by the time the sun starts setting, I'm ready to start crying my damn self.

The moment I spot Mia coming down her steps and rounding the side of her house, I turn to Jordy, who's sniffling on the couch, trying to rock Ole in submission. He's not having it. Right. That's enough of that. By the time I get to her cottage, her dog is waiting; his tail wagging and his tongue lolling out of his mouth. For a moment, I forget why I'm here when she comes around the corner at a stiff clip, almost bowling me over. Okay, not quite, given I'm about twice her size, but I wobble. A little. I tell her to be careful, but have to steady myself holding on to her and end up steadying her instead. The smell of strawberries warmed in the sun wafts up from the basket she has clutched in her hands, and the sight of her clear green eyes, in a much healthier-looking face than last time I saw her, has my breath catch. She's quite pretty, with that halo of short, unruly curls framing her flushed cheeks.

It takes me a minute to respond when she asks why I'm there, but before long, I have her walking back to my place beside me. From the occasional glances I direct her way, she's not at all unhappy about it. I can't quite figure her out.

"Hey, honey," she says softly when we walk inside to find Jordy, still with tears coursing down her face. They only increase at Mia's gentle inquiry and before I can blink, she's sitting beside my sister, wrapping her and the baby in her embrace. I grab the chicken she abandoned on the coffee table and carry the lot to the kitchen, wishing for the first time I didn't have an open concept house. What I wouldn't give to be able to close a door and maybe watch some TV or something. Instead I mindlessly wash and rinse Mia's harvest as I listen to the soft murmur of her voice from the living room.

"Could you put on the kettle for tea?"

I turn around to find Jordy apologetically eyeing me from her perch on the couch. Alone.

"Where's Mia?"

"Changing Ole's diaper."

That puts a smile on my face. I've had that unpleasant task the past couple of days and let me tell you, my gag reflex is alive and well.

"You're so transparent," she accuses me with a smirk. "Don't think I haven't noticed your distaste for my son's excretions." I shrug. No use in denying the obvious. I love the way his little warm body smells snuggling under my chin, but when he produces, the stench is overwhelming. My sister swears it'll get worse when he starts eating solids, and I sure as shit hope that won't be for a good long time. Or at least until Jordy's able to do her own baby's damn diaper changes.

She looks a little better. Still flushed and her face a little swollen from crying, but her eyes don't look lost.

"You okay, Pipsqueak?" I ask, as I put the kettle on the stove and pull down a couple of mugs and her teabags.

"Better," she says. "Mia's going to help me feed. She says the baby looks a little jaundiced."

"Do we need to take him to the clinic?" I'm instantly on alert.

"No need," Mia says, as she comes walking into the living room, carrying my nephew face down on her crooked forearm like a football, his little legs dangling on either side and his face resting on her upturned palm. Totally relaxed. I'm taking mental notes for next time he decides to bring down the house with his little temper. "I was just telling your sister it's not unusual for babies to turn a little yellow. Her milk is just coming in and it's not quite as rich as the colostrum, so he'll need a little more to get the same satisfaction. It's just a transitional phase."

I have my hands up when she starts talking about milk and whatever the hell that other thing is.

"Whatever," I mutter dismissively, drawing a chuckle from my sister. "Want some tea?" I ask Mia, promptly changing the subject to the women's amusement. Mia just nods and I'm struck at her ease around Jordy and Ole. No sign of the pale anguish I've seen on her face more than once. Instead, she looks almost serene as she expertly positions Jordy before placing Ole in her arms. I quickly turn when my sister flips down one side of her ugly ass nursing bra, exposing her breast so Ole can latch on. It's getting easier, but I'd be lying if I said it didn't make feel a little weird. Not that I can't see the beauty of it, a mother nursing, I just need to get over the fact it's my sister.

Jesus. If my teammates could see me now, I wouldn't hear the end of it. Changing diapers, burping, washing spit rags and onesies—making fucking hot beverages. Yeah, they'd get a good chuckle out of it.

By the time the tea is ready, Ole is nursing contently and both girls are watching him with tender expressions. I need to see if there's a good action movie on TV tonight. I have a sudden craving for something rich in testosterone.

The baby is peacefully sleeping on the couch, surrounded by pillows to hold him in place, and I've put his little cot by the window, as per Mia's instructions. Apparently the kid needs sunlight and frequent feedings. Makes sense to me; that's enough to get me through my days as well. Maybe babies aren't as complicated as I thought. He certainly doesn't look complicated, he looks relaxed as his little tongue pokes out and his mouth still makes those little sucking motions. I lean my head back and absentmindedly scratch Griffin's head.

I let the dog in to feed him the leftovers of our impromptu dinner, while Mia is helping Jordy take a shower. Griffin had scarfed down the chicken and some leftover rice, before he sauntered over, sniffed the baby and plopped down in front of the couch. He lifted his head when I sat down, before dropping it down on his front paws and closing his eyes.

This is nice.

I must've dozed off, when I feel my hand, which I'd put protectively on Ole's stomach to prevent him from falling off, lifted and placed on my leg. My eyes shoot open to find Mia carefully lifting the baby up, trying not to wake him—or me apparently.

"I'm just going to put him in his crib and head home," she whispers when she sees I'm awake. "Jordy's resting and you should grab a nap as well." She disappears toward Jordy's bedroom, where we've temporarily set up Ole's crib.

I rub my hand over my face to clear the sleep from my eyes and push myself upright.

"I'll walk you back," I tell her when she returns.

"No need," she says with a sharp shake of her head. "I'll be fine, and besides, the baby could wake up any time. I suggest he feeds on demand for now. I'll pop back over tomorrow morning to check on Jordy. I'm more concerned about her, she running a low grade fever. Might be an infection, so she needs to drink lots. Every time she nurses, she should do so with a glass of water beside her."

Once again I'm taking mental notes of everything she says, realizing how terribly unprepared and uneducated I am on the subject. Talk about a steep learning curve.

"I'll just sleep here on the couch where I can hear them," I suggest, following her and the dog to the door, where I reach past her to open it, and flick on all the outside lights at the same time. "And I'll watch from here until you get inside."

She slips past me out the door, with her head turned away, but I don't miss the roll of her eyes. I silently watch as she makes her way down the trail, occasionally disappearing behind a tree or some brush, with Griffin following faithfully behind her. When she emerges on the other side, walks up her steps, and raises a hand in my direction before disappearing inside, I finally close the door and turn off the outside lights.

I fall asleep the moment I lie back down on the couch, only to be woken up what feels like mere minutes later, to the sound of my nephew's lusty cries.

I guess this diaper is mine. *Shit.*

EIGHT

Mia

It's been a busy week.

I smile when I catch myself thinking that. I don't think I've had a busy anything in a decade. It feels good, being needed, feeling useful.

I've spend almost every day at my neighbours', checking up on Jordy and Ole. The baby's getting a bit better; no longer quite as yellow and he appears to be a strong little boy. Other than the first few days, when she was sore and her boobs were leaking like faucets, Jordy's feeling a lot better too. She's becoming more confident and the little one seems to be able to sense that.

As for me, it feels nice to have a friend right across the bay. Especially when I only see Steffie a few times a year. My fault, clearly, since there's no way I could envision heading to the big city any time soon. A shiver runs down my spine at the thought. Any visits are dependent on her.

I jot down eggs on the grocery note I'm compiling. I haven't been since my little meltdown in the store and am not particularly looking forward to heading out. But Griff's food is almost gone, and I'm down to stale crackers and homegrown veggies, which frankly, isn't cutting it. Jordy asks me almost daily to stay for a meal, but since I brought over that chicken and salad a week ago, I've avoided it. It's tempting enough to come here every day and snuggle with Ole's little warm body, while chatting with Jordy. It's the kind of contact I've been missing, which is why I have to be cautious not to latch on to them.

I haven't seen much of Jared the past few days, he leaves before I get there, but he's been home at night. I've seen his car come back—not that I am looking. Yet another reason to keep some distance; I'm not good at hiding my fascination with him.

Anyway, I promised Rueben, who is away for a few weeks visiting his daughter in Colorado, that I'd try to keep up my weekly visits to town. When I checked with Jordy yesterday, to see if she needed anything from town, she practically begged me to get some proper pads. Apparently Jared's brought home a dozen boxes of panty liners, telling her he bought in bulk because he had no wish to repeat the experience. She didn't want to point out panty liners wouldn't do the trick, so instead she'd been making do…with three or four stacked at a time. She mentioned Jared was going to take her and the baby into the clinic for an appointment this morning, but she wasn't sure if she was going to feel up to making any more stops, so I told her not to worry; I'd pick up some pads on my run.

Having delayed long enough, it's almost noon, I tuck my list in my purse, grab my keys, and my grocery bags, and determinedly ignore the bite of anxiety in the pit of my stomach. As an afterthought, I pick up the bucket with kitchen waste, destined for the compost bin beside the shed, and step outside.

"You stay, buddy, I'll be back soon," I reassure Griffin, who tries to follow me outside, and quickly close and lock the door. I glance across the water to the other side to notice Jared's car already gone, and make my way to the shed. With the waste emptied into the bin, I close the lid and leave the bucket to rinse out and take inside when I get back. I'm about to toss my bags in the car, when the crunch of gravel has me turn around to find a familiar car driving down the hill.

"Hey," Jared calls out through the rolled down passenger side window. "Need a ride into town?" I lean down to see if Jordy is in the car with him.

"Where's your sister?" I ask, when I see the back seat is empty.

"Back home. She and Ole are taking a nap. She was tired after her appointment," he explains. "Anyway, when I told her I'd run out to grab some supplies, she mentioned you were heading into town. Thought I'd see if you were still here. We can save on gas." He's leaning over the centre console, smiling easily.

The anxiety that had been building up in my gut, eases slightly at the prospect of not having to brave town alone, but another type of tension fast takes its place. Being in his proximity is creating its own brand of anxiety, which I'm not sure I'm able to ignore. He catches my hesitation and leans even further to shove open the passenger door. Not wanting to make an ass of myself, and secretly relieved for the company he's offering, I tuck my bags under my arm, and get in.

"What did the doctor say?" I ask, as he turns the car around and starts driving toward the road.

"The baby's lost a little weight since birth but he says that's normal."

"It is," I interrupt. "He'll put it back on, and then some, in the coming weeks."

"Yeah, that's what he said. Anyway, other than that, he seemed pleased. Assured Jordy the baby looked good and said she was healing well. Was curious about you, though," he says, and I can feel him turning his eyes on me. "He admitted never having heard of you, when Jordy mentioned you'd been taking care of her. Said he was surprised, since he knows every midwife in the region."

I detect a hint of accusation in his comments and try not to let it sting. Of course, he has every right to question the validity of my claim, given that I've been in and out of his house, taking care of his family. I take a deep breath.

"I got my degree at McMaster University and practiced in Toronto for seven years before moving here." I'm leaving out huge chunks of information, spanning about thirteen years, but what I do give him is enough to check my credentials. To my surprise, he reaches out with his free hand, covering my folded ones in my lap and gives them a light pat.

"I wasn't doubting you," he says, his voice dipped low, and I can't help glancing up at him. His eyes, peeking at me from under his ball cap, hold the middle between blue and gray, and show no suspicion at all. "And I don't think the doc was either, given the way you had things firmly in hand during the delivery. It's just curiosity," he assures me, and I feel compelled to give him just a little more.

"I had to give it up years ago," I admit, turning my head to glance out the window, or maybe I just don't want to give myself away with my eyes. "I just never knew how much I missed it."

My words are met with silence and when I finally take a peek at him, I notice he's staring straight ahead, his mouth in a firm line.

"Yeah, I hear you," he finally says. "I wish I didn't know what that feels like."

His words intrigue me. My first reaction is to ignore it for the platitude it might appear to be, but I can tell from the look on his face he's dead serious. He may not know my story, but he clearly has one of his own—lost something he loved as well. I'm the one curious now, but the set of his jaw keeps me from asking. I'm not ready to share—not sure if I'll ever be—so I can hardly ask him to open up.

The rest of the drive takes place in silence, but it's not unpleasant. Each of us is lost in our own thoughts, and I don't even feel the familiar pounding of my heart when he pulls into a vacant parking spot in front of the grocery store.

Jared

"I, uhh…have to grab something here," she says, nudging her head in the direction of the feminine products aisle. Her voice is tight and the fact her knuckles are white as she hangs on to her cart, like it's her anchor, doesn't escape me. Still, I nod for her to go, pretending to be interested in the sale items on the end display, just so I can keep an eye on her.

When Jordy mentioned Mia was planning to head into town this morning, I was hit with guilt. All week, I've been using and abusing her kindness by leaving Jordy in her care, while taking care of some medical appointments in Toronto and a long awaited sit-down with my agent, Brian, in Barrie. Loose ends I'd planned to take care of the last few weeks before the baby was born, but the little bugger decided to come early. It took me less than forty-eight hours to realize that with a baby in the house, time is no longer yours. I grabbed the opportunity and told myself it had nothing to do with the fact I was trying to avoid my very attractive, and confusing neighbour.

I'm not a fool. I know there is something going on when someone is confident, taking charge, one minute, and is a scared little mouse the next. I've seen both sides of her, and while the one intrigues me, the unpredictability of the other scares me witless. Avoiding her seemed easier. I was wrong. I may have avoided seeing her in my space, but her smell lingered, instantly triggering thoughts of her.

Seeing how frazzled she was the first time I saw her coming back from town, and how panicked she was at the hospital, I'm guessing being out in public is not easy for her. Which is part of why I swung by to pick her up. The other part being that I'm an ass for disappearing on her, when in all reality, I'd like nothing more than to find out more about her.

She took me by surprise when she spoke of her profound sense of loss since giving up her calling. The words rang true for me in a way that was uncanny. I recognize the feeling because I've lived it every day this past year. But this past week, tying up those loose ends, I think the finality of it ultimately hit me. Yeah, I feel that loss.

My eyes wander back to where Mia is scouring the shelves, with her eyes darting in the direction of anyone passing her in the aisle. I start moving toward her, tampons be damned, when she squeezes her eyes shut, drops her head down, and sways on her feet. *Shit*. She's barely hanging on. The shallow breathing, buckling knees, and death hold on her cart tell me I'm not wrong. I quickly step up behind her, bracing her between my body and the cart. To anyone looking, we hopefully look like nothing more than a loving couple.

"I've got you," I whisper, with my lips against the shell of her ear. My arm wraps around her waist and bears her weight as I tuck her tight against my front. "Breathe, baby," I encourage her, when she starts gasping for air and fighting my hold. "You're okay. You can do this, Mia. Breathe with me."

I quickly glance around, hoping no one saw her brief struggle and got the wrong idea, but the aisle is blissfully empty. Slowly I feel the tension sliding from her body as she struggles to match her breath to mine.

"I'm sorry," I barely hear her say.

"Nothing to be sorry about. Now, what was it you needed here?" I try to set a normal tone when I slowly release her, making sure her legs are once again steady. She turns her head with an incredulous look on her face.

"I have to go."

"Nope," I say firmly. "We're not done getting our groceries."

"But…what if I…" Her eyes are almost panicked when she looks at me, so I lean in once again and bracket her in against her cart. This time front to front.

"What *we're* going to do, is finish picking up our groceries, grab a nice couple of steaks from the butcher, and casually browse the bakery on the way to the register. And *if*, by chance, you feel another one of those coming on, we're gonna breathe right through until it passes," I enforce on her, almost nose to nose. "Now, like I said, what is it you need in this aisle?" I watch with interest as the fear in her eyes is replaced with the fire of indignant anger. Oh yeah, the lady is pissed.

"Kotex maxi pads," she says, an evil little smirk on her face when she catches my flinch. "A small pack of heavy flow and a large package of medium flow.

They're for your sister," she points out with some venom. "And you can help me find the nipple shields. Her breasts are leaking through her bra." I feel like she just nailed me in the gonads with an oversized pair of steel-toed boots.

I swear she's snickering as she walks away, pushing her cart. At the end of the aisle she looks over her shoulder.

"I'll be *casually browsing* the bakery if you need me."

With a toss of her wild curls, she disappears from sight, leaving me to gape after her.

Nothing left to do but peruse the gazillion choices of feminine products. It takes me way too goddamn long to find what I need, so I ask a passing grocery clerk, who smiles at me sympathetically as she points me in the right direction.

The entire exercise is uncomfortable as hell, and when I find Mia at the counter in the bakery, I quickly dump that shit in her cart. I glare at her, but it doesn't stop the corner of my mouth twitching up in a smile, when I'm met with the mischievous sparkle in those green eyes.

-

By the time I pull into her driveway after our otherwise uneventful grocery run, the trunk and back seat filled with bags, we're chatting easily. I was stopped by a fan while we were loading up the car and had to smile at the confusion on Mia's face, when she was asked to take a picture of us. Apparently she didn't have a clue who I was, something I found oddly refreshing. Apparently she's not a big hockey fan, by her own admission.

I just finished giving her a very brief synopsis of my career when I hear her gasp beside me.

"Sonofabitch," she mutters under breath, before turning to me. "Stop the car."

I'm about to ask why, when I see what got her attention and slam my foot on the break. Before I have a chance to react, Mia is already scrambling out of the car.

"Honk the horn," she instructs me as she bends down, picks up a loose branch, and starts waving it in the air.

She looks fearless as she takes a few steps toward the black bear, who is taking notice. Half his body had been stuck in a bin beside her shed, but it's big head is now turned toward Mia, who is yelling and getting a little too close for comfort. I get tangled in the damn seatbelt when I try to climb out of the car, and it takes me a second to get free.

"Horn!" she yells again, when the bear rears to its hind legs, from what I understand, not a good sign. I dive back in the car and lay on the horn. That draws his attention away from Mia as he drops down on all fours and calmly lumbers into the trees beyond, casting a last glance behind him.

I'm pissed when I stalk around the car to give her a piece of my mind.

"Are you out of your fucking mind?" I roar, making Mia jump a foot in the air before she swings around, dropping her stick in the process. The only thing she manages is a choked protest as I pull her tight in my arms, my focus on the tree line beyond.

"Your heart is racing," she points out, her hands splayed on my chest, and I drop my eyes to her face.

"Ya think? You scared the crap out of me," I admit. "What were you thinking, getting out of the goddamn car?" I'm still shouting even as she pats my chest with her hand.

94

"This is not my first rodeo, Jared," she replies way to calmly. "You'll get used to them. It's worse in the early spring when they're starving." She looks back at the trees before facing me again, a reassuring smile on her face. "It's just a little unusual he showed up in the middle of the day, but it's my own fault. I left my compost bucket out, the scent must have drawn him in," she says, pushing back from my hold. "Besides, he was just a young one, more brawn than brains. He doesn't know who's boss here."

I've got nothing to say as I watch her pick up the bucket before she walks to her cottage.

It's only then that I notice the dog frantically barking inside.

It takes me a second to get over the fact that the same woman who, less than an hour ago, was trembling in fear in the grocery store, just went head-to-head with a bear with nothing but a skinny little branch, and cojones the size of bowling balls.

She's something all right.

NINE

Mia

"Thanks," Jordy says with a smile, when I hand her an iced tea. "It's getting pretty steamy out here."

I drop down in the second deck lounger and put my own glass on the small side table.

It's hot all right. Has been for a few days now and doesn't show any signs of letting up. I haven't slept much. There's no air conditioning in my cottage and the nights haven't cooled off like they usually do. The last cool one we had was Tuesday, when we found the bear in my compost bin.

Today is Friday, and as usual, traffic on the lake has picked up since midafternoon. Weekenders driving up from the city to enjoy their little corner of heaven for a few days, before heading back to the rat race.

I take a sip of my drink and watch a boat, pulling a tube with a bunch of screaming kids behind it, going by. A little breeze coming off the lake makes it bearable to be out here, under the large umbrella, and I sigh as I lay my head back.

"Tired?" Jordy asks. I turn my head to face her, smiling.

"I am," I admit. "But I'm pretty sure not as tired as you are."

Ole had hit a bit of a growth spurt, and with Jordy still feeding on demand, she's been up every two hours or so during the night. Both her and Jared looked a little the worse for wear when I came over to check on her. I watch as a little smile tugs at her mouth.

"Exhausted," she shares. "But I don't mind. I sleep when he does. It's harder on Jared. He can't sleep during the day."

"I don't need sleep." The subject of discussion walks up to our loungers, setting the baby monitor on the table between us. "The kid is diapered, burped, and down for the count, however long that is. I'm going for a dip. Anyone game?"

Without waiting for an answer, he saunters to the end of the dock, giving me full view of his large body, clad in just his swim shorts, with a towel draped around his neck. He drops the towel beside him before stretching his arms above his head, the muscles in his back moving—mesmerizing. His legs push off as he dives into the water with a splash. The memory of that body protectively wrapping around me recently has goosebumps rising on my skin, despite the heat of the sun. It's been a long, long time since I've been touched by someone other than my best friend, and even those moments of brief connection have been few and far between. So being held by his big body, firmly placing himself between me and the world, had a greater impact than I've been comfortable acknowledging. It's been on my mind—especially in those sleepless moments the past few nights.

"He likes you, you know."

98

My head whips around to Jordy, who is staring after her brother, before turning to face me with a glint in her eyes.

"Okay?" I hesitantly say, not quite sure what to do with that information. It makes her chuckle.

"He always has his eyes on you," she clarifies. "My brother is—or maybe I should say *was*—a bit of a manwhore, never lacking for female attention, but I've never seen him ogling anyone quite as closely as he does you. You're nothing like the groupies he's used to. I think it's throwing him off his game." If that isn't the understatement of the year. Despite the blush heating my face, I can't help snort, remembering the stacked blonde of my first encounter with him. She's right on that account, I am nothing like what he's used to. "What?" she prompts me.

"It's just that I think you're a little delusional," I tease her. "I've seen his *usual,* and believe me, I saw more of it than I cared to." I feel a little pang of guilt at the partial lie. I *have* seen his usual, but I've also come to the conclusion that I had him pegged wrong. He's done nothing but show me that every day since. And I haven't seen enough. Not nearly.

"Pray tell," she urges me, as she leans over her armrest, smiling like the Cheshire cat.

"Fine," I bite off with a sigh. "Your brother was buck-assed naked, the first time I saw him." I tamp down a laugh when Jordy's eyebrows shoot up in her hairline. "Right here, on the dock, in the middle of the afternoon. She was tall, blonde, and carried around her own impressive, built-in, floatation devices."

"No way!"

"Way," I confirm, smiling at her shocked expression. "The second time I saw him was when he was hugging a brunette in his driveway, and I just knew he was a player."

Jordy's loud laughter bounces off the water as she throws her head back and lets loose.

"Oh my God," she gasps, holding her stomach. "You thought he was stepping out on me?"

"Well, yeah," I defend myself. "What else was I supposed to think, when one moment he's making waves on the dock with the leggy blonde, and the next he's welcoming his very pregnant woman home?"

"I'm so gonna torture him with this," Jordy snickers, before turning to me with a serious expression on her face, putting her hand on my arm. "You know he's a good guy, right?"

"I've come to that conclusion," I reassure her with a smile. "But it doesn't change the fact I know that whatever you think you've seen is a figment of your imagination. I'm pretty much the polar opposite of his type."

She doesn't respond, but simply leans her head back on the chair and closes her eyes, a little smile playing on her lips, when the baby monitor crackles to life.

"I'll get him," I tell her, with my hand on her arm when she makes a move to get up. Ole's angry cries indicate he's not likely to fall back asleep, and I quickly make my way inside.

"What are you making such a fuss about?" I coo as I lift him out of his crib, his little legs pumping in frustration. "Oh, good grief. You're soaked right through, kiddo." His little romper is drenched and judging by the smell, I'm bound to find a mess when I peel it off him.

Instead of putting him on the changing table, I grab a clean towel from his dresser, and take him straight into the bathroom. The trough sink is perfect for his baby bath, as we've come to discover. In no time I have him stripped, sinking him carefully in the warm water. Before long, his crying stops as he floats contently, his little head firmly in my hand, and his eyes intently on my face as he appears to enjoy the nonsense I babble.

A noise from the door has me lift my head to the mirror, and a little gasp escapes my lips as I watch Jared push away from the doorway in the reflection. I don't know how long he was standing there, but his hair is still wet, and he's wearing only the towel he brought outside earlier. With his eyes focused on me, he walks up behind me, placing a hand on my shoulder as he leans his chin on the other.

"He smells," he concludes, a smile in his voice as he looks at his nephew.

"That he does," I confirm. "It was up his back. I had no choice but to dunk him."

"Thanks," he rumbles in a low voice, his breath warm against my neck. "Appreciate all your help." I feel him press a kiss where my neck meets my shoulder, before he backs away, leaving me swaying a little on my feet. I concentrate on not letting go of Ole when I hear his voice behind me, and I look up at his reflection by the door.

"For the record; I know you saw me. As fucked up as it is, the thought of you watching me—getting off on it—has been sweet torture since."

I suck in a breath at his crass confession, and I want to turn away from the mirror as I feel heat flushing my face, but his eyes won't let me go.

"So you see, you're dead wrong. I can't seem to help watching you, which makes you very much my type."

Jared

I caught enough of their conversation when I leisurely swam back to the dock. I suppose the gentlemanly thing to do would have been to alert them to my presence, but my interest was piqued at what I was hearing.

"You're a sneak," Jordy says, when I pull myself out of the water. Her mouth is set in a straight line but amusement dances in her eyes.

"And you're meddling," I fire back, before picking up the towel and drying myself off.

We hear Mia's soothing voice over the baby monitor, along with Ole's pitiful cries, when Jordy reaches over and shuts it off.

"She's nice."

I look at my sister, who is clearly not ready to let it go.

"Yes, she is, Pipsqueak, but she—"

"Who's the blonde?" she cuts me off, squinting her eyes at me.

"A distraction." I look toward Mia's screened-in porch before turning back to Jordy.

"Clearly." Her distaste drips from that single word. "On the dock, Jared? Christ…what if…never mind." She waves her hand dismissively. "I was gonna say what if someone saw you, but it seems a moot point. Someone *did* see you. Poor thing probably had to rinse out her eyes with bleach."

I smile at that. I'm pretty sure Mia hadn't been thinking about bleach.

"You know…" my sister starts, but I've had enough.

"Let it go," I tell her firmly, before she can finish that sentence. "Not kidding, Jordy, drop it."

Without waiting for a response, I head to the house, tying the towel around my hips. Instead of taking the hallway to my own side, I find myself heading left— toward Jordy's quarters.

Mia's focus is on Ole, murmuring soothingly as she holds him firmly in one hand and washes him with the other. She doesn't notice me and I use the opportunity to let my eyes wander. She's wearing cutoffs and one of her man-sized T-shirts, her standard getup, with little but her strong, firm legs visible. I've watched her move, though. Enough to know she hides generous hips and a full ass, and she rarely wears a bra.

I've caught myself staring, more than once, quickly lifting my eyes to her face. A more appropriate focus of attention, but no less appealing, with her slightly slanted, expressive green eyes—cat eyes— and full lips. Not a lick of makeup on her. No attempt to hide the fine lines on her forehead or around her eyes. No expert colouring job, masking the sparse silver threads running through her hair, either. Completely natural and uncomplicated, and fuck if I don't like it better than the carefully put together women I'm used to.

Not my type—my ass.

I must've made a sound, because I suddenly find myself looking at those green eyes in the mirror.

-

When I walk into the living room after my shower, Jordy's feeding Ole on the couch. There's no sign of Mia.

I'd taken my time in the bathroom, needing to get a grip on my body's response to Mia's proximity earlier. The scent of her skin lingered in my nostrils; warm from the sun and fresh, with a hint of lemon. The brief taste, when I pressed my lips to her neck, only making me want to taste more. From the startled look on her face, I could tell I shocked her. Hell, I shocked myself. But it's one of those things, once it's out there—once that line is crossed—there's no taking it back. I have a feeling there's no way I can ignore the stirring of my cock whenever she's around any longer.

"Where did she go?"

Jordy looks up as I plop down beside her on the couch, trying hard to hide my disappointment.

104

"Home. Did you say something to her? She just shoved Ole in my hands and took off, mumbling something about some work she had to finish."

"You think he'll let us get some sleep tonight?" I peek over her shoulder and swiftly change the subject to one I know my sister can't resist. As expected, her face softens as she immediately turns her eyes to her baby, who is fighting to keep his eyes open while lazily nursing. She's clearly observant enough, she doesn't need more cause to get up in my business, especially since my anatomy is quickly rising to attention at any talk of Mia.

"He'd better," she says, a smile in her voice. "He's going to go from hand-to-hand tomorrow, he won't get much rest."

Jordy invited a couple of her friends for a BBQ tomorrow. A couple of girls she'd known since high school and the three of them had stayed close friends since. They'd been blowing up her phone since Ole was born, wanting to come see him, until finally a few days ago Jordy declared she felt up to it. I don't mind. This is as much her house as it is mine. Besides, Lesley's husband is a good guy. The few times I've met Phil, we've hit it off. It helps he's a bit of a sports fanatic, it always makes for easy conversation.

Tina, her other friend, is apparently newly single and heavily on the prowl. Doesn't surprise me, even when she was married, she put out some strong signals. Yeah, I wasn't particularly looking forward to fending her off all afternoon. I was hoping Ole would prove to be enough of a male distraction for her.

"Did you have a chance to see if Mia wanted to come?" Jordy cuts into my thoughts.

"I forgot," I lie.

I didn't exactly forget, but something tells me spending an afternoon among people she doesn't even know, would not be her thing. She clearly likes her solitude, and after witnessing her reaction both in the hospital and the grocery store, I'm starting to understand why. We haven't exactly shared life stories. The focus has been on Jordy and the baby, and there hasn't really been opportunity for much sharing, but still I'm surprised how at ease she's become around us these past few weeks.

I hope I haven't just fucked it all up.

TEN

Mia

Okay, so I'm a coward, but we'd already established that.

I was afraid I'd let Ole slip from my shaking fingers when I pulled him from the water, and he wasn't pleased when it took me way too long to get him dressed. Luckily Jordy was already inside, waiting for him, and I unceremoniously dropped him in her lap. With a quickly mumbled excuse about work, I hightailed it out of there. It wasn't until I was halfway around the bay that I allowed myself to think.

About the electric charge of his body right behind me.

About the deep vibrations of his voice against the shell of my ear.

About those confusing and tantalizing words he said.

Most of all, about the burn on my neck, where the heat of his lips marked me. *Holy heart failure*. I was glad he left right after or I might never have drawn my next breath.

Of course, I haven't been able to think about anything else since I got home. Those changes to the designs I was pretending to be so eager to get back to, have not been touched. The ratatouille I was planning to make with the last of the zucchini has not even been started. Instead, I've been staring out the window, not wanting to miss a single glimpse of him as long as it's from the safety of my house. *Pathetic*.

"Hey, honey." Steffie's voice is almost a surprise when she answers, I'm so used to leaving a message.

"How are ya?" I jump in, unnaturally chipper. There's no hiding my scrambled mood from Steffie because she comes right back.

"Maybe I should ask how things are with you? You sound funny." She knows me too well. "What happened?"

"Nothing much. I've been busy. Just gave the baby a bath, he'd shit all over himself. Nursing is going well. He's quite the little bruiser, feisty as all get out, but he turns to mush when you dip him in water." I'm rambling, I know it, but I can't stop myself. "Then Jared said some stuff and threw me off. Anyway, I got those edits back and need to finish the designs, so I came home. What are you up to? The kids okay?"

"Not so fast. What was that about your neighbour? What did he say to you?"

"He knows I saw him," I blurt out. "That time on the dock? When he…"

"Banging Barbie. Yes, I remember, Mia. Hard to forget," she adds sardonically.

"Right. Anyway, he overheard me telling his sister I'm not his type, and one thing led to another."

"You told her?"

"It kinda slipped," I confess guiltily. "He came inside when I was bathing the baby and told me I was wrong. And he kissed me."

I have to hold the phone away from my ear, she squeals so loud.

"Kissed you, kissed you? Like on the mouth?" Apparently this makes her happy, since I can hear the grin in her voice.

"Well, no. More like a...friendly kiss, I guess."

"Cheek?"

"My neck, actually."

"Damn, that's hot. I love the neck," she almost purrs. "And don't be an idiot," she adds sternly. "That's not a friendly kiss and you know it."

I do. That's the trouble. That kiss was far from friendly, and so were the words that followed. More of a challenge, actually, and one I'm not quite sure what to do with. I feel my resolve not to get too attached slowly melt.

No longer playing coy, because what's the use with the cat already out of the bag, I end up telling Steffie what happened verbatim. Word for stinking word, firmly lodged in my memory. I feel twelve years old, telling my best friend the boy I was crushing on looked at me. Except Jared hadn't just looked, and I wasn't aware I'd been crushing. Denial will do that to you.

"He likes you." Steffie ironically uses the exact same words Jordy said to me earlier. I denied it then—I'm no longer denying it now.

"But why?" The question flies from my mouth before I know it. It sounds needy, but I really just can't wrap my head around it.

He doesn't know me. Not really, just that I'm a little nuts, he's been witness to that a few times now, to my utter horror. I'm pretty positive I have at least a few years on him and for Christ's sake, *look at me*.

"Does he need a reason?" she fires back at me. "I mean other than the obvious: you're gorgeous, intelligent, unbelievably kind, and refreshingly earthy." I can't hold back the snort at her summation.

"You started off so well," I convey with a chuckle. "But kind and earthy? Those are adjectives usually reserved for when you're desperate to find something nice to say. Not exactly flattering."

"Depends on your point of view," she argues. "If you've always been blinded by fake and self-absorbed, earthy and kind might be the most flattering thing someone could call you." Annoyingly, as usual, my friend makes a point, but I'm not ready to concede.

"How would you even know that? The fake and self-absorbed bit, who says that applies to him?"

"Hellooo, blonde on dock?" she sneers before softening her tone. "Besides, I may have looked your hottie neighbour up. Most of the women he's pictured with are all tits and teeth—and not a real one in the bunch."

"You did what?"

"Googled him. He looked familiar, and the other day when Doug was watching the sports news, they

110

announced Jared Kesla had confirmed his retirement. He's a hockey player." I'd like to say I'm shocked, but I'm not really. I spotted enough paraphernalia around his house to know he's a sports guy, but I was thinking along the lines of a hobby rather than a career. It makes sense though, I had a hard time imagining him in any kind of corporate setting, and over the past week, there'd been some things Jordy had let slip that suddenly fit. *Jared Kesla*. His name even sounds like that of a hockey player.

"…was injured pretty bad last year, according to Doug. The rest I found on the Internet." Steffie, who hasn't stopped talking, interrupts my thoughts.

"Sorry, what was that?"

"I said that apparently he was known as a tough as nails defenseman. Pretty good too: he won the Calder Trophy, his rookie year, and was awarded the James Norris Trophy, five years ago."

"I don't even know what those mean, but I'm assuming that's good?"

"God!" Steffie blurts out, clearly exasperated. "I can't even believe you call yourself Canadian."

"Whatever," I dismiss her, having had this argument before. "Tell me about the injury?" I'm pretty sure it's his knee, since I couldn't help but notice the scars, but it's not something you just casually ask.

"Last regular game of the season, last year, he got nailed in the boards. Took out his knee. Pretty ugly too, from what Doug tells me. He says his retirement isn't really news, anyone who watched that play could see it was a career-ending injury. Especially given his age." I wince at her description before my mind focuses in on one piece of information.

"His age?" I ignore Steffie's chuckle as I'm starting to realize I know little to nothing about him. I've spent some time with Jordy, know she's on maternity leave from the advertising agency she works for. She also mentioned the guy she'd been seeing had bailed, when he found out she was pregnant, which is when big brother stepped up to the plate. I know she's thirty-six, something I overheard in the hospital, but that's about it.

"Thirty-nine, birthday coming up in September, so then he'll be in his forties as well," she teases. Okay, so he's younger like I thought, but not by that much. It makes me feel a little less...cougar-ish. "He's never been married, and from what I could find, he's got—"

"No more, honey," I cut Steffie off. It suddenly doesn't feel right, listening to her giving me whatever background she was able to dig up off Google. "I think maybe I should just wait until he wants to tell me."

"Yeah," she gently says after a pause. "That's probably a good idea."

By the time we end the call, the sun is a pretty, deep orange, low in the sky, and the lake has quieted down. I glance over the water to his house, where some lights are already on, when I spot movement on the dock. Leaning forward in one of the deck chairs, his elbows settling on his knees and his chin propped up on his hands, is Jared. His gaze unapologetically in my direction, and even though I'm pretty sure he can't see me, his eyes seem to be locked on mine.

112

Jared

I put the bottle to my lips and throw back the last sip of beer.

Funny, for someone who'd found solace in beer a little too easily in the past year, tonight is the first night, since Ole was born, that I actually craved it.

After an easy dinner, Jordy went to her bedroom to feed and announced she'd likely crash afterward. With the house quiet, I finally turned off the boring baseball game, grabbed a bottle, and parked myself in the chair at the end of the dock. It's a pretty night, the last of the sunlight disappearing at the horizon and except the occasional laughter bouncing off the water from one of the cottages on the other side, the lake is peaceful. It always amazes me that the moment the sun goes down, the ripples over the lake seem to smooth right out, leaving a mirror-like surface behind.

Not that the lake is the only thing holding my attention. The cottage, only a few hundred yards away, and its intriguing owner, catches my attention more than a few times as well. It isn't until I clearly feel eyes on me that I focus there. I don't see her, none of the lights are on yet, but somehow I know she's watching as I lean forward in my seat. Part of me is tempted to give her another show; take my already stiffening cock from my shorts and stroke myself. Knowing she's watching—knowing I have the power to turn her on—would probably have me off in a heartbeat.

Fucking hell.

It's not even completely dark out yet, and although my sister went to bed, it just seems wrong. Plus, I obviously freaked Mia out this afternoon—I whip out my cock, I'll never see her again. That would be counter-productive.

So instead, with one last look at her window, I head inside to grab another beer and try the baseball game again. I know I've fallen asleep on the couch when Ole's angry screams have me almost rolling off the cushions. Only a little disoriented, I make my way to the nursery to find him kicking furiously at his blanket. I've just picked him up when Jordy walks into the room, her hair mussed as she rubs the sleep from her eyes.

"Go back to bed, Pipsqueak. I'll clean him up and bring him to you." Uncharacteristically obedient, and without a word, she turns right back around. The baby's settled down a little now that he has my undivided attention. It helps that I'm relieving him of a heavily soaked diaper, which can't be comfortable. I've actually become quite handy at these diaper changes, and I don't even mind them that much. Gives me a chance to bond with the little guy.

I drop him off with Jordy, and tell her I'll be back to put him to bed in a bit. I manage to catch the last two innings of the game that apparently turned into something worth watching while I was asleep, since they needed extra innings. When the final out is called, I notice it is after eleven, so I shut off the TV and head back to my sister's room. She's half-asleep when I come in, but still throws me a sweet smile.

"Thanks for being there for me," she whispers over the sleeping form of her son. I bend down and kiss her forehead.

"Always," I whisper back, before carefully picking up the baby and carrying him back to his crib.

Always.

It has been that way since our parents died. We're the only family the other has.

Ole doesn't even flinch when I put him down, but still I sit down in the rocking chair for a bit to make sure. My parents would've loved having a grandchild to fawn over, and I'm sad they're not here anymore to enjoy him. Most of the time, I'd say I'm used to not having my mom and dad around, but there are some days when I really miss them. I would've loved to have been able to talk to my dad when I was told my career was over. It would've been great to have him clap me on the shoulder and tell me in his loud, boisterous voice, that it's not the end of the world. That no son of his worth his salt would hang his head in defeat. He'd been a fiercely proud man; not just of me, but my sister as well. He'd worked hard his whole life. Came to Canada from Norway, when he was just nineteen years old and could leave the foster care he grew up in. He'd put himself through school, met my mom, who was French-Canadian, and married her within months of meeting her. Dad had always dreamed of a big family, with lots of young ones running around. Probably because he never had that as a child. It makes me sad to think he missed out on this. That *they* missed out on this.

I gently kiss the baby's almost hairless head and carefully leave the room. I'm a little sad and not quite ready for bed.

My feet carry me to the sliding doors. The moon is reflecting off the water, casting a blue hue over everything. The window across the water is dark and I think about Mia. Wondering what her story is. Where her family is. Why she is living alone, a virtual hermit, with only a dog for company? Is she thinking of me?

No sooner has that thought formed, and I'm sliding the door open, stepping outside. A splash draws my attention and my eyes find the ripples on the water. To my surprise I see a head bob up. Even with her hair wet, she is familiar enough. Keeping my eyes fixed on her leisurely stroke through the water, I make my way down the dock, sitting back down in the chair I left there earlier. I don't think she's seen me, as I watch, only able to see her head and shoulders as she swims out toward the open lake. A bit irritated she'd be stupid enough to swim into the potential path of a boat, in the middle of the night, I'm about to jump in the boat and haul her ass out, when I see her turning back toward her dock. She doesn't appear to see me and when I watch her pull herself up, water sluicing down her naked body, my breath catches in my throat. Her skin looks pale in the moonlight, almost translucent. As she bends over to pick up a towel she had tossed in her kayak, her lush, ripe ass is on full display. She shakes out her hair, sending droplets flying before running the towel over it. Then she wraps it around herself and walks toward her house, not looking in my direction even once.

Moments later, I hear the sliding door open and watch as her shadow steps onto the porch.

Whatever restraint I might have felt before, is now gone. Life is too short. I keep my eyes on her as I unzip and free my cock, lifting my shirt up my torso. It feels hard and hot in my hand, and I brush the pad of my thumb over the tip where a drop already formed. I slide up my hand and roll my palm over the crown, wetting it before fisting it firmly around my shaft. My hips come up involuntarily, seeking friction, as I slide my grip firmly up and down. A low groan rumbles from my chest, as I imagine her small hand on my skin. A firm squeeze when my thumb hits the ridge and back down to the root. I scoot my hips lower in the seat, so my other hand can slip out my balls and tug them, as I feel the tingle at the base of my spine. I knew it wouldn't take much. My hand jerks faster and my mouth falls open, trying to get more air. I almost miss the soft moan bouncing over the water, but I don't miss the slight movements of her shape, since I've not removed my eyes from her since I came out.

My fist is moving at lightning speed, and I have to bite my lip to keep from yelling out when I come hard over my hand and belly. I tug off my shirt and wipe my hand and my stomach, as I watch her shadow move and disappear into the house.

The last thing I hear is the click of her door.

ELEVEN

Mia

I force my eyes open, blinking at the bright sun streaming in, and notice the banging is not part of my dream. There's someone at the door.

Scrambling out of bed, I locate my comfy, flannel PJ pants I'd kicked off in the middle of the night, and quickly tug them on. A quick glance at the clock on my nightstand stops me in my tracks. It's fucking eleven o'clock? Sleeping in for me is eight, tops. Granted, just as I watched the sun go down last night, I watched it come up early this morning as well, before finally falling into a restless sleep, but dammit, I hate sleeping the day away.

I'm out of sorts, and it doesn't even occur to me to wonder who is at the door until I yank it open, still rubbing the sleep from my eyes.

"Long night?"

If not his suggestive words, the sound of his voice is enough to send a charge through my body. Straight between my legs. I gingerly lift my hand away from my reddening face and my eyes travel up his body. I can't help it. They get caught on his crotch. That part of his anatomy I've been able to ogle from afar twice now.

But that's not even the most embarrassing part. *That* would be his clear indication he knows I was watching, and he is clearly calling me on it.

"No air conditioning," I evade, not yet able to look him in the eye, so mine are stuck straight ahead, where his V-neck T-shirt shows the hair on his chest. "Took a while for the night to cool off."

I immediately realize the mistake when he chuckles at my unintentional innuendo.

"It sure did. Didn't it?" he teases.

It fires up a hefty dose of indignant anger, since he was the one who cranked up that heat in the first place. I squint my eyes, pissed off enough to finally lift them to his face. The smug smile there only stokes the fire.

"You're an ass, you know that? A gentleman wouldn't whip his...his thing out in public."

"Thing?" he retorts, lifting an eyebrow. "You mean my cock? If I recall, there wasn't a single part of you covered when you decided to parade your naked ass in front of me. Come on now, Mia."

The heat of embarrassment wins out. I'm pretty sure I'm beet red from my hairline down to my toes. He's right; at least partially. Skinny-dipping, when the nights get too hot for me to sleep, is something I do occasionally to cool off. I didn't go down to the water in just a towel for his sake, but I can't deny the remotest possibility he might see me had occurred to me. It wasn't until I turned back to the shore that I'd noticed him sitting in that chair again—facing me. I had a choice; I could scurry back on land, cover myself quickly, and rush inside to hide, or...I could pretend I never saw him. I opted for the latter, although my body was shaking as I pulled myself out of the water, exposing myself completely. There'd been something liberating about it.

"I didn't..." I barely have the beginnings of a lame excuse out of my mouth when his hand comes up and his fingers cover my lips.

"Don't," he threatens. "Don't make excuses, don't apologize—I sure won't." He takes a step closer, making me painfully aware of the ratty old men's undershirt and PJs I'm wearing. Not to mention the state of my hair, which most mornings resembles a bird's nest, or the brutal morning breath I'm sure I'm sporting. "I knew you were there. I could feel your eyes on me earlier in the evening, too. I was tempted then, but then I saw you sliding through the water..." he trails off, shaking his head. "When I heard you come out on the porch, I knew you'd seen me out there. I liked it. I like the idea of you watching me." I push back on his chest abruptly and walk back inside, feeling completely overwhelmed and not just a little turned on.

"What do you want, Jared" I bite off over my shoulder, desperate to change the topic. I'm not surprised to see he's followed me inside. He looks even bigger, standing in my living room, looking around.

"Why are you here?" I prompt, when he bends down to scratch Griffin behind the ears. Some watchdog, he never even left his bed at the banging on the door.

I try not to appreciate the view when Jared straightens up, rubbing his hands on his legs. *He's nervous.* The realization is oddly calming.

"Actually," he starts, with a crooked smile and a casual shrug of his shoulders. "Jordy's been bugging me. She has some friends coming up from Toronto today, to meet the baby, and this morning some of my friends announced they plan to come up as well. Looks like it'll be a crowd. We'll be having some drinks, firing up the BBQ, and wanted to see if you'd like to join us."

There's so much I'm getting out of that invitation, but what stands out most is the almost reluctance in its delivery. It makes my answer easier.

"Thanks for the invite, but I have a lot of work to catch up on. I think I'll pass."

Jared nods, apparently not surprised by my answer at all and almost resigned. With a few steps, he closes the distance between us and reaches out with his hand to brush a stray curl from my face. His eyes follow the movement intimately, making me squirm a little.

"That's what I told Jordy you'd say," he says, before he completely throws me off by pressing a kiss to my forehead, and turning for the door.

It takes me a minute to register that he's being awfully presumptuous to think he knows me so well. I almost call after him that I've changed my mind, but I let him walk out without opening my mouth.

-

I hate to admit I regret that decision five hours later.

I did everything to distract myself; had a long shower, cleaned my bed linens, took the dog for a long hike, finished my edits and sent them off, and I've just turned the burner down to let the ratatouille I finally got

122

around to simmer. Unable to ignore the stifling heat of the cottage or the sounds coming from the lake, I finally step out onto my porch.

The sound of revving boats, screams of excitement and water splashing is much louder out here. People are out in full force, enjoying the water in this heat, and I have to say I'm tempted to join them. Not that I will. One glance across to my neighbour's dock cures me on the spot.

The first person I spot is Jared, in only board shorts, manning a smoking grill. There are two more guys, similarly attired, with beers in hand, hovering over his shoulder. Probably telling him how to properly cook the meat, since I've learned every man is an expert when it comes to grilling. Jordy is easy to spot, lounging on one of the chairs. She's the only one with dark hair, and something more than just a few scraps of fabric covering her body. The others? *Jesus,* they look like they came straight from a Barbie convention: tall, slim, blonde, stacked, and wearing impossibly tiny bikinis, all three of them.

Yeah…so not my style.

Even if my skin didn't crawl at the thought of being stuck in a crowd of people I don't know, I'd still rather be sitting here, in the safety of my porch, wearing my slouchy cutoffs and tank. Not a bikini kind of girl, more of a utilitarian Speedo suit person.

I quietly sip my iced tea and observe, pretending my eyes don't slide over in Jared's direction more than is probably healthy. I therefore don't miss Red Barbie getting up from a lounger, sticking her feet in what look to be colour coordinated mules—*I kid you not*—and sway her way over to the BBQ. Part of me wishes her silly heels get stuck in the deck boards, and I'm almost disappointed when she makes it to the men, without at least stumbling awkwardly.

I really, really hope she's with one of the two guys, but when she saunters up behind Jared and slips her arms around his waist, splaying her hands on his abs, it's clear who she has her claws into.

I don't allow myself to feel anything but resignation. I knew he was a player, and just because he chose to play with me a little, when there weren't any other distractions around, doesn't make him any less of one.

Without giving the scene another look, I resolutely grab my glass, my book, and head inside to check on my stew.

Jared

"Hey, handsome. How's your meat?"

I feel Tina's hands move lower on my stomach and have to fight not to stick her with my meat fork. Brian and Phil chuckle at her very obvious, and frankly, unattractively crass, come on. As I feared, she's been on my case since she got here earlier. Jordy's tried to quietly intervene on my behalf a few times, but Tina has her head

124

too far up her own ass to recognize rejection, unless it slaps her in the face. That may still happen, if she continues to put her hands on me uninvited. I've had enough.

I've kept an eye on the screened-in porch across the water, sure that at some point, Mia would take up her favoured spot. She didn't disappoint, I can feel her eyes on me now. I pushed her earlier, irritated that she suddenly played coy. She'd clearly had a rough night but was apparently more than willing to deny it had anything to do with me. Instead of taking a step back, I took it as a challenge, almost forgetting to deliver Jordy's invitation; the reason I stopped by in the first place. When Brian called this morning, announcing he wanted to come up with his wife, Sandy, she'd managed to finally convince me it would be rude not to ask Mia as well.

As I expected, it was awkward. Made even more so because I'd just accused her of being a tease, of swimming naked with the sole purpose of getting a rise out of me. Of course she did get a rise out of me, but I don't really think she went skinny-dipping on my account. Not in the middle of the night.

So it was awkward, she declined, which was no surprise, and I didn't know how to make it better, so I kissed her forehead. Her fucking forehead, when there clearly are other parts of her I would've much rather kissed. I ended up cutting my losses by leaving rather abruptly, cursing myself all the way back here. And of course Mia hid out all day.

Until now, right at the very moment this octopus of a woman has her tentacles wrapped around me.

I put down my fork and grab her firmly by the wrists, pulling her hands away from the danger zone she's approaching. I let one go and pull her aside by the other. Apparently thinking she's about to score, her now free hand immediately comes up to toy with my nipple. *Sonofabitch*, the woman is shameless. I quickly disable both her hands by pulling them behind her, grabbing them both with one hand, while forcing her at a distance by the shoulder. She still thinks I'm playing, judging by the come hither look she sends me with her eyes and the coy lick over her bottom lip.

"Ooo, I like a little play," she whispers and I repress a shiver.

Oh yeah, time to give it to her straight.

"I've tried to be polite because you're a good friend of my sister's, but seriously, Tina, this shit has to stop." I get some satisfaction from the confusion washing over her face, but I need to hammer this shit home, so I lean my face a little closer. "I've known you for years. The fact that despite your desperate attempts to get your hands down my pants—regardless of your marital status—I have not ever taken you up on your blatant offer, should tell you something. I am not, nor have I ever been, interested in you in any way other than that you are Jordy's friend, and I'm forced to tolerate you on occasion. That does not give you permission to put your hands on me. Fuck, woman, if the roles were reversed, you'd be screaming sexual harassment."

When I see tears pooling in her eyes I immediately regret my harsh words. I'm about to apologize when I see her face steel over and a tight little smirk form on her lips.

"Your loss," she hisses. "Because trust me, I can do better than washed-up, hockey *history*. I was just being compassionate, giving you one last go at something spectacular, now that your career has tanked. Call it a pity fuck." With that, she tosses her hair over her shoulder and struts into my fucking house.

"Ouch," I hear Brian's voice behind me, as I watch her slam the door shut, rattling the windows.

Ouch is right. Even though I know she meant to injure to cover her own embarrassment, I can't deny she managed to find the sorest of spots with alarming accuracy.

A woman scorned and all that.

"Had to be done," I tell him, turning back to the grill. My eyes find Jordy, whose worried gaze is lingering on the door before she turns to me. I hope my eyes convey my apology. I know she was looking forward to this afternoon, and I'd hate to spoil it with drama, but she easily shrugs her shoulders and mouths, *"Oh well."*

Dinner is a casual affair, with paper plates and Tupperware containers, and the massive amounts of food surprisingly disappear in no time. Must be the outdoor air. Afterwards, I suggest a sunset run of the lake, which Tina passes on, offering to stay with Jordy and Ole instead. I'm not arguing. Brian, Sandy, Lesley, and Phil all climb aboard, and we cruise until the sky is almost red with the last remnants of sunlight.

To my knowledge, Mia never took out her kayak or canoe for her daily paddle. By the time everyone leaves for home, and Jordy heads to bed for the night, I find myself once again on my chair at the end of the dock,

127

watching a dark cottage, waiting for any sign of movement.

There's none.

TWELVE

Mia

It's Sunday night when my phone rings.

I've stuck close to home, spending most of my day cleaning, doing my laundry in the tub, trying not to think about the fully outfitted laundry room I noticed on the other side of the lake. When that was done, I rearranged my bedroom out of boredom, since I was too restless to do any reading. I thought about going out on the lake a few times, but decided against it.

This weekend has been emotionally exhausting. First the sexual tension between Jared and me, building right across the inlet, feeling so tangible, the burn of his eyes felt like fingers stroking my skin. Knowing he had the capacity to arouse me with a few hundred yards, and a body of water separating us, left me questioning my own sanity. I barely had a chance to recover from that encounter when I let him inside my sanctuary, where his words were both a challenge and a caution, and he left me feeling out of sorts. When I finally couldn't resist a glance across the water, I watched as another woman proprietarily put her hands on him, and I couldn't watch anymore.

I don't blame him, oddly enough. I've known exactly the kind of man he is from the first time I clapped eyes on him. No, I'm more disgusted with myself. I'd been jealous; an emotion I'd opened myself up to. I let myself spin fantasies around him. Allowed myself to be lured, well outside of my comfort zone, with sexual innuendo and visual stimulation. I needed the distance to sort myself out.

Sleep last night had been no better than the night before, with my mind spinning in every direction and the temperature in my bedroom stifling. I'd ended up on the couch on the screen porch, in an attempt to catch whatever small breeze on my clammy skin. Surprisingly, there hadn't been any movement from the other side of the bay. None that I've seen.

Which is why it shocks me to see Jared's number on my screen. We'd exchanged numbers at some point, in case of an emergency and in a feeble attempt to keep some distance, I'd entered it as *neighbour* in my contacts. Like that would make him less real. I consider letting it go to voicemail, but what if something is wrong with the baby?

"Hello," I finally answer, a little out of breath.

"Mia," Jared starts, a little abruptly. "Jordy's been running a fever since last night. She doesn't want to take anything because she's nursing, but she's cold and can't stop shivering. It's still fucking thirty degrees out, and she's curled up under the covers, soaking with sweat."

I'm already sliding my feet in some flip-flops and slap my thigh to call Griffin, who's been snoozing in his bed in front of the fireplace. Still he gets to the door before I do.

"On my way. How's the baby?"

130

"He's a bit fussy, but not warm. I'll turn the outside lights on, and meet you on the path."

I tuck my phone in my back pocket, grab my flashlight, and head outside. Dusk has set in and the remaining mosquitos, hiding under the cool canopy of the trees, come out in full force, feasting on every sliver of exposed skin. Forgot to spray the damn repellent, I'll be a pincushion by the time I get there.

I'm slapping at the buzzing cloud when I see Jared approaching from the other side, doing much the same.

"Fuck, they're thick tonight," he swears as we close the distance.

"Guess you didn't spray either?" I state the obvious as we make our way toward his house.

"Didn't think," he mumbles, before turning to me. "She says it hurts when she nurses. Wants me to go get some formula. I was going to do that while you're here. If you don't mind."

"Don't do that yet. Let me have a quick look first."

He slides open the door and lets Griff and me pass before following in, quickly shutting it before the bugs get in. I head directly to Jordy's bedroom, quickly peeking inside the nursery to find Ole awake but quiet, so I leave him in his crib for now.

"Hey, honey," I greet her, when I walk in to find just her hair sticking out from under her duvet. The temperature in the room is nice and cool, but not cold.

"Hey," she croaks weakly.

"Let me have a look at you," I suggest, peeling the covers down. Poor girl is drenched, but her teeth are chattering. "Let's take this off, okay?" I pluck at her wet T-shirt and start pulling it off when I hear Ole start fussing.

"I've got him," Jared's voice comes from the doorway and seconds later can be heard over the monitor on Jordy's nightstand.

I don't need to look far; her right breast is red and swollen. Gentle palpitation with my fingers finds a hard disk under the surface of her skin, close to her breastbone.

"You have a breast infection, honey," I tell her, when she winces at my touch.

"Should we take her to the clinic?" Jared asks, walking in with Ole on his arm.

"There are some things we can try before we need to do that. First order of business is to let that little bruiser drink as much as he can manage." I smile into Ole's curious eyes as I reach out and take the baby from Jared's hands. "If you can grab two bowls, one with ice cold and one with hot water. Oh, and two washcloths, please," I instruct Jared.

"It hurts when he latches on," Jordy complains.

"I know, but what you have is likely a backed up milk duct. The more he drinks, the looser it gets. We'll do some hot-cold compresses; hot before, to soften things up, and cold after nursing, to soothe." I unwrap Ole while I'm talking, until he's only in his diaper. "Roll on your side, Jordy." I place the baby next to her on the bed, cozied up against her skin, his little mouth already searching for the nipple. When Jared walks in, I take one of the washcloths from him and wet it in the hot water, squeezing out the excess, and draping it over her breast, leaving the nipple free. "What you need to remember is that the strongest pull of his mouth is from his bottom jaw, so you want to position him with his chin in the direction of any hard spots." I grab the edge of the duvet and tuck it under the baby's legs and butt, so his head is angled down a bit and help him latch on.

"Should she be doing this if it hurts that much?" Jared says over my shoulder on hearing his sister's sharp hiss and seeing the tears rolling down her face.

"Yes," I answer resolutely when I see Ole suck deep and Jordy visibly relaxes. "Come with me," I order Jared, pulling him out of the room behind me, straight to the kitchen. "Do you have apple cider vinegar?"

"Pantry," he says, immediately moving in that direction.

"Good. And I'll need a bit of honey to if you have it. If not, syrup will do for now."

When he's set everything on the counter, he looks up at me expectantly.

"The vinegar has anti-inflammatory and antibacterial properties, so we're gonna use that to battle her fever from the inside. One tablespoon of that and half of one of honey to a cup of water. She needs to drink that three times a day and keep it up for a full two weeks. It's just like antibiotics, it won't have it's full effect unless you finish the course," I explain, as I mix the first batch under his watchful and dubious eye. "I also need you to run over to my place, take my flashlight, and grab me a green cabbage from the garden. They're still small, but will do the trick."

"You sure this is all gonna help her? Sounds more like the makings of coleslaw or something."

133

"Cold cabbage leaves will bring down the swelling," I tell him with a smile. I can see the disbelief all over his face, but I'm not worried, he'll be a believer soon enough.

"Anything else," he says with a hefty dose of sarcasm. "Cucumber? Tomato? Root of hemlock?"

I throw my head back and laugh. It's not like I've never encountered a cynic. Plenty of them. I've also never encountered one who didn't ultimately become a believer after seeing the effects of some simple home remedies. His reference to a potion, albeit jokingly, is not unusual either. Midwives were at some point in time viewed as witches, until finally common sense prevailed. Just as I'm positive Jared will come around as well.

"You'll see," I tell him, handing him my flashlight.

Jared

"She's asleep and Ole is tucked in with her."

I turn my head over the back of the couch to see Mia slowly approaching. Without a word, I pat the seat beside me, watching her come around and bend to give Griffin, who's curled up on the other side of the coffee table, a scratch. She finally sits down, kicks off her flip-flips and tucks her feet up on the couch, leaving quite a bit of distance between us.

I'd been staring blindly at reruns of *Criminal Minds*, yet listening to the soft murmurs coming from Jordy's bedroom, my thoughts on Mia. It's like watching two different people; the confident, self-assured, composed midwife, versus the skittish, insecure, withdrawn hermit. Yet both are all Mia, which makes her even more intriguing. Her kindness, empathy, passion, and intellect are clear in both sides of her. Intriguing, complex, beautiful, and fascinatingly irresistible.

"Do you want something to drink?" I ask, in an attempt to break through the fast building tension, as I watch her hands wring in her lap.

"Just water is fine," she says on a whisper.

"I can make some tea?" I offer, getting up from my seat.

"Water's fine. I should be getting home soon anyway."

"Why?" flies out of my mouth before I can check it. "I mean, what if she needs you later?" I lamely add as I fill a glass with cold water. "Besides, you haven't slept much in the heat, by your own admission. You can crash in the spare bedroom, it's nice and cool." I hand her the glass before sitting down beside her again. I watch her throat work as she swallows a sip, before she sets the glass down on the table and turns to me, folding her hands in her lap.

"Maybe I will," she says so softly, I have to watch her lips form the words.

"Come here." I watch as her eyes flash and her body goes rigid, yet she doesn't move. She also doesn't resist, when I lean over and pull her closer, arranging her so her

135

back is tucked against my side, her butt pressed against my hip, and my arm is loosely curved around her shoulder. Close but not restraining. "What do you want to watch?" I ask, pointing at the TV.

"*Criminal Minds* is fine," she says, her body still tense against mine.

It isn't until a new episode comes on that she finally relaxes into my hold. About five minutes after that, her head is on my chest and she is fast asleep. The moment I lift her up, to carry her to the spare bedroom, Griffin is on his feet, his ears up and alert as he follows me down the hallway. I've just loosely covered her with the sheets when he jumps on the bed and curls up against her back. I leave the door open a crack, and turn on the bathroom light, so she can find her way around in the middle of the night. Then I cross the hall to my bedroom, leaving that door open as well, strip off my clothes, crawl in bed, and close my eyes.

-

A creak of a floorboard wakes me up, sometime during the night. For a second I'm disoriented, until I remember Mia across the hall. I stretch out, tuck my arms behind my head, and listen to the sound of muffled voices coming from the other side of the house. Footsteps moving around, cupboards opening and closing, and the sound of the tap running in the kitchen—before it goes silent once again. A sense of craving, deep in my gut, keeps me restlessly alert

Finally, when I hear the slight shuffle of bare feet coming down my hallway, I roll out of bed. Mia jumps when I open my door all the way, whipping around with her hand pressed between her breasts.

"God, you scared me," she whispers, closing her eyes.

By the time she opens them, I've closed the distance between us. I tug her close with my hand on her hip and my other arm wrapping around the small of her back. Her eyes widen, as do her lips as I lower my head and take her mouth.

Soft, warm, and deliciously wet, with a rich flavour the brief taste of her skin a few days ago only hinted at. Her body presses closer to mine involuntarily and I release her hip, only to slide that hand up her side and around to her neck, holding her head in place as my tongue explores deeper.

She feels good. So good that if I don't release her now, I'll lose all control. Reluctantly, I pull back from her inviting mouth, leaving her with a soft press of my lips against hers. Her eyes, luminescent in the dim light of the hallway, are confused, but she doesn't say a word. She moves obediently as I lead her into her bedroom, peel back the covers to let her climb in bed, and tuck them back over her.

"Get some sleep," I tell her, leaning in to press one last kiss to her mouth before heading back to my own bed.

This time, I close my door. Not so much to keep anyone out, but more to keep myself in. Because the moment I give in to the temptation on the other side of a hall, I will lose myself.

THIRTEEN

Mia

I love this time of day.

It's early enough that the light from sun is just peeking through the treetops. Narrow beams filter through and hit the smooth surface of the lake, evaporating the fine fog rising up from the water. Some rustling a little further along the shore catches my attention, but it's just Griffin, who's poking out from the underbrush, out on his morning explorations.

I was a little disoriented when I woke up, and a lot surprised that I'd so easily fallen asleep again. That kiss. A touch, once so casual, so commonplace, had felt preciously intimate and completely revealing. The mechanics of it instinctual, despite the length of time I'd been without, yet the rush of need it evoked felt unfamiliar. There had been no thought to whether I should or shouldn't, in fact, I'm pretty sure my mind was a complete blank. I don't know where it would've ended, if not for Jared pulling back. I certainly had no sense of self-preservation in that moment. When he walked me to my bed, part of me expected him to crawl in with me. I don't think I would've stopped him. But he didn't, and this morning I can't help feeling grateful for that. It didn't feel like a rejection when he tucked me in, kissed me gently, and walked out of the room. It felt more like a promise.

The house had still been silent when I snuck outside behind Griffin, wrapped against the morning chill in the quilt off the bed. The sound of the sliding door opening behind me had me shoot a glance over my shoulder.

"Morning," Jared says from the doorway, dressed in shorts and a wrinkled shirt. It takes him a second to navigate closing the door behind him with two mugs in his hands, before he walks up to me, handing me one. "Milk and a little sugar, right?" I accept the coffee with a smile, taking a sip right away.

"Morning," I finally reply, earning a smile back as he sits down in the chair beside me. "Just what I needed."

The sound of paws on the deck announces Griffin's return. He ignores me and goes straight for Jared, shoving his big head under his hand for attention.

"Hold on, buddy," he says, putting his mug safely under his chair before giving the dog a sturdy two-handed rubdown. "How did you sleep?"

"Good," I answer immediately. "Really good, actually."

"You sound surprised."

"I am, a little," I admit. "I didn't hear the baby once. He must've slept a good stretch. I should probably go in and check." I move to get up, but Jared stops me with a hand on my arm.

"They're fine. He woke up ten minutes ago, I changed him and Jordy's feeding him now."

140

"Oh, okay," I mumble, sitting back down, trying hard to ignore the goosebumps rising on my skin from the feel of his touch. It feels nice. Even nicer when he doesn't let go, instead slides his hand down and casually tangles his fingers with mine. I glance at him from the corner of my eye, to find him staring out over the lake.

We sit like that for a while, sipping coffee and silently enjoying the lake coming to life. I'm reluctant to admit that the view from his dock is better than from my porch, and watching the sun come up together is infinitely more enjoyable than doing it alone. Even if neither of us says a word.

Just as my reservations start resurfacing about the wisdom of what is happening here, he gives my hand a squeeze before letting go.

"Another one?" he asks, getting up and indicating my now empty mug. He catches my quick glimpse at the house. "I'll check on them."

"Okay, then sure." I smile up at him, expecting him to head inside. Instead he stays put, looking down at me. "You look beautiful," he says in a low voice that has my muscles instantly turn to Jell-O. Before I can react, he puts his free hand on my armrest and leans down, pressing his mouth to mine. He opens enough to pull my bottom lip between his, stroking it lightly with his tongue before letting go.

Oh my. I'm sure my mouth is hanging open as he turns and heads inside. It isn't until I hear the door slide shut that sanity returns, and with it a panicked reach for my hair, which as usual, has matted into my customary morning bird's nest. *Shit.*

141

For someone who has gotten by the past years by carefully guarding herself and controlling her environment, I sure seem content to go with the flow; Jared's flow.

-

"I want to take a quick shower," Jordy says, swinging her legs out of bed. "I'm rank." Her nose curls up as she sniffs her nightshirt. "Nothing like the combination of sweat and sour baby milk."

"Go," I urge her with a wave of my hand. "And use the handheld to spray directly on your breasts, alternating hot and cold."

Jared had insisted on cooking breakfast, and I'd gone to check on his sister, finding her snuggling with Ole, but awake, clearly a lot better. Although still too warm, she no longer had chills and her eyes were a lot clearer.

The little one is cuddled up contently against my shoulder. I can just make out his downy cheek and softly pursed little mouth. Every so often, his suckling instinct will surface and I can hear the soft smacks as his tongue presses against his palate. I love that sound, just like I love hearing the little sighs and groans as he stretches and settles again. I become aware of a feeling I recognize from a long time ago as I carefully put Ole down in his crib, instantly missing his warm little body against me.

Longing.

There'd been a time when Blair and I had talked about having children. After 9/11 we actually started trying, having both come to the harsh conclusion that life was too short to wait for perfect moments. It had become all too obvious that for some that perfect moment might

142

never come. I'd had one miscarriage early in the pregnancy, something that took a while to recover from, emotionally. Rationally, I knew that quite often miscarriages occur because for one reason or another, the baby is simply not viable. But working with pregnancy and childbirth, being constantly exposed to it, there were times I felt resentment. Especially since I didn't succeed in getting pregnant again. Not before things started going south.

Here I am, forty-two years old, and by most standards, too old to even contemplate the possibility, but still feeling the longing for something I won't ever have.

"Pancakes!" Jared yells from the kitchen, and with a quick peek to make sure Ole is still sleeping, I walk out, leaving his door open a crack.

"Jordy should be out of the shower shortly," I tell him, sitting down at the kitchen island. He turns around from the stove with a plate in his hand, setting it down in front of me.

"Good," he says, leaning over and surprising me with a swipe of his thumb along my lips. "She was starting to smell," he adds with a chuckle, completely oblivious to the fact he just scrambled my brain again with that simple touch.

"I heard that!" Jordy bites off, sliding into the seat beside me.

I hadn't even heard her come in. I give her a quick smile, trying to gauge if she'd witnessed her brother's intimate little touch, but she gives no indication.

"It was bad," Jared pokes back. "I was afraid you were going to spoil my appetite." He teasingly pulls a strand of her hair as he sets a plate in front of her, too. She grimaces at the sight of a short stack of blueberry pancakes on her plate.

"Not sure I can handle this," she protests.

"Nonsense," he states. "You haven't eaten since Saturday."

I sit and take it all in, both entertained by and slightly in awe of the easy way these two interact. I was an only child. A surprise for my parents who, already in their late thirties, had given up hope of having children. Despite the fact I sometimes wished for a sibling, I had a wonderful childhood. They loved me to bits and I was devastated when they passed away within a year of each other, eight years ago. Mom went first from a massive stroke and Dad simply didn't wake up one morning, eight months after that. I'd been in rough shape then, and although I managed to struggle through my mother's funeral, having my father by my side, I couldn't make it through his.

Steffie had been with me, since Blair was working on a project in Beijing at the time. He wasn't able to make it back. The anxiety had been high before we even left the house, but it became unbearable when I saw only a handful of people gathered at the brief service at the funeral home. The thought I had no family left, no blood ties to another human being, was too much for my already overwhelmed emotions.

"Hey…" Jared's voice cuts through the painful memories, and I'm mortified to feel a tear trickling down my cheek. He cups my chin in his big hand and with the fingers of the other, wipes under my eye. I force a smile on my lips.

"I'm good," I lie through my teeth. "I'm starved, actually." I gently push away his hands and grab my fork, pick up a bite, and shove it in my mouth. "It's good." I nod encouragingly and give a worried-looking Jordy what I hope is a reassuring smile.

"It's really good."

Jared

Not sure what happened over breakfast. One moment Mia was smiling at the banter between Jordy and me, and the next she is somewhere else, her eyes unseeing. For a minute there, I thought she was maybe having an anxiety attack, but when I touched her face and her eyes focused on me, all I could see was intense sadness.

She tried to brush it off, and I chose not to push it at that time, but I will try to get it out of her. She looked actually relieved when Ole announced he was hungry. Urging Jordy to finish eating, she was on her feet and off to the nursery in a flash.

Both women are now holed up in Jordy's bedroom with the baby. With the kitchen clean again, I head to my office to call Brian. He didn't have a chance to go into detail when he was here, but had urged me to call him first thing Monday morning about some interesting prospects he wanted to discuss.

"Morning," I greet him when he picks up.

"So what are the chances of you flying to Miami with me, first thing tomorrow morning?" He gets to the point.

"Depends," I tell him. "What's in Miami?"

"Curt Forbes resigned on Friday, listing family reasons. It'll be announced on Wednesday."

"Assistant coach for the Panthers? No shit?" A little twitch of excitement has me shift in my chair. "They looking?"

"Management called me Saturday morning, when I was driving up there. They're looking alright. Wanted to know if you were in the market."

"How'd they know? I mean, I've only just received the final verdict on my career," I grumble, saying that out loud still smarts.

"That's why you pay me the big bucks. Been putting discrete feelers out here and there, just in case," he says, sounding smug. "They've got you on the short list and are looking to get the lay of the land from all their options before the announcement on Wednesday."

"What do you think?" I ask him, trusting his advice above anyone else's. He's been my agent for the past ten years or so, give or take, and has never steered me wrong.

"I think you should drive down tonight, crash at mine, and get on the 4:30 a.m. flight to Miami with me tomorrow. We'll see what plays out. Look," he adds. "Like I've said before, the only good decision is an informed one. I know your circumstances have changed with Jordy and the baby, and Miami would not be your first choice, but if anything, a meeting like this might be educational."

"About Jordy, she's hit a bit of a rough spot, health wise," I inform him. "I'm gonna have to see what I can do to have her covered while I'm gone."

"I'm sure Sandy would love nothing better than to get her hands on that baby," he offers his wife's services, making me chuckle.

"I'm sure, but I may be able to organize something locally. Mia, my neighbour, has been helping out a lot. Let me check with her first."

"Sounds good. I'll book the flight, you talk to…Mia?" he confirms, but I can hear the curiosity in his tone.

"Later," I cut him off, knowing he'll grill me later anyway. I can still hear him chuckle as I end the call.

Christ.

The Panthers—I'm not sure how I feel about Miami. Actually, that's not true, Miami is probably the last place I'd want to settle, but damn it feels good to be wanted anywhere.

I take a few minutes to try and settle the churning in my stomach, before I go find the girls. By the time I walk into her bedroom, Jordy is curled up on her side, fast asleep. The soft mumble of Mia's voice comes from the monitor on her bedside table, and I turn toward the nursery.

"Hey," I inadvertently repeat the last word I said to her. She's bent over Ole's crib, her head turned to watch me come up behind her.

"He just settled down," she says, as I peek over her shoulder to find my nephew sleeping with his mouth open.

"Looks like he's out for the count," I observe, taking a step back when she straightens up.

I follow her out of the nursery and into the living room, where she stops in front of the sliding doors, staring at her own place.

"I should get home."

"Stay," I whisper, brushing my hand along the side of her neck and down her shoulder. I'm close enough to feel the warmth of her body against my front. Ignoring the slight stiffening of her spine, I lean my chin on her shoulder. "Stay and talk to me." A shudder runs down her body before she turns around to face me, putting one hand in the middle of my chest. I immediately cover it with mine.

"I don't know if I can." Her voice is soft and torn.

"Try."

Taking her hand, I lead her to the couch and with a gentle tug, pull her down beside me, never letting go.

"I was remembering my parents." Her eyes are focused on our hands, where my thumb softly strokes her skin. Her words, suggesting she no longer has them, slice me. Noticing she's gone silent, perhaps struggling with her emotions, I decide to share as well.

"Our parents died in a traffic accident," I start, feeling her hand twitch in mine. "They were driving down to see friends in Rochester, when they were sideswiped by a tractor-trailer."

"I'm so sorry," she whispers, briefly lifting her eyes brimming with tears. "Mom died of a massive stroke and Dad was gone eight months later," she explains. I tuck a stray curl behind her ear and almost imperceptibly she leans her head into my touch.

"You miss them," I conclude and she nods.

"Every day."

"The other day I was thinking…" I lean back in the couch, bringing her with me so she's resting again my chest. "Other than the initial shock of not having them around, I never felt their loss quite as sharply as I do now. They would've doted on Ole."

"Be hard not to," she mumbles, her fingers toying with the buttons on my shirt. "He's adorable."

I want to ask her more. Want to know what happened to her, why she's practically shut herself off from the world, but I figure it's been emotional enough for today. I sit like that for a while, my arms keeping her anchored, each lost in our own memories, but with the comfort of the other's touch. I could stay like that all day, but eventually the need to get my life sorted takes over my thoughts.

"I have a favour to ask." Her head comes up and she looks at me questioningly. "I talked to my agent this morning; I need to head into town tonight. We have to fly to Miami tomorrow morning for a meeting. I was hoping you might be able to stay here…with Jordy, while I'm gone." I watch the surprise on her face and quickly add, "I wouldn't ask, or even go, if it wasn't important."

"Okay," she agrees easily, before tilting her head to one side. "You have an agent? I mean…Steffie mentioned you used to be a hockey player…" she mutters, a little

149

embarrassed. "I'm sorry I didn't know who you were." I bark out a laugh.

"I'm sorry," I immediately apologize when I see her wince, cupping her face in my hands. "I actually love that you don't. I'll admit, I'm so used to it, I kind of assume everybody does. It's refreshing," I reassure her with a smile, before setting her back and pulling the leg of my shorts up, to show her the surgical scars on my knee. "My career officially ended a few weeks ago when I found out my knee won't hold up. Brian, that's my agent, is helping me figure out what to do next."

"That's why you're going to Miami?" She wants to know.

"Yeah," I say hesitantly. "I don't want to leave, especially with Jordy not one-hundred-percent, but I feel better about it with you here. I can tell you more about Miami when I get back."

"It's not a hardship," she smiles. "I'm happy to stay."

"Good," I tell her, pressing a kiss to her lips. "Because it won't be a hardship for me to come home to you." I watch her face flush, thinking how true that statement is.

Coming home to Mia in my house will not be a hardship at all.

However, it does make Miami even less attractive.

FOURTEEN

Mia

"I'm just gonna run to over and grab that lasagna from my freezer," I call out over my shoulder, as I step out the door.

Jordy is doing much better today. Even said she was hungry, but didn't feel like the chicken and steak Jared has stockpiled in his freezer.

He left last night, and called briefly this morning when he arrived in Miami, to let us know he'd arrived safely. I did some laundry that was piling up, taking the opportunity to get my hands on that sparkling new washer dryer combo in his laundry room. It was hard not to be jealous when I have to resort to washing by hand at home. While I was taking care of Jordy's and the baby's, I figured I could grab Jared's laundry as well. It felt weird, going into his bedroom. Almost voyeuristic. There's that word again.

I tried not to be too curious, but I couldn't seem to help myself. The first thing that struck me was the size of his bed. It must be what they call a California King, longer than a regular one. I guess it makes sense, seeing that Jared is a tall man. A tall, *big* man. It was perfectly made, without any visible creases. Come to think of it, there was nothing in his room that seemed out of place. He clearly likes things tidy.

Catching myself gawking, I quickly looked for his laundry basket, which I found in the en suite bathroom, equally spotless. With my arms full of his laundry, I hurried out of his room.

The last time I did a man's laundry was on the rare occasion Blair asked me to take care of his. We usually did our own, something that had evolved since we each had pretty unpredictable working schedules. So sorting through Jared's things felt a bit illicit.

In between loads, Jordy and I bathed Ole, chatting easily the whole time. She really was doing much better. She mentioned how she'd enjoyed having her friends visit, although she'd seemed irritated with one named Tina. When she told me Tina was annoyingly persistent in her pursuit of Jared, I clued in quickly that she must've been the one I saw wrapped around him the other day. I tried to hide the relief, but found Jordy watching me with obvious interest anyway. I avoided any further conversation, on that subject, by getting up and clearing away the laundry. Except Jared's, that I left folded on the foot of his bed, not comfortable opening his dresser drawers.

My cottage is hot as hell. I leave the front door open and Griffin, who'd faithfully followed me around the trail, distractedly sniffed his empty bowl before heading straight back outside. I pull a few things together, crack the kitchen window facing the lake a little, to get in some fresh air, and head to my garden.

With two grocery totes filled with some dog food, a few groceries, along with the lasagna I'd frozen a few weeks ago; loaded up with some fresh veggies, I start my way back around the inlet. I'm just rounding the bay when I hear a car door slam. Looking up, I spot a man standing in front of Jared's house, beside a shiny luxury sports car, a bit out of place in the Canadian North. I'm not sure what makes me pick up the pace, but Griffin appears to sense my urgency, beginning to growl low in his throat. I keep my eyes focused on him, ignoring Griffin, who is rushing ahead. I watch him as he walks up to the door and rings the bell.

I'm almost to the end of the trail where it runs into the driveway, when I see the door opening and Jordy sticking her head out. I can't hear what she's saying but see her firmly shake her head, before closing the door on the guy. Except she doesn't get a chance to close it all the way. His hand shoots out and shoves the door back open, sending Jordy stumbling back. I'm running now, rounding the car as I watch Griffin creep closer to the man, the hackles on his back up. His raised voice can clearly be heard now.

"You can't keep me from him!" he booms. "He's mine!"

"Hey!" I yell to get his attention, and he swings around, just as I reach out to pull him away from the door. His arm comes around and hits me square in my shoulder, knocking me right on my ass.

"Mia!" I hear Jordy cry out as Griffin charges, stopping just short of the guy, but squarely in front of me. I don't know what I was thinking, charging up like the damn cavalry.

"I'm okay," I call out to her, my eyes still firmly focused on the angry looking, well-dressed man, as I scramble to my feet. "Can I help you with something?" I direct at him.

"And who the fuck are you?" he snarls back, causing Griffin to take a threatening step toward him. I quickly reach out a hand to hold my dog back. I don't want to add to an already volatile situation.

"Get out of here, Nick," Jordy answers for me, stepping outside with a phone in her hand. "I called the cops."

That elicits a snarky laugh from him, as he spreads his arms and dramatically gestures around him.

"Out here? You're in the middle of nowhere, sunshine. Besides," he adds, taking a menacing step closer to her. "I have every right to be here; that's my son you have in there."

With Griffin's collar in my hand, I pull him along as I step a little closer to Jordy, who by now has smoke coming out of her ears.

"You're delusional!" she yells. "That is *my* child! You lost any and all rights when you tried to force me into aborting him. Now you show up? Demanding to see him? Are you nuts? For your information, I was pregnant for nine months, where the fuck were you?" she says, squinting her eyes as she leans forward. "Get the fuck away from here, and stay away!"

Hoping to calm the waters before things get completely out of hand I turn to Jordy.

"Honey, go see to Ole," I tell her, giving her an encouraging nod. She looks back and forth between me and her ex before heading inside.

"*Ole*? She named my son, Ole?"

I swing back around to face him.

"Look," I start carefully. "Maybe it's better—"

"Not going anywhere," he cuts me off. "And you—whoever the hell you are—can save your fucking advice! None of your goddamn business!"

Griff starts growling again and straining against my hand. He's clearly not a fan either. With a firm yank on his collar, I pull him with me, backing into the house and quickly slamming the door shut and engaging the lock.

"Is he gone?" Jordy asks, walking into the living room with the baby on her arm.

"Nope," I tell her, letting go of Griff, who sits down in front of the door like some sentry, before I head to the sliding door, flicking the lock on that. "Windows locked?" I ask casually, after sneaking a glance at the driveway. He's still there, leaning with his back against his car, talking on a phone. It gives me an uneasy feeling.

"Should be," Jordy answers from the couch, flipping up her shirt to feed a fussy Ole.

Still, I quickly do the rounds, making sure every last one is latched.

"Did you really call the cops?" I ask, when I return to the living room.

"No," she says, her bottom lip trembling. "I thought it might scare him off. Nicholas Quarles is the passive type. Under his daddy's thumb," she snorts derisively.

155

"I'm calling them," I announce, grabbing the phone from the coffee table. "He doesn't seem so passive now, and he's not leaving."

"He's not?"

"Out there staring at the house, talking on the phone. At the very least he's trespassing, honey." I don't remind her that it's just the two of us here, and that the man was pretty angry. I can handle a bear, their behaviour is mostly predictable, but I'm out of my element with a pissed off asshole.

I briefly explain the situation to the nine-one-one dispatcher, and she assures me they have someone on the way and to stay inside. *No shit, lady*. Another glance out the window shows him pacing back and forth, still on his phone, when my eye catches the grocery totes I must've dropped in the driveway. *Well dammit*.

"Why would he show up now?" I ask, sitting back down beside Jordy.

"I'm surprised he found us at all," she says, lifting a half-sleeping Ole to her shoulder and absentmindedly patting his back. "I never saw him or spoke to him again after he bailed. There aren't many people who have this address, Jared wanted to maintain his privacy. The press went rabid after he was injured. They were constantly on his case, to where they would stalk his surgeon's office, and even the physiotherapy clinic, to try and get information on his recovery." She half-smiles at me. "Jared was kind of a big deal in the world of hockey," she says with a hint of regret. "It's been a tough year for him."

"I can understand that," I sympathize. I do get it. I may not have had a job in the limelight, but I lost something I was passionate about; something that gave my life meaning. "So how did he find you? Your ex, I mean?"

"Like I said, only a handful of people know where we are. Heck, even my friends didn't know until I invited them up here and gave them directions."

The sound of an engine outside has me shoot out of my seat and over to the window. An SUV, the familiar black and white of the OPP, the Ontario Provincial Police, comes rolling down the driveway. Jordy's ex, who apparently got into his car at some point, gets blocked in when the SUV pulls up, right behind him, leaving him nowhere to go but the lake.

"Cops are here," I tell Jordy over my shoulder, watching as the officer steps out of the vehicle, his hand resting on his sidearm as he approaches the driver's side door.

"What's he doing?" Jordy asks from behind me, Ole nursing on the other side.

"Talking," I report, when I see the car door open and Nick get out, placing his hands on the roof. I watch as the officer pats him down, before stepping back, and crossing his arms over his chest. Nick is doing the talking now, getting more agitated by the minute. The other man takes a step closer, and he immediately drops his hands, which I think is a good idea given the policeman's size.

Another OPP vehicle rolls in behind the first, and a second officer gets out to join them. I watch as the first one turns this way.

"He's coming to the door," I tell her, as I watch him bend over to pick up my grocery bags before walking up to the house. I turn away from the window to see Jordy covering herself and the baby with the receiving blanket.

"Afternoon," the officer's pleasant voice greets me when I open the door, "Are these yours?" I grab the bags from him with a smile, surreptitiously glancing over his shoulder. "He's looked after," he says, smiling at me reassuringly. "Can I come in?" He gestures past me, his eyes clearly landing on Jordy when I see them widen slightly.

"Come in," she calls out, nodding at me.

I step aside and close the door behind him.

"Sergeant John Leblanc, ma'am," he says, walking straight through to the living room.

"Have a seat," she offers, and he sits down across from her, never sparing me another glance.

-

"Do you wish to press charges?" his voice startles me. I've only half-listened to the conversation since he sat down. Instead, I've made myself busy in the kitchen.

"Sorry?"

"Ms. Kesla mentions he shoved you to the ground?"

I shoot a quick glance in her direction before answering.

"I don't think that was on purpose. I startled him and he swung around. I wasn't hurt." *Much.* I might have a bruise on my ass. LeBlanc's dark eyes squint a little as he studies me.

"You sure? My colleague has sent Mr. Quarles home, with a stern warning, but I've offered to take Ms. Kesla to file a restraining order tomorrow. I'll be able to help her

158

get one on an emergency basis, but it would help if you came along as well. Give your statement directly to the judge."

Immediately I feel the irrational panic overwhelm me: tingling in my hands and feet, itchy skin, lightheaded, shallow breathing. I grab onto the edge of the counter for stability as I start swaying on my legs, the full impact of events suddenly robbing me of air.

"Are you okay?" I hear concern in his voice, but still shrink back when he tries to touch me.

"She's fine," Jordy's voice pipes up as she walks up. "Hold him," she says to the man, before shoving Ole in his hands. If I weren't gasping for air, I'd laugh at the startled look on his face as he holds the baby like it could attack any minute. I feel Jordy's hands grab me firmly by the upper arms.

"Look at me," she snaps. "Eyes up here. In through the nose, out the mouth. Just like me."

I struggle but manage to follow her lead. It doesn't stop the urge to come out of my skin, or puke up my guts, but at least it stops me from passing out. When she sees I'm regaining control, she lets go with one hand and turns to the officer.

"You can take Mia's statement here," she announces as if I'm not even in the room. "There's no need for her to come in."

I'm about to open my mouth to object when the front door slams open and a very angry Jared comes in.

"What the hell is going on here?"

Jared

I'm exhausted.

I spent last night strategizing with Brian until close to midnight, slept until the blasted alarm woke me up a scant three and a half hours later, and walked into a meeting in Miami at ten o'clock this morning. I passed on the Panthers' offer of box seats at a Heat game and the penthouse suite at the Four Seasons. Instead, with Brian complaining all the way, I opted to head straight back home.

The meeting had been good, the offer on the table nothing to sneeze at, but understandably management had wanted an answer right away, and I wasn't ready to give one. They grudgingly gave me a week.

"You're going to turn them down, aren't you?" Brian said, as the first class flight attendant slid dinner in front of us.

"Probably," I admitted, feeling like I was letting him down. Brian just nodded and proceeded to eat his meal.

"Tell me," he asked, putting his fork down when his plate was empty. "Before your career took off, what did you use to dream of doing down the road?"

"Other than make the NHL? Coaching kids," I recall easily. I'd been fortunate with parents who supported every step I made in my career, but I'd also had some pretty awesome coaches growing up. Coaches that spent a good amount of time not only honing my hockey skills, but my personal development as well. Kept me on the straight and narrow, forcibly at times. I'd been nineteen the last time a coach plucked me off the streets of Sault St. Marie one night, after I snuck out of my billet's house, and benched my ass for five games. In the eyes of the law, I might've been an adult, but as my coach reminded me, the law didn't make the rules, the team did. I smiled at the memory. "If not for all of this," I waved my hand around the first class cabin, "I'd be coaching kids."

"Okay." Brian slipped the tray back into his armrest, when the flight attendant cleared our plates and turned in his seat to face me. "Let's talk OHL."

Turns out Brian had maintained some pretty decent connections in the Ontario Hockey League. Despite the fact none of those salaries would come close to the earning potential in the NHL—which meant Brian's percentage would take a hit as well—he didn't flinch when discussing amounts less than half of what my income might have been. The years have made him into a good friend.

I'd thanked him when I dropped him home and waved off his offer to crash there and drive home in the morning. I just wanted to get home tonight. Check how Jordy's doing, get a snuggle in with Ole—fine, and see Mia. If I had any doubts left about my decision to turn down the Panthers, I expect my need to see all three of them would've taken care of that.

What I didn't expect is OPP cars in my driveway.

I slam the car in park and ignore the officer trying to block my way into my own damn house.

"What the hell is going on here?" I roar, pushing through and seeing a very pale Mia, a perfectly fine Jordy, and my nephew in the arms of another good-sized OPP officer.

"I'm sorry, sir," the cop pipes up, having come in behind me. The one holding Ole is clearly his superior.

"Jared!" Jordy calls out, a smile on her face.

The big guy looks from my sister back to me and his face visibly relaxes.

"It's fine, Jenkins. Why don't you head back? On your way out, make sure Mr. Quarles hasn't decided to linger around somewhere after all. I'll finish up here."

I hear the door click shut behind me, but I don't take my eyes off the man, who is smiling at my sister as he hands her the baby. I don't like him.

"I'm OPP sergeant John LeBlanc, Mr. Kesla, " he says, coming at me with his hand outstretched, which I choose to ignore until Jordy walks up and stabs me with a pointy elbow.

"*Jared*," she hisses.

Grudgingly I reach out and take the man's hand, letting him know he may be big, but I'm still bigger, as I force a grin on my face and put some extra force in the handshake.

"Let me explain what's going on," *John* offers, pissing me off when he doesn't even flex his fingers when I let him go.

"One minute," I snap, turning my attention to Mia, who hasn't said a word. I walk straight up and cup her face in my hands. "You okay?" I ask, searching her eyes, that looked wild when I first walked in. They're a lot calmer now as she gives me a wavering smile.

"I'm fine now," she softly says, lifting a hand to cover one of mine.

"Okay. We'll talk after."

After a quick kiss on her forehead, I take her hand and lead her into the living room, where LeBlanc is observing us with interest, and Jordy wears a grin from ear to ear.

FIFTEEN

Jared

"I'm thirty-six years old, Jared," my sister whines. "I have a child, it's not like I need you to protect my virtue."

The argument I thought I'd settled last night, when I told Jordy there was no need for OPP sergeant LeBlanc to pick her up, since I would be taking her into Bracebridge myself, is apparently not over.

"You're my little sister, Jordy," I echo her tone. "And I don't care if you're seventy-six years old, I'll always look out for your virtue." I try to keep a straight face when I hear Mia's soft giggle.

I'd been ready to go charging out the door after LeBlanc filled me in on that son of a bitch showing up here yesterday, scaring my sister, and knocking down Mia. LeBlanc calmly informed me that although he didn't want to, he wouldn't hesitate to arrest me before I made it out the door, regardless of my reputation as 'enforcer.' So he knew who I was. I didn't like the guy, but couldn't help respect his quiet confidence and calm control of the situation. I held Mia's hand as he finished taking her statement, only letting go when he was ready to leave, and I showed him to the door.

But when he casually addressed Jordy, telling her he'd be by first thing in the morning to pick her up, my bristles went up. I pulled open the door, told him thanks but no thanks, I'd drive my sister myself, and practically slammed it in his face. Jordy did not like that. Thus started the argument. One I thought was over when she stomped down the hall to her bedroom.

I insisted Mia stay here, although she seemed to need little convincing. Even though I really wanted to crawl into bed with her, I just gave her a chaste kiss outside her bedroom door and opened my own. I looked inside, turned right back around and knocked on her door, which she opened immediately. This time, when I took her mouth, I did so thoroughly, thanking Christ for years of developing iron control. When I finally pulled back I was happy to see the slightly haunted look that had remained in her eyes all night, replaced with dazed heat.

"You did my laundry," I pointed out, and a little smile tugged at the corners of her mouth.

"It was piling up," she said with a shrug. "Besides, you have a kick-ass washer." I grinned at that; I bought top of the line appliances, and I love my industrial-sized washer.

"Can't remember the last time someone did my laundry," I confessed, before giving her mouth a brush with my thumb. "Thanks."

I'd slept like the dead after that.

I don't particularly want to leave Mia alone, but as she calmly pointed out, she lived alone and off the beaten track for more years than I have.

"I'll make sure the door stays locked," she says, patting me on the arm. "Ole and I will be fine. Besides, we have Griffin."

"If you hadn't stomped all over the perfectly good plans that were already in place, in your testosterone driven need to…" Jordy interjects and throws in a couple of dramatic 'air' quotation marks for effect. "…*protect*, I'd be on my way into town with a frickin' OPP escort."

I grab her arm as she tries to squeeze past me out of the door, swing her around and into my arms. I tuck my head down by her ear.

"I wasn't there when that cocksucker tossed you and my nephew away like yesterday's garbage. I wasn't there when he decided, for whatever fucked up reason, to stake a claim on your son. I didn't have the satisfaction of kicking his ass or planting my fist in his face, so give me this."

Jordy's arms wrap around my waist and give me a squeeze, before she leans back and looks up at me.

"Okay," she says. "I can give you this."

"Thank you." I kiss the top of her head and let her go.

She grabs her bag and scoots out of the door, tossing out in passing, "But you better not throw a fit the next time a hot guy asks me on a date."

I turn big eyes to a snickering Mia, before following my exasperating sister outside. "First of all, he is an OPP officer, not a *hot guy*—and since when is taking you to get a restraining order a date?" I call after her.

"Same difference," she fires right back, before getting in the car.

I open the driver's side door and am about to continue the argument, when I spot Mia in the doorway, laughing with her arm wrapped around her middle and her head thrown back. I can't help but smile. When her eyes land on me, she gives her head a little shake, but smiles back broadly. So I do what I do best. I protect.

"Get inside, Mia. And lock that door."

Mia

"How's my favourite patient?"

With the house quiet, and Ole still sound asleep, the silence and inactivity gives me time to think. The past weeks seem to have passed in a blur, and the changes to my comfortable routine had been pretty substantial. My boring, safe, predictable life had come off its moorings with the birth of Ole. Or perhaps it had been even earlier, when Jared moved in. Regardless, instead of spending my life securely anchored, these days I seem to be on a rudderless raft getting bounced around by rapids. I'm not going to lie, it makes me feel alive, but also terrified of being washed under.

My world, which had been small and self-contained, has grown exponentially. Before I had two people I'd regularly interacted with, because it was easier, and now there are new faces to deal with all the time. And I don't know if I'm *dealing*. To be honest, I'm afraid I may have

168

simply hooked my raft onto someone else's by way of anchor.

"Confused," I admit to Rueben, whom I called when the tumbling thoughts unleashed my anxiety.

"I see," he states calmly. "Is that why you're calling and not here?"

"Sorry?" My question is met with a long pause before he speaks.

"You *are* confused," he says, with humour in his voice. "So much so, you forgot we have an appointment this morning."

Shit. It's Tuesday and Rueben was back from holidays.

"I'm so sorry!" I blurt out. This is exactly what I mean, I never forget these appointments, they're the only thing I have on my calendar. The calendar that is on my fridge at my cottage, my sanctuary, where I've barely spent any time in recent days.

"Don't be," he chuckles. "I've been waiting for a day where you'd be too busy or too preoccupied to remember your standing appointment with me. It means you are living." My earlier anxiety flies out the window with those words, and instead I feel like I've just been given a gold star by the teacher. "Now, why don't you fill me in?"

The next half-hour I tell him everything. Well, almost everything, I'm purposely vague about the night I watched Jared on the dock, but other than that he gets it all.

"You've certainly been busy," he points out.

"I feel like I could get washed under at any moment," I confess.

"A change in tide."

"A what?"

"A change in tide," he repeats. "When you get caught in an rip current or strong tide, the best way to prevent getting pulled under is to ride it out. You can struggle against it, but you'll only exhaust yourself, and eventually drown. Just ride it out, Mia, pace yourself, but ride it out. It may get bumpy, but there is always, always calmer water on the other side."

When I finally hang up the phone, with a promise to actually come into his office next week, I feel much better. Rueben's analogy makes sense.

I don't have much time to mull it over further, when Ole, right on cue, announces himself. I quickly put the emergency bottle of breast milk, I'd shown Jordy how to pump, in hot water. Sitting on the couch, with my feet up on the coffee table and the baby's warm body snuggled in my arms, I let myself enjoy the moment. The little sounds he makes as he gets used to the bottle, the smell of baby shampoo and fresh laundry, the feel of his downy soft cheek under the pad of my finger. It occurs to me, and not for the first time, that I've really missed this.

-

"Can we talk?"

I open the door to Jared and let him in.

Over any objections, I headed to my cottage the moment he and Jordy had gotten home. There was stuff I wanted to do; laundry, a bit of cleaning, tend to my garden, and maybe take my kayak out for a spin. Groceries would've been on that list if they hadn't gone grocery shopping already, bringing home most of the basics already. I protested, but not a lot. I was trying not to fight the current, but I was pacing myself.

I had a nice day. Accomplished a bit, had a good paddle that left my shoulders a little sore, and was not at all surprised when there was a knock at my door as I was clearing away my dinner dishes.

"Do you want to sit outside?" I ask him, pointing in the direction of my porch.

"Sure," he shrugs, but I notice the teasing glint in his eyes. "Seems like a good spot to get out of the heat."

"Drink?" I offer, trying to ignore the blush I can feel creeping up my face.

"I'm good," he says before sitting down.

Strange how easily we move around each other in his house, yet here, things feel a little awkward. Maybe because he's on my turf now? It doesn't help that after that kiss in his hallway last night, he hadn't touched me again today.

"What's up?" I try for a light-hearted approach.

"First of all," he says scowling, apparently not appreciating my efforts. "I'd like to know why you're all the way over there instead of here? How am I supposed to talk with you?" I had chosen to sit down in the chair, after he picked the couch. Rather than argue, I move over to sit beside him.

"This better?" I can't hold back the hint of sarcasm in my voice.

"Much," he confirms, looking pleased with himself as he drapes his arm over the couch behind me. We sit like that, watching the last of the boaters disappear off the lake, as the sun disappears behind the trees. The shared silence is nice.

"I'm thinking of turning down Miami," he says finally, and I shift slightly to watch his profile as he stares out over the water. "They gave me a week to think, even though the official announcement they're looking for a new assistant coach was made tonight. I just watched the news conference." His eyes turn to me. "It's a good offer. Great money. Unbelievable opportunity."

"But?" I prompt, when he falls silent, searching my face.

"But it's there, and not here," he says a little cryptically before explaining, "I went a little nuts after I was injured. Wild. I was drinking too much, partying too much. Not sure what that was all about, but I was in a bad place. Then I found out my sister was pregnant and facing it alone, I smartened up. Bought this place, had them build on a separate wing for Jordy and her baby, and proceeded to work on convincing her to live out here with me."

I listen, without saying anything, but I'm affected. Instead of speaking, I reach over for the hand he has resting on his knee, flip it over, and press my palm to his, lacing our fingers.

"My life has been chaotic, to say the least. Rewarding, but chaotic. Never knowing where you'll end up, once your contract runs out. Living a life that is designed so it's easily picked up and moved elsewhere, whether it's another hotel in another city, or another apartment and a new team. I'm tired of that. Tired of constantly making sure all is organized and in its place, so I'm always prepared for everything. I just want to kick off my shoes and leave them where they drop."

"I get it," I acknowledge, and I do, I totally get it. Different situations but a similar crossroads.

"I think you might," he softly says, tugging at a curl by my ear with his free hand. "Anyway, now with Jordy's ex crawling out from the rock he lives under, it's a good reminder there is more to life than snatching up a lucrative contract. There's my family to look after. Time for me to step up to the plate."

"Sounds like you don't need to think about it, your mind's pretty much made up," I point out.

"Guess it is."

"You do realize that honourable as it is for you to 'step up to the plate' as you say, Jordy is very much a capable adult who might want someone, other than her brother, in her life eventually?" I tease him.

"Don't remind me," he groans, making me snicker.

"I won't need to," I tell him. "Your sister will make sure you don't forget."

The words have barely left my mouth when I'm lifted from my seat and pulled on his lap.

"Enough talking," he growls, before his mouth seals in my protest.

The comfortable awareness I'd been feeling suddenly flares up into a heated charge, as his tongue plunges deep between my half-open lips. A single thought of concern that my ass on his lap and my tongue tangled with his

173

might not exactly constitute 'pacing myself,' evaporates as quickly as it develops, before my body takes over. My arms come up, wrapping around his shoulders and a hand slides involuntarily into his shaggy hair. I feel like the bone-dry grass at the end of summer, lighting up at the single touch of a random spark. Flaring, all encompassing, and hungry.

"*Jesus*, I could live off the taste of you," Jared mumbles, tracing his lips along my jaw and down my neck. I wantonly tilt my head and moan softly as he accepts the invitation and sucks the soft skin in his mouth, while his hand slips under my shirt, stroking its way up to cup my breast. The callused pad of his thumb swipes over my nipple, the friction even through the fabric of my bra, enough to send a shudder through my body.

"Cold?" he asks, pulling away, clearly misinterpreting my reaction.

"No," I breathe in protest, but it's too late, he's already pulling the quilt from the back of the couch, wrapping me up. I didn't want him to stop, but I don't say anything else as he tucks me close, his breath against my cheek.

We stay like that, and watch as the moon comes up and draws a line of light over the surface of the water. The fire subdued, but not out. Simply waiting for a breeze, a touch, to bring it back to life.

SIXTEEN

Jared

I feel a little stupid, knocking on her door again the night after.

Hell, I've felt stupid since leaving her last night. Not sure what the fuck I was thinking, putting the brakes on like that. Not usually my style, taking it slow. Especially not after a prolonged drought, like this current one.

For some reason it seems important with Mia.

Last night, I had her on my lap with my hand up her shirt so fast, she didn't know what was happening. I don't want that. I want her to know *exactly* what is happening. More than that, I want her to see it coming.

I haven't seen her at all today, although Griffin came out on the dock this morning while I was having my coffee. I had an appointment in Barrie this morning with a local lawyer, Marie Blumberg. One that LeBlanc recommended yesterday, when we left the courthouse in Bracebridge. LeBlanc had been waiting for us when we arrived, and while I'm hesitant to admit it, if not for him, we likely wouldn't have walked out of there an hour later with a temporary restraining order. The judge had suggested we make sure to consult with a good family lawyer to help us sort out what, if anything, we needed to have in place, in case that asswipe gets the urge to put in a claim for custody or something ridiculous like that. I have a lawyer on retainer in Toronto, but all he does is look over contracts and such. Not much help in this case.

I almost walked right back out of the office when Marie Blumberg introduced herself. I'm not sure what I expected, but it certainly wasn't the bohemian grandmother, about five foot tall, wearing a butt ugly, floral tent and with her long grey hair in a thin braid down her back. Sure wasn't like any lawyer I'd ever encountered, but the moment she opened her mouth, I could hear her bite. A terrier. Not only that, she was sharp, to the point, and by the time I left her office with a notebook full of homework and a stiff retainer lighter, I was feeling pretty good about her.

My good mood lasted until I got home to find out Mia had been by, while I was gone. In and out, Jordy said.

"Again?" Mia says, opening the door.

"If I were a lesser man, my feelings would be hurt," I start, calling a spade a spade. "Gone for no more than half an hour and you pick that time, out of the entire day, to pop over?" I watch as her cheeks flush, and her mouth opens and closes a few times, as she's working on a comeback. Before she has a chance to formulate a response, I slip my hand around the back of her neck and pull her close. I wait for a beat until her eyes focus on mine before I close the distance, pressing a close-mouthed kiss to her lips.

"Gonna let me in?"

She steps aside to let me pass.

"So I've decided I'm shit at this," I announce, sitting down at the small dining table, watching her pull out the

176

chair across from me. "I fully intended to proceed with caution, since I really don't want to fuck up, but it's messing with my head," I confess. "You see, one minute it feels like you can't get close enough, and the next, you go out of your way to avoid me. It's denting my ego." I draw an intended snort from her.

"I'm thinking your ego is dent resistant," she finally speaks, if only to jab at me.

"Pretty much," I admit with a shrug. "But here's the thing, I like you. You're great with Ole, Jordy adores you, you're a quiet neighbour, and your dog is *da bomb*." I hide a smile when I see her eyebrow hit her hairline. "But you're also great with Ole, my sister worships you, you're the perfect neighbour, and did I mention, I really dig your dog? Do you see my dilemma?" I watch with interest when one corner of her mouth starts tugging up and the tip of her tongue pokes out. "See? That, right there; your mouth moves, and all I can think of is my next taste of those lips, and when you sit down and tuck your leg up underneath you like you do now, I can't help wonder how soft the skin is on the inside of your thigh. You're great to talk to. Smart and funny. And that hair." I shake my head as her hand instantly reaches up to check her curls. "My fingers ache to dive in there to see if I can mess it up more."

"More?" she questions me.

"Stay with me here, I was going somewhere with this."

"A point would be good." There goes that eyebrow again.

177

"You're also complicated, beautiful, and so closed off and skittish, I'm constantly worried I'll say or do the wrong thing and send you running."

She immediately lowers her eyes and stares at her restlessly moving fingers.

"Like that," I point out softly.

"I'm not running," she snaps, raising her eyes. "I'm just…thinking."

"Okay, well could you maybe do it out loud? Since I'm kind of sitting here with my guts spilled all over the table, and the exposure is killing me." I'm relieved to hear her laugh at that, her eyes lit with humour.

"I adore Jordy back. Love Ole. I enjoy being at your house, hanging out." She smirks when I growl, and quickly adds, "And I like you, too. It's a lot for me. A bit overwhelming and I want to share more. I think I owe you that, but I'm going to need a stiff drink first."

"Then let's get comfortable." I push my chair back, while trying to downplay the urge to pump my fist. "And I'll take one of those stiff drinks, too," I add over my shoulder as I make my way out on her porch.

I don't have to wait long before Mia follows me out, carrying two tumblers and what looks like half a bottle of scotch.

"This okay?" she wants to know, holding the bottle up for my inspection. A nice single malt Glenlivet.

"Perfect. You clearly like your scotch," I conclude. Mia chuckles as she pours us both a generous two fingers.

"Actually, I got it for Doug. I may have had a taste at some point, but I don't drink much."

178

Doug? I'm not a jealous man. At least I haven't been so far, but I haven't heard that name before. I overheard her mention something about her ex-husband, but I'm pretty sure she didn't call him by that name. I wait until she sits down, this time not immediately beside me, but on the other side of the couch, like she needs a little distance.

"Doug?" I can't stop myself from asking.

"Steffie's husband," she answers, observing me over the rim of her glass as she takes a sip, with a twinkle in her eye.

I hide my relief by taking a drink of my own before putting my glass down, leaning my elbows on my knees, and whispering, "Tease."

Mia

Yes, I definitely needed some liquid courage.

Sometime between yesterday and today, I'd already decided that I was going to 'ride it out' like Rueben had suggested. Last night when he'd shown up, I was toying with the idea of opening up a bit more, but my good intentions were blown to bits by just a touch of his lips. This morning, I woke up after a restless night and started doubting myself again. Ironically, for mostly similar reasons to the ones he just brought up.

I am a tease, pulling Doug's name out of a hat, but if I'm not mistaken, he's a bit jealous and that, plus the swig of alcohol, is enough to force the words from my mouth.

"I get panic attacks," I start, not really telling him anything he doesn't know yet. "Mostly when I'm in public. I'm better than I used to be, living here helps, but I still struggle when I have to go out in public. My official diagnosis is agoraphobia."

There—I jump right in and wait for some reaction from him, but he hasn't shifted uncomfortably. Hasn't even so much as blinked.

"What happened?" he gently asks instead. "I mean, I know you worked as a midwife in Toronto, so I assume this is not something that already developed in childhood. What happened?" he repeats, tilting his head slightly.

"I don't know," I answer honestly, letting my gaze wander out over the water. "One minute I was on a full subway train on my way home from the clinic, when the lights went out and the train screeched to a halt. The next thing I know, there was yelling and screaming, people piling on top of each other." I wrap my arms around my body to stop the shaking, and keep my eyes open on the lake so I remember where I am, fighting hard to keep the tendrils of panic from taking hold. I shake my head sharply when I sense Jared leaning in. I want his touch, but then I don't know if I'll be able to finish. "From what I hear, we were down there for close to six hours, but I only remember the first few minutes of it. The rest is gone. I don't remember EMTs finding me, curled up, and wedged under a couple of seats on the floor. I don't remember people stepping on me, breaking my arm. I don't even

180

remember feeling pain until they set it in the hospital I was transported to."

"*Jesus.*"

"They thought maybe I'd hit my head, that I didn't remember, but tests came back clear. I was kept overnight, in case I had a concussion, and was sent home. Three months later, I had another one in a movie theatre. Months after that again, that time in line at the grocery store. And then another one, and another one. Over the years, the attacks came more frequently. At first only when I was in crowded, enclosed spaces, but with time, it happened on almost every occasion I'd step outside my house. Then finally, about five years ago, I couldn't leave the house at all. Steffie had been carrying the load by herself for so long, I sold my half of our midwifery practice. Blair finally left. He couldn't cope, and I can't blame him."

"Christ, Mia," I hear Jared say, and I finally turn to look at him.

"Do you remember where you where August 14, 2003?" I ask him, but I don't wait for an answer. I barely notice the shift in his body. "I do—I don't think I'll ever forget."

"The blackout," he mumbles, and I suddenly notice his face has turned pale as he closes his eyes.

"Jared?"

"That day is etched in my memory." His voice is rough, as he suddenly stands up, looking down at me with pain clear in his eyes. "I was running a hockey camp for inner city kids in Cleveland when the lights flickered and then went dark in the arena. I didn't get my sister's phone call until I got back to the hotel. That semi that plowed

181

into my parents' car? He barrelled through an intersection when the traffic lights stopped working. What are the odds?"

I'm frozen on the spot when he turns and heads inside, a sick feeling in the pit of my stomach. What are the odds, indeed. A painful coincidence. One that hits me with a force of a sledgehammer. For years, I've claimed that date as my cross to bear. The day my life was irrevocably changed. Like some kind of virtual grave marker, August fourteenth was mine to mourn.

How selfish. How utterly self-involved. So mired in my own life falling down around me, as a result of that day, I never even considered any possible impact it might have had on others. I don't think I've ever felt quite this small in my life.

I'm not sure how long I've been sitting here when I hear the door slide open and Jared steps out. I thought he'd left.

"I'm sorry," I blurt immediately, when he crouches down in front of me.

"For what? It's not your fault," he gently says, swiping at the tears on my face.

"I thought you'd left."

"Nah...I just needed a minute to wrap my head around it." His fingers slide into my hair, cupping the side of my head, and I lean into his palm.

"Quite the coincidence," I find myself saying.

"Quite." Slipping his hand from my hair, he moves to sit right beside me on the couch, his arm around me, and instinctively I pull up my legs to snuggle into his side. "It amazes me sometimes how small the world really is," he says in a low voice, as his hand finds my hair again, playing with a curl. "How indelibly intertwined we all are. Invisible connections that surface under strange or extreme circumstances, and somehow seem to confirm a higher force at play. I don't necessarily believe in God, or at least not in the traditional way, but I believe there is something that links us all."

"A universe with plans," I contribute, feeling his words resonate inside me.

-

Funny—I kept expecting the soft stroke of his fingers on the tender skin of my neck and shoulder to lead to something more, but Jared seemed content just to touch me and frankly, so was I.

We talked a little, off and on. Nothing quite as deep or revealing; I guess we both were left a little raw and exposed and were happy with the comfort of the simple intimacy. Simple, but almost more profound than as if we'd been stripped naked.

Although I have to admit, lying in my bed, after he'd gently disentangled himself from me and left with a soft kiss on my lips, stripped naked sounds pretty good right about now. I close my eyes and concentrate on the touch I can still feel on my skin, the scent of him I can still detect lingering with me, and the sound of his rich, deep voice vibrating in my ears. It doesn't take much to give myself relief. Already primed by his proximity, a few lazy strokes over my clit and an almost distracted tweak of my nipple, is enough to tumble into a warm, gentle orgasm.

183

With my hand still tucked between my legs, and a heart rate that is yet to return to normal, I fall asleep, feeling a lot lighter and much less lonely than I'm used to.

SEVENTEEN

Jared

"Morning."

My sister comes shuffling into the kitchen, looking as if she's still half-asleep. Not a surprise since the sun is only just getting up.

She had been last night, when I got in. Just as she had been the night before. She hadn't asked me any questions about my whereabouts yesterday, but from the squint she's directing at me, I have a feeling I'm in for it this morning.

"Morning," I rumble back, doing my best to ignore her observant eyes.

"Rough night?" she asks, pulling down a coffee mug and grabbing for the coffee pot that just finished gurgling.

"Do me one, too?"

I have my hands full of the dough I started making in the middle of the night, after I got tired of restlessly rolling around in my bed. You'd think Jordy would've inherited the Suzy Homemaker gene in the family. My mom had been a great cook and a fabulous baker. Growing up, we never lacked for friends just 'popping' in, who mostly walked right by us and straight into the kitchen, where Mom always had something on the go. I was only seventeen when I was moved around to billet

185

families, depending on what OHL team took me on, and I missed my mom's cooking something fierce. That's when I started asking her for recipes of some of my favourite things. When I finally was drafted by the Sabres, I made sure the condo I moved into had a state-of-the-art kitchen. My teammates found it odd, preferring to eat out or order in, but I didn't give a shit. I liked cooking, and they liked eating it. Even if they gave me a hard time about it. After they died, it became a way for me to connect with Mom.

"Are you making Mom's cinnamon rolls?" Jordy says when she sets down my coffee and leans on the counter, looking at me.

"Mmmm," I grunt, trying to avoid the question I know is coming. My sister knows me too well.

"Did something happen?"

And there it is, she doesn't beat around the bush.

"Not really," I try. "I was up early and hungry."

"People who get up hungry usually make eggs. Takes all of two minutes. They don't make Mom's cinnamon rolls, which take a couple of hours beginning to end. Try again," she snaps, and this time I look at her.

"They were on my mind. I couldn't sleep. I still miss them," I tell her honestly, watching her face soften.

I'd been staring up at the ceiling, with all these thoughts tumbling through my mind, and wished I could pull up a stool in my mom's kitchen and talk to her about it. The way I used to.

Instead, I'm elbow deep in the flour I use to roll out the dough, with Jordy wrapped around my midsection, her arms squeezing tight.

"I miss them, too," she mumbles against my shirt. "Days would go by that I only thought of them fleetingly, but since Ole was born, it feels like the loss is sharper again."

She's right, it does. My parents should be here. My dad would be sitting at the end of the dock, with his fishing gear, yelling out for someone to bring him another beer, but would drop everything to hold his grandson. Mom would love caring for my sister, pampering her, and loving on that baby. That is if she wasn't in the kitchen, preparing every meal either of us ever liked.

Instead, I'm in the kitchen, like a poor surrogate, trying to find comfort in Mom's food.

"But why couldn't you sleep?"

My sister is a terrier. All she needs is a whiff of something, and she'll put her teeth in and not let go until she gets it out.

It's not my place to tell Mia's story, but the odd connection to that one point in time has been plaguing me all night.

"Grab me that bowl with the sugar mix?" I point Jordy at the mix I prepared earlier, before turning back to rolling out my dough. The bowl lands on the counter with a bang, and I look up to find her standing with her fists on her hips.

"Jared," she says, the threat clear in her tone.

"Okay," I sigh, resigned. "I'm not gonna tell you everything, because that's Mia's to share, but the day we lost Mom and Dad? It's the same day Mia's life irrevocably changed."

"The blackout?"

"Yeah. I guess it's not that strange to consider there were more people impacted in some significant way on that date, but when she told me last night, it threw me off. Been chewing on it all night," I admit, as I carefully roll the filling into the dough. "Hand me the chef's knife?" Jordy automatically reaches for the knife block and hands me what I want.

"Did she lose someone, too?" Jordy asks, as I slice the roll into thick disks, placing each in the waiting muffin tin.

"In a way," I admit, setting down the knife, and dropping the last roll in the tin, before covering it with plastic to rise one last time. "She lost herself."

Ole chose that moment to let us know he was awake and hungry, by crying so loud, we didn't need a monitor to hear him. The boy has some lungs on him.

"Drink your coffee," I tell Jordy, who is standing there, looking lost in thought. I step around her to wash my hands. "I've got him."

When I walk up to his crib, Ole immediately quiets, looking up at me with big wet eyes, his mouth already working in anticipation of food. Typical boy. I pick him up and snuggle him in the crook of my neck, where he enthusiastically starts rooting around. I rock back and forth on my feet, inhaling the soothing scent of baby soap and feel the world settle around me.

I would've been comfortable staying like that indefinitely, but my nephew has other ideas. His little legs pump for traction and his little head bobs around in search for milk, which clearly, I'm not properly equipped for. An angry cry lets me know that snuggle time is over, and I quickly lay him down on the commode to change his diaper before taking him to his mom.

With Jordy nursing Ole—something that took some time for me to get used to, but is a beautiful thing to observe—I slide the cinnamon rolls in the oven. When the smell of cinnamon and butter starts filling the air, I grab my coffee and sit down on the couch, lifting my arm around my sister's shoulder.

Through the windows, I can see the sun coming up over the water. It's promising to be another beautiful day. But when my gaze drifts over to Mia's cottage, that promise evaporates.

Mia

I slept like a baby, but I wake up like a bear.

There's a reason I don't drink. I'm a lightweight. Normally one glass of anything and I'm already happily sozzled, but last night, Doug's half bottle of scotch got annihilated between Jared and myself. I don't remember feeling drunk when I kissed him goodbye at the door near midnight, or when I rolled into bed just minutes after that. There's no doubt this morning that I was. My head is throbbing and my mouth feels like I licked the inside of an old barrel: raw and funky.

It's still early, judging by the soft light I manage to distinguish with one barely cracked eye, but Griff makes it very clear there will be no rolling over for me. He's restlessly pacing between my bed and the front door, indicating the need to relieve himself. *Wonderful.*

I tumble out of bed, fighting a wave of nausea when my second eye opens and the light hits it. Instant dizzy spell, with the accompanying surge of stomach contents, reminding me once again that drinking is evil. Normally I'd say riding a roller-coaster is top of my list of things never ever to do again, but this morning it's been eked out by the consumption of alcohol.

My feet blindly find my flip-flops and I grab my oversized, zip up hoodie from the back of the door. In the kitchen, I quickly put a fresh pod in my single cup coffee maker and jam a mug underneath, before shuffling to the front door, where Griff is much too excitedly jumping up and down.

"Please, buddy," I plead uselessly. "Have some mercy."

It clearly falls to deaf ears, because the moment I open the door, Griffin barges out, barking at the top of his lungs. I immediately cover my ears and squeeze my eyes shut against the light. This much sensory stimulation is not working for me. The fact that my dog is out there causing a ruckus is not something that has priority right now. Coffee does. It's probably a chipmunk or bunny anyway, that has his tail in a twist. I'm not too worried about my only neighbours, since as I discovered, their place is pretty much soundproof. Something that makes me more than a little envious right now.

My Advil bottle is empty, so instead I down as much water as my stomach can handle, before doctoring up my coffee. Mug in hand, I work up the courage to go see what has Griff all riled up outside; I freeze the moment my foot hits the first step down.

The first thing I notice is the white van, sitting in my driveway and clearly the object of my dog's attention, since he's jumping against the driver's side door, making a lot of noise. The second thing I notice, is the huge lens of a camera, sticking out the driver's side window, aimed in the direction of the cottage. Where I am standing in flip-flops, my favourite ratty pyjama pants, slouchy tank, and a men's XXXL hoodie, with hair that I'm sure this morning resembles a tumbleweed.

The third thing I notice, as shock seems to have frozen me on the spot, is a familiar figure charging toward the van, bellowing, "Hell, no!"

This is too much for my fragile condition this morning, and I barely manage to bend over the bushes on the side of my steps as the meagre contents of my stomach comes surging up. *Did I say wonderful?*

"Mia!" I hear Jared yell and before I embarrass myself even more, I rush inside and slam the door behind me. The loud noise makes me wince as I hurry to the bathroom.

That's where Jared finds me, maybe fifteen minutes later, still hanging over the sink, splashing cold water on my face every so often. He bends down to pick up the hoodie I dropped on the floor and tosses it in the laundry basket, before placing a hand in the middle of my back. I should probably be upset, or even mortified, that he just walked into my house and barged into my bathroom. Especially when I look like I crawled out of a hole in the ground. Instead, I just let his hand comfort me, realizing that the damage was probably done when he saw me hurl into my *Euonymus Alatus*, the burning bush I've been struggling to keep alive for five years because it turns a such a pretty vibrant red in the fall.

"I'm sorry."

"Why are you sorry?" I want to know, lifting my head to look at him in the mirror. "And who was that?"

"Get some clothes on. We'll go over to my place and I'll fill you in." He avoids answering my question, but raises another.

"Why over to your place?" I whine, I don't want to get dressed, I don't want to go back outside, and I don't want to go over to his place. Wait, the last is a lie. I do want to go home with him but not when I'm feeling like poo.

"Because that creep I just chased off might be finding his way over to my house as we speak, and Jordy is alone. Just get dressed, please?" I can't ignore the urgency in his voice and instead of wasting time arguing, I splash my face with water, one last time, before squeezing past him into my bedroom, and pulling on some clothes. I'll have to forfeit my shower, but with Jared pacing in the living room, I'm not going to push it. Maybe I can grab one after.

-

When we step outside, the van is gone from the driveway and the light is much brighter, but I can handle it. Jared had been on the phone when I walked into the living room just now and seemed to quickly sign off. All he said was, "Let's go," and ushered the dog outside.

Jordy is waiting by the door, Ole on her shoulder and looking herself like she's just rolled out of bed. It makes me feel a little bit better about my overall state.

"Was it Nick?" she asks Jared the moment we walk in.

"No," he answers curtly. "But I bet it was his doing." With that, he marches through to the kitchen and yanks open the oven.

"Took them out ten minutes ago," Jordy calls after him, as I pull a sleepy Ole in my arms for a snuggle. That's when the smell hits me—sweet warm cinnamon— and if I hadn't just appropriated the baby, chances are good my stomach would've done an encore. As it is, the warm little bundle provides enough distraction to get me over that hump.

"Have a seat." Jared walks up with a glass of water and a bottle of extra strength Tylenol.

I sit down, shift the baby onto my shoulder, so I have one hand free, and pop back the two pills he shakes in my palm. Once I've drained the water, I hand him back the glass, and wait for him to sit down across from the couch where I sit next to his sister.

"It looks like maybe your asswipe ex was served with his restraining order," he directs at Jordy. "That was a reporter from *The Sun*, here on an anonymous tip, he said. Appeared pretty pleased to find his lead pan out. He left, but I'm sure it's not for long. Put a call in to police." Then he turns to me. "Last thing I wanted was for you to get pulled into this."

193

"Pulled into what, exactly?" I want to know, although, I have a sneaking suspicion.

"Since I got injured I've kept a low profile, managed to avoid the press for the most part. This place was kept pretty much off the radar for Jordy's sake but also mine. My life is no longer public property but my own and nobody's business. A few weeks ago, Brian publicly confirmed my retirement and has been fielding more than the usual phone calls from the media since. They're looking for an interview, but my head's been elsewhere. I was hoping once things settled down here, I could do one media day in Toronto to get everyone off my back. Seems that someone decided to point the press in the right direction."

"You think it's Jordy's ex?"

"I *know* it's Nick," Jordy confirms. "He doesn't play nice when he's crossed. Plus, he never liked Jared."

"I never liked that asshole either," Jared says, making Jordy snort. "Why don't you get some clothes on before the cops gets here." He gestures toward her oversized sleep shirt. For a minute I think she's going to protest, but apparently decides to let this one pass. Shrugging her shoulders, she turns to me and plucks her son off me.

"I'm just gonna put him down." She smiles apologetically when I whimper a little at the loss of his little warm body.

"You ready for food yet?" Jared asks when she's gone. "Made my mom's cinnamon buns this morning."

"Thought that's what I smelled," I confess, gauging the state of my stomach. "Although I'm not sure I'm quite ready for that."

"I'll get you some toast and scrambled eggs then," he says, getting up from his chair. I follow him to the kitchen and hop on a stool.

"You seem intent on feeding me," I point out, finding this need of his as much endearing as it is curious.

"It's what I do," he says, pulling a carton of eggs from the fridge. "Besides, you're gonna need it."

"Why?"

"Because the guy this morning? Is only the beginning."

EIGHTEEN

Jared

"You cooked, I'll clean."

I watch as Mia takes my plate and hers to the sink and proceeds to hand-wash them. I guess I could tell her she can just drop them in the dishwasher, but I'd rather just sit here and watch her move around my kitchen. No need to speed things up.

"Perv," Jordy hisses in my ear when she walks up, dressed, thank God, and hops up on a stool beside me. I shoot her an unapologetic grin before quickly looking at Mia, but she doesn't appear to have heard her over the running tap.

What started off as a quietly reflective morning, propelled downhill fast when I noticed Griffin jumping up on a van in Mia's driveway. In hindsight, rushing out there might not have been the smartest thing to do, given that they guy was likely looking for me, but I hardly took time to think it through. I know how these guys work. I'm used to having my every move scrutinized, and perhaps, I should've cared more before. I didn't, and they ended up with plenty to write about. The bad boy image had worked for me, both on and off the ice, but not anymore. Coming here, invading my privacy, and worse, Mia's sanctuary? Yeah, that's not okay.

"Why did you call John?" Jordy interrupts my thoughts, and it takes me a second to clue in to who she's talking about. Then I follow her gaze out the window, where a black and white OPP SUV is rolling down the drive.

"Because he's local law, and I want to know what can be done to make sure shit like that doesn't happen again. That guy was trespassing, and there'll be more," I answer, getting up from my seat and walking to the door. "Besides, I think he likes you, which hopefully means he'll take this seriously." Without waiting for a response I open up for LeBlanc.

"Morning."

I step aside to let him in and note his eyes immediately searching out my sister. It takes all I have not to follow my instincts and trip him as he moves right past me to where she's perched at the kitchen island, but the shy smile on my sister's face holds me back. I don't want to see her hurt anymore, but I also don't want to hold her back from maybe finding something, or someone, that makes her happy. Right now, watching the big man bend close and talk softly to my sister, making a blush stain her cheeks, it looks like there could be something there. I guess she could do worse. Even the dog seems comfortable in his presence, he just sniffs his pant leg in passing before slumping back down by the coffee table.

By the time I've shut the door and joined them in the kitchen, Mia has already taken on the role of hostess and is sliding a steaming coffee in front of LeBlanc. She seems relaxed in his presence, too. He's taken up a position on the other side of Jordy, leaning his elbow on the counter and a foot on the rung of her stool. Very close. Very protective.

"You want another coffee?" Mia's sweet voice breaks through my observations. I turn a smile on her and nod.

"So what happened?" LeBlanc asks me, his eyes all business when they meet mine.

It doesn't take long to get him up to speed, with the help of Mia. His questions are quick and all business, except when he addresses Jordy, then his voice softens perceptibly. I wonder if I'm as obvious when I'm around Mia.

"Why the interest in you?" LeBlanc wonders out loud. "Why now, I mean?" I shrug at the question, and hesitate to answer in front of Mia, but she's already seen that part of me so it won't be a surprise. Still, I step a little closer behind her stool and rest my hand in the crook of her neck, stroking her throat with my thumb.

"I guess I've always been an interesting subject for the press." Jordy snorts and I shoot her a glare. "Especially when real news was slow."

"What he means to say is that his escapades rarely failed to rate interest. Not just from sports journalists, but also from mainstream paparazzi," Jordy adds helpfully, with a smirk on her face. "Sex and violence sells. And my brother knows how to sell both." I roll my eyes to the ceiling as the cop chuckles softly, while Mia's body noticeably tightens. I give her neck a little squeeze.

199

"I've been off the radar since my injury and they've mostly left me alone, until my agent made the announcement a few weeks ago; I definitely would not be returning to hockey. Guess that sparked up interest, since his phone's been ringing off the hook, looking for sound bites. The number of people who know I moved here is very small," I explain.

"If that's so, how was Quarles able to find you?" he wants to know. Good question. Both our eyes focus on Jordy.

"Don't look at me; I'd be the last person." She shrugs her shoulders dismissively.

"I'm sorry to interrupt," Mia, who's been rather quiet, says. "But is it possible one of your friends let it slip?" She addresses me when she asks, but she flicks a glance over at my sister before her eyes come back.

"Brian wouldn't," I point out.

"Lesley and Phil wouldn't, they hated Nick. And Tina…" Jordy's voice trails off before her eyes snap to me. "Tina," she whispers. "I never would've thought…"

"You're shitting me!" I drop my hand from Mia's neck and start pacing. "I thought she was your friend? Why…" I stop talking when Jordy hops off her stool, snatches up the phone and stabs angrily at the numbers. "Jordy," I try to get her attention, but she bats me away with her hand.

"Tina? Yeah, it's me," she says, the knuckles on the hand holding the phone turning white. Her voice sounds deceptively innocent. So far. "Why? Why would you do such a thing?" she demands to know before I'm sure Tina has even had a chance to speak. "Why what? Are you serious right now? You are the only person, who still has occasional contact with Nick. Are you telling me it wasn't you who gave him my address?—Right, like I believe that.—You know what, Tina? You're a sore loser. Like I told you many times before, Jared's not interested. But maybe you need to hear it a little clearer: he doesn't want you because he can barely stand to be in the same room with you. Besides, he already has a gorgeous, intelligent, successful woman, why the fuck would he even look at you?" She slams the phone down with a bang, wiping the hair out of her face with a jerky motion, her face red with her temper. In the background, Ole starts crying and this time it's Mia who jumps up and rushes to the nursery, while Jordy is still huffing and snorting like an angry bull.

"Remind me never to piss you off," LeBlanc remarks softly, taking his life in his hands. My sister, not one to be poked when she gets like this, swirls around and pokes her finger in his chest.

"You just did!" she yells, before turning away from him with her hands in the air. "I can't even."

I've never really known what that means; *I can't even*. What? Can't even what? Comprehend? Manage? Believe it? Whatever it is, I'm not about to ask for clarification. I value my life.

"She says it may have slipped, when she ran into him last week. Not bloody likely. She probably got her panties in a twist and called him right when she left here."

Best thing to do is to let my sister blow off steam, in my experience, so I fold my arms over my chest and only nod occasionally while she does. LeBlanc seems highly amused by the drama. Something that I hesitate to admit,

201

bodes well for him. It doesn't escape me either, that when Mia walks in and hands Ole to his mom, the guy's features soften.

"You okay?" Mia says, sidling up to me with her eyes on my face.

"Better, now that Jordy got that out of her system," I respond dryly, making Mia giggle.

Mia

Surreal. This whole situation is so far outside my frame of reference, I'm not quite sure what to do with it.

Instead of agonizing over it, I busy myself in Jared's kitchen, listening with half an ear, while the other three talk. I can't help but pay attention when Jordy starts yelling into the phone, and I shoot a quick glance at Jared when she mentions Jared already has a woman. He is looking straight at me. *Yikes*.

I'm grateful to hear Ole cry, it gives me something to do, because I'll start wearing down the granite if I wipe the counters any more.

"Hello, little man," I coo, walking into the nursery and lifting him from his crib. A quick diaper change later, I bring him to his mom. The boy is hungry.

"Okay," John Leblanc starts, his eyes still on Jordy. "Your properties start at the top of the hill, where the road splits into your respective driveways. I suggest starting with a gate. It's not going to stop everyone, but at least the cars won't be able to get down and it may deter the fainthearted. I can't afford to assign someone to you, but I can include regular patrols in the schedule. I have no idea how bad this can get, you're the better judge of that." He nods at Jared. "But I suggest maybe hiring your own security, in the short term. Until things settle down. If you need recommendations, I have a few contacts of security firms that work around here. You're not the only celebrity with a place here."

My head is spinning, listening to him talk, and I can feel anxiety rising in my body. Apparently so can Jared, because I suddenly feel his arm slip around my waist, pulling my back tight against his front.

"Set me up with your best suggestion," Jared says over my shoulder. "As soon as possible. Mia will stay here so we're easier to cover. I'm sure it'll blow over soon enough. Not like I'm that newsworthy anymore."

I freeze when I hear him simply decide for me, but I'll keep my lip zipped until John is done saying his goodbyes. My heart warms a little when I watch him bend over Jordy and rub Ole's bald head. Jordy flushes a little when he says a few words to her, still bent close. I almost laugh when I feel the protective brother growl from behind me.

"Give me twenty to get back to the office and I'll call you with details," John promises Jared.

"Sounds good," is his rather brusque response.

The moment the door closes behind him, I step out of Jared's hold and swing around.

"I will *not* stay here," I snap, my temper flaring even more when I encounter the smug grin on his face. "And I don't find this in the least amusing. I'm not some kind of hapless creature, who'll let herself be bullied around." I know the instant I see Jared's lips press in a thin line and his eyes go dark, that I've hit a nerve. Inadvertently I take a step back.

Jordy, who chuckles softly behind me, apparently finds all this very entertaining. I don't, and apparently, Jared doesn't anymore either.

"Let's get some facts straight here, shall we?" he bites off with a heavy dose of sarcasm. "You freak out when some lowlife comes to invade your carefully guarded privacy, because he's after some juicy intel on me. This after you jumped in, delivered, and cared for my sister's baby, been roughed up by her asswipe ex, and been questioned by police, and you don't think I should take some responsibility for you? You're far from a hapless creature, and you damn well know it. Just like I'm not a bully: I'm protecting my family in a situation I created," he says, slapping his hand on his chest for emphasis.

"Actually," Jordy pipes up. "Tina and Nick created it."

"Hush," he tells her, but his eyes stay on me.

"I didn't freak out," I offer meekly, my temper duly deflated, and watch Jared grab his neck and tilt his head back, his eyes rolling up to the ceiling.

"Fuck me," he groans, before turning his attention back on me.

204

"That's what you got out of that? Mia—you were blowing chunks in your plants, for Christ's sake. Tell me that's a standard reaction you have to visitors?" I struggle to hang on to my snit, but Jordy makes it really hard when the sound of her giggles follows her as she walks out of the room.

"*Euonymus.* It's a shrub, not a plant. Burning bush," I mutter defiantly, when I'm suddenly bent back in a pair of strong arms and kissed stupid. Tilted precariously backward, all I can do is grab onto Jared's wide shoulders for balance. As his tongue slips in my mouth and slides along mine, his hold keeping me steady, my arms snake their way around his neck, and my fingers tangle in his hair. Any thoughts I had disappear under the onslaught of his lips on mine, and I can't help the groan that slips out when he slowly straightens me and releases my mouth. By the time I'm set back on my feet, my lips are bruised, my legs can barely hold me, and I'm sure my brain is leaking from my ears.

"Only way to shut you up," Jared growls, giving me a little shake.

Since I appear to have misplaced the last of my facilities, and no longer have the capacity for independent thought, I guess there's only one thing to do—give in.

"Okay."

NINETEEN

Jared

"Thanks again," I call after the retreating back of the foreman of the crew, who'd been working at the head of the driveway all afternoon.

It had been surprisingly easy to get the local company, who did most of my renovations, to come and install gates on a Saturday. Money still talks, and luckily I have plenty of it.

I know we're not going to keep everyone out, but at least the gates will be a bit of a deterrent.

As promised, LeBlanc came through with his private security connections and already there was a guy stationed at the gate in his truck. His responsibility is to turn those that make it that far around, reminding them this is private property. Hopefully, it will discourage at least some.

It was sure easier dealing with the press when I didn't have the added responsibility of my sister, my nephew, and Mia. Perhaps it had been naive to think I could just phase myself out, without anyone the wiser. In a lengthy conversation with Brian this afternoon, he pointed out that trying to stay off the radar completely would only add to the curiosity. Right now, with no active hockey season to distract them, these guys are clambering for a story. Any story. When I suggested a news conference, he indicated it might be a good idea, but that it would be even better if I had some solid plans for the future to impart. He had a meeting to attend, but said he'd call me later.

I close the door after seeing the construction crew off and head to the kitchen, where Mia is already pulling stuff together for dinner. Normally the kitchen is my domain, but I don't mind sharing it, or anything else for that matter, with the woman currently occupying it.

"Hey," I warn her, as I walk up behind, slip my arm around her middle, and dip my face into her neck. I like how she doesn't stiffen up at my touch anymore. At least not when Jordy's not around, which she instantly confirms, twisting her head to look into the empty living room. Jordy went to lay down with the baby after the last feed. Told me to wake her for dinner.

After coercing her into agreeing to stay here for now, I didn't waste any time getting her to drive over to her place with me, pack up all she would need for a few nights, and get her and Griffin settled into the spare room. I figured it might be presumptuous to clear space for her in my closet. Especially with my sister keenly scrutinizing every move.

"Chicken pot pie okay?" she asks, relaxing into me.

"Sounds great. What can I do?" I ask, just as my phone starts ringing. "Hold that thought," I tell Mia, pressing a quick kiss on her shoulder before pulling my phone from my pocket.

"Brian," I answer, after checking my call display.

"Got a minute?' He doesn't waste time with platitudes.

"Sure, shoot."

"Look, I know Miami isn't it," he offers. "But I thought about what you said, about coaching kids, and I may have a lead for you. If I can set something up for this week, would you be able to make a meeting in Barrie?"

"Barrie?"

"Colts are looking for an assistant coach. Pay is shit and Dale is in there pretty solid as head coach, so there won't be much movement in that regard any time soon, but you'll be on the ice with the kids."

"Do it," I answered. "The money doesn't matter, the politics that come with being head coach is something I can do without, and on the ice with the kids is what I want. Set it up." Brian chuckles at my instant reply.

"No need to think on it? Put down some requirements of your own?" he teases.

"Fuck no. It already meets all of them; working with the young guys, minimal headache, and only an hour travel time. It's perfect." I watch as Mia regards me with growing interest.

"Do you at least have a preference for days?" Brian wants to know.

"End of the week. See if we can hammer something out on the spot with them. If that works, use the weekend to write up a press release and news conference for Monday."

"Maybe we can do it at the Colt offices, have management in attendance. Would get some welcome positive exposure for them, too. It could be a good incentive to make this happen fast," he suggests, proving once again why he's my agent. Quick thinker, master negotiator. "Any way we can do it sooner?"

"Need a few days to make sure everything here stays quiet. I won't leave my family unless I know they're looked after." I'm talking to Brian, but my eyes never leave Mia's face. She turns back to the vegetables she started chopping, but not fast enough to hide the smile tugging at the corner of her mouth. "Gotta go, my friend. I promised to help with dinner. Call me when you know more." I end the call, cutting off Brian's chuckle. The man is not stupid.

I choose not to say anything to Mia when I lightly bump her hip to stand aside and grab a knife to help her slice carrots. She stays quiet as well, our hands and shoulders occasionally brushing as we silently move alongside each other in the kitchen.

I wipe my hands as Mia slides two good-sized pot pies in the oven and hang up the towel when she turns around to face me. Jordy hasn't surfaced yet, but even if she had, it wouldn't stop me from reaching out and drawing Mia in my arms. She doesn't resist, just puts her palms flat on my chest and tilts her head back to look me in the eye.

"Forty-five minutes," she offers in a soft voice.

"Long enough to get into trouble," I tease her, watching her eyebrows lift a fraction. "But not nearly long enough for what I have in mind for you." She blows a puff of air through pursed lips and my gaze locks in on them. Not enough time to get her naked and finally get a chance to explore that mysterious, moonlit body I can't stop thinking about. But there's always time for an appetizer.

Her mouth opens in invitation the moment my lips touch hers. Every hair on my body stands to attention when her tongue tentatively tastes, sliding along mine, and becoming bolder with each stroke. I let her lead, content to be on the receiving end of this kiss, but when a small groan escapes her, my patience comes to an end.

My hand slides up between her shoulder blades, pressing her torso harder against my chest, before finding purchase in her wayward curls, tugging her head back for a better angle. I take over, exploring every corner of her mouth before sliding my lips and tongue down her chin and along her jaw. She tastes like lake air: warm, sweet, and a little salty, yet fresh with a hint of lemon or juniper. My mind instantly makes its way down her body, wondering whether her pussy would taste the same. If so, I could easily get addicted.

Most of the time going down on a woman, or even kissing her, is simply doing my part in making sure she's taken care of. Kissing Mia is something else altogether. It fills a basic need I don't think I was even aware of before the first taste I had of her.

My lips find hers again, and her fingers tighten on the small hairs at the nape of my neck, adding a little sting that's not unpleasant.

"I can just take a plate to go," Jordy's smart mouth sounds behind us. "Looks like you're ready for a different kind of dinner entirely."

Mia tries to break free of my arms, but I'm not about to let her. I turn her in my arms, holding her back tight to my front as I eye my sister, who is looking too pleased with herself, bouncing a very awake Ole on her arm. I never heard him wake up.

"Can I just remind you that any torture you subject us to, I will make sure you receive tenfold when your time comes?" I point out with a grin that only grows bigger when I see realization wash over her face.

That's right, Pipsqueak.

Mia

"So what's the difference between the NHL and the OHL?"

Both brother and sister turn to me at once, the same incredulous look on their faces.

After that…awkward moment earlier in the kitchen, Jared tugged me along to follow Jordy to the living room. I was ready to sit on the couch beside her while she fed, but Jared had other ideas. He sat down in the comfy club chair, pulling me down on his lap. Before I could protest, he started talking, letting us know that the gates were installed, security was in place, and that he was working with Brian to draw attention away from here. I was silent, all through his argument with Jordy, who felt he was being a little paranoid with all the precautions. To which Jared fired back that she should check with her OPP officer to see if he felt Jared was being overprotective.

Although both got heated, the bickering never got ugly. It was easy to see the love. And every time Jared would say something about 'his family' or 'his responsibility,' Jordy sent a telling smile my way.

It's clear from his words and his actions, he considers me part of that equation and as much as it apparently pleases Jordy, it both thrills and terrifies me equally. It feels amazing to realize he cares, but I know my baggage. Therefore, I realize all too well, the impact my limitations can have on another person. Blair couldn't hack it, and we'd been together for years. It had decimated me.

Opening myself up to Jared, to this almost idyllic family he apparently sees, has the potential of annihilating me. Yet, I can feel myself slipping further under his spell, and I do nothing to stop it. Mild as this may seem to anyone else, I feel like I'm standing on the edge of a cliff, enjoying the breathtaking views around me, and yet painfully aware of the deadly precipice, only a hair's breadth away.

I'm half-listening to their conversation during dinner, when I hear Jared mention the Colts again, and I start paying better attention. I'm not, nor have I ever been a hockey fanatic. Proof being that I had never heard of Jared Kesla before. Now I know he is a pretty big deal in the sports world. I still don't know much, though, evident from their reaction to my question.

"NHL stands for National Hockey League, and OHL stands for Ontario Hockey League. The OHL is one of the stepping-stones for kids with talent and proper coaching, to make it to the NHL," Jared patiently explains.

"Jared played for the Soo Greyhounds. Sault Ste Marie?" she adds, when I look a little lost. "Wayne Gretzky played there, too," she says proudly. Now that's a name I know well. No self-respecting Canadian doesn't know it.

"So you want to coach for these Colts? In the OHL?" I direct at Jared, who smiles back.

"It's the best of both worlds," he says with a shrug. "Showing kids the ropes, sharing what I have in experience, and at the same time staying close to home. To my family."

That word again.

He's clearly happy at the prospect, and I'm happy for him too. It's also a stark reminder how different our lives are. It doesn't feel like an obstacle as much as it does a challenge. Jared obviously knows how to ride the change in tide, he seems to adapt easily and quickly to each new twist in the road. It's something I gave up a long time ago, sticking instead to the safety of my limited world, but it's definitely something I'd like to win back.

I get up to clear our plates, making a mental note to set up an appointment with Rueben for next week, and one with the nail place next to the clinic for after. It's been over a decade since I've had a proper pedicure. Maybe Jordy will want to come with me?

The thought is both exhilarating and frightening.

-

"Where did you disappear to tonight?" Jared asks from close behind me.

Jordy went off to bed a while ago, and I'm just letting Griffin back inside, while Jared turns off lights. The only light on is from the hallway to his bedroom, and I guess mine. His body is partially blocking its reflection in the sliding door in front of me. Not that I need to see him to know he's there; my body seems to know instinctively, the energy zapping my senses.

"I was thinking," I answer, leaning my head back against his shoulder when he closes the gap between us.

"I hope it was good," he mumbles, his lips moving against the sensitive skin behind my ear.

"I think so," I sigh, quickly adding, "I hope so. I've atrophied—allowed my world to shrink—it was easier at the time, but I want to have choices again."

"Choices are good," he rumbles, skimming the pads of his fingers along my shoulder and down my arm, sending shivers up my spine.

"It'll take time," I caution, but I'm not sure if it is for his benefit or mine.

"All the time in the world, Beautiful." The gentle seduction of his touch and the soft timbre of his words have me turn around in his arms.

"Be careful with me," I whisper, wrapping my arms tight around his neck and pressing my face there.

"Is that an invitation?"

I'm surprised to hear a touch of uncertainty in his voice, and it oddly gives me a touch more confidence.

"If you want it to be."

Instead of answering me, Jared bends at the knees, folds his arms under my ass, and lifts me right off the ground. I instantly wrap my legs around his waist as he quickly carries me to his bedroom, flicking off the light as he goes. Poor Griffin gets the door slammed in his face when he tries to follow. But only moments later, I'm not thinking of Griffin.

I'm not thinking about anything much as Jared's large hands make quick work of removing every last stitch of clothing from my body. I barely have a chance to feel self-conscious when he tosses me on my back onto the large bed. I've never seen someone strip so fast, and before I have a chance to properly admire his large body, he covers me, lowering his hips between my legs.

"I want to go slow. Want to drag this out as long as I can, but right now I have to be inside you," he groans, as he slides a hand down my body and straight between my legs.

Oh, I'm ready. I'm readier for this to happen than I may ever have been. Weeks and weeks of sweet build up have me so eager, I almost rip the condom he pulls from his nightstand from his hands. I'm barely conscious of the whimpers escaping me as I watch him sit back on his heels, fists his perfectly proportioned cock, and pumps a few times, before sheathing himself.

Instead of covering me once again, he dips his head low between my legs and completely blows my world when he runs his tongue along my crease, giving my clit a flick before he climbs back up my body.

"I needed to taste you," he mumbles with his lips against mine, "I'll do better later, but I need to feel you." He effortlessly finds my opening with the tip of his cock. I'm prepared for pain, but I didn't expect the gentle rocking motion of his hips, as he carefully works his way inside me, distracting me with his lips and his hands discovering my body. I feel full, I feel stretched to the max, and more than a little emotional, but I don't feel any pain.

"You okay?" he asks softly, brushing at the tears on my cheeks. His tenderness only makes them fall harder.

"Better than okay," I assure him with a watery smile.

With his hands framing my face, his lips occasionally brushing mine, and his eyes locked on me, he slowly pulls back his hips before sliding home. Slow and steady at first, again and again, until the tension in my body is wired so high my limbs start shaking. My hips lift, desperate to feel every last inch of him, and our hips grind together on every stroke. When his movements become erratic, he slips a hand between our bodies and rolls his thumb over my clit, detonating my body.

I'm so wrapped up in my own sensations, I barely notice when his body readies for its own release. But I know when he's reached it, because his beautiful face is thrown back, exposing the solid column of his neck as he comes, my name a groan on his lips.

"You knew. Thank you," I whisper when he carefully lowers his body to rest on mine. A welcome weight that feels anything but constricting.

"I figured," he grunts, as he lifts his head and looks down on me. "And being the one to take you there? The gratitude is all mine."

I swallow hard. I'd seen him fuck. I wouldn't normally label it as such, but I realize now that was fucking.

217

What happened here, just now, that was something else entirely, and his words suggest I'm not the only one to understand the difference.

TWENTY

Jared

"Did you see it?"

It's not uncommon for Brian to forfeit a greeting when he calls, but this morning I detect anxiety in his tone that's not normally present. He has me at a loss; I have no idea what he's talking about.

Could be because my mind is still filled with the sound of Mia trying to stifle her cries in a pillow, after I made her come with my mouth, early this morning. Or the time after that, when she was pressed up against the shower wall, her moans drowned out by the water as I plunged into her from behind. It's like these weeks of restraint have ramped up my hunger for her to a point where I've become insatiable. In these past two nights, I've easily made up for my recent lack of action in that department. Still, it's not enough. I'm afraid it'll never be enough. Not with her.

The only reason I'm not still in bed with her is because I noticed her wince walking out of the shower, reminding that as much as it's been a while for me, it's literally been ages for her. So instead of letting her get dressed, I urged her to crawl back in bed while I saw about some breakfast. She didn't argue, just curled up under the sheets I covered her with.

I snatched up the phone, without checking caller ID, the moment it rang, not wanting to wake anyone. It takes me a minute to process who's talking, and another to try and clue in to what he's saying.

"See what?" I finally manage.

"The spread in *The Sun*. Page twenty-three. The entertainment section."

I'm already walking toward the office before his words are out. *Fucking journalists*. Although, in all honesty, the asshole from *The Sun* can hardly be called a journalist. More like paparazzi, lying in wait for a juicy tidbit he can exploit for maximum sales. It's not the first time he's done it.

"How bad?" I ask as I boot up my computer.

"For you? Mild. Although being relegated to the entertainment section instead of sports might be considered a direct hit. For your neighbour? Let's just say it didn't take him long to dig up dirt."

His words burn sour in my stomach as I pull up the paper's website and flip to page twenty-three. Bile crawls up my throat when I see the headline and the collection of images the dirt bag managed to get. *Fallen Hockey Hero Hideout*.

Right below is a grainy picture of Mia's porch, taken at night. It shows the barely recognizable image of me holding Mia on the couch. We're set mostly in shadow, just backlit with the lights from inside. Despite the poor quality, the caption makes it clear who is depicted, including Mia's full name. It appears that prick had been busy before he showed up in her driveway.

There's one of Mia in front of her cottage, her arms wrapped around her middle and shock on her face, with the caption *Slumming it.* And one last one of me opening the front door, shooting an angry glare back at the photographer. No caption on that one, just an insulting piece with a small thumbnail image from a gala event I attended two years ago, with Trinity Hall. At the time, the rumour mill was buzzing about my supposed involvement with the insufferably annoying model. It had been played up like some version of Beauty and the Beast. But that one date had been the total sum of our perceived relationship. One night of listening to that woman had been enough.

Now this guy, Taylor Torrence, is dragging that up again, but putting a new spin on it. What the fuck kind of name is Taylor Torrence anyway? Sounds like a sleazy character in a bad daytime soap. The small caption below the gala image reads: *From Beauty To Beast?* The story they spin is one that makes my blood boil. Boasting sources who reveal Mia Thompson as a local woman, whose mental problems have forced her into seclusion.

"Sue them," I bark at Brian. "I don't care what the cost. I want the newspaper sued for slander, and I want to know who's been talking to that scumbag."

"Easy, my friend. The newspaper is one thing, but before you start ripping up the locals for talking, let's look into it. It may have been an innocent remark twisted out of context. We know that's been done before." As always, Brian manages to keep his head when I'm losing mine.

"What the hell?" Mia's voice sounds from the doorway behind me, and I immediately slap my laptop shut.

"Is that her?" Brian wants to know.

"Yup. Gotta go," I say, as I turn to find a pale-faced Mia, with her arms once again wrapped around her middle. "Get legal on this."

"Done. Go do some damage control," he suggests before he ends the call.

"Come here." I toss the phone on my desk and hold out my hand to Mia. "Beautiful, come here," I repeat gently.

"What's going on?" she demands with more fire in her voice than in her body language.

When she doesn't make a move toward me, I lean forward, grab her arm, and pull her between my legs. My hands on her hips hold her in place.

"I'm sorry," I start. "I guess the asshole from your driveway didn't give up, as I kindly suggested. Looks like he was busy. He posted a bullshit article with some pictures of you. Of us."

"I want to see," she says, her hands reaching for my laptop.

"Mia, it's bullshit. I'm taking care of it." I try to stop her, but she already has the screen open. I can hardly wrestle the computer away from her, so instead I twist my seat around to where I can pull her down on my lap as she reads.

I don't have to see what she's reading. I can feel it in the way her body responds. By the time she reaches the end of the ridiculous piece of garbage, she's shaking. To my relief she doesn't bolt, but instead leans her weight back against me. I slip my arms around her waist, covering her own.

"I'm sorry," I repeat, to which she gives her head a sharp shake.

"It's okay," she says, her voice a little wobbly, and I worry she's crying. I can only see the side of her face, but it's turned away from me. I follow her gaze out the window, where her cottage is visible on the other side of the water. "I have nothing to hide. Not anymore." The wistful tone of her voice cuts me.

"My lawyers will get them to retract the story. It's all bullshit," I enforce, giving her body a squeeze.

"Not all," she says so softly, I can barely hear her.

"Mia..."

She doesn't let me finish; with sure movements she pushes off my lap and turns to face me, a high blush on her cheeks and red-rimmed eyes, but no tears, just an unfamiliar firm line to her mouth.

"It doesn't matter," she dismisses firmly. "You mentioned something about breakfast?"

Not wanting to push things when she looks like she's hanging on by sheer willpower, I stand up, reach for her hand, and lead her out of the office.

"Bacon and eggs okay?" I ask over my shoulder.

"As long as it comes with coffee, it's perfect," she answers, unnaturally bright.

223

Mia

"Did you see this?"

I've just struggled to down a perfectly good breakfast but feel it surging back up at Jordy's shrill question. She slams a tablet down on the kitchen counter, in front of her brother, and plants her fists on her hips.

"We saw," he says, throwing a quick glance my way before turning back to her. "Brian's on it."

We'd consumed breakfast in silence. Every time he started saying something, I stopped him. More than anything I want to run to my place and hole up inside until I can process this, which is my usual modus operandi, but it's clear after yesterday's events and this morning's discovery, I'm better off here. Doesn't make it any easier. When you spend years, basically on your own, you start living inside your mind. You have discussions with yourself, even arguments, and you process shit at your own pace. Of course, I've had Rueben to drag me out of my head, but it's still a place where I'm most comfortable. Especially when my emotions are firing off all over the place—like now.

God, I already felt raw after the past few nights with Jared, and I don't just mean physically. I care. I'm also terrified, unsure, excited, and a whole lot turned on, but most of all I actually care. For the past two days, in this joint seclusion, the world has been kept at large, our only

224

concern the people inside these walls. The nights felt like a vacuum, where Jared and I were each other's single focus. Nothing breached that bubble. I had no reason to doubt what was happening, what he was saying and making me feel. I *was* beautiful and special. Right up to where he tucked me back in with a kiss this morning, leaving me to snooze in his soft bed, the tender reminders of his touch putting a smile on my lips.

Reality can be brutal. And it hit me with the force of a Mack truck when I saw those images on his computer. Those words, my God. So crushing and painful. But the truth often is.

I'm surprised I haven't had a panic attack yet. If there was ever a good reason, I believe this might constitute one. Although the familiar tingles in my arms and legs were there, they never progressed, just petered out when Jared wrapped my body against his. Even now—trying not to listen to the heated communication between siblings, the glaring evidence of my shortcomings staring up at me from Jordy's tablet—there is no shortness of breath, just a deep sad feeling of loss.

When the baby starts crying, I'm the one who gets up, the other two still talking.

Ole stops complaining the moment I pick him up from his crib. He spit up a little, which probably means Jordy fed him not too long ago. Instead of cleaning him on his change table, I take him, and his towel, straight to the bathroom. He likes his baths and as soon as his little ass hits the warm water in the sink, any strain left on his little face smoothes right out. I love the silence, only broken by the occasional little splash as his hand hits the water. It gives me the mental space I need to sort things out.

It bothers me that Jared keeps apologizing. It's like he expects me to blame him for having my privacy invaded. I don't. I can't even imagine what it's like to live under the kind of constant scrutiny he's been exposed to most his life, but this at least gives me a better idea. I know he feels responsible somehow, for the ugly things that guy writes about me, but he's not. What would it say about me? He has shown to accept me, including the storage facility of mental baggage I drag along, so how hypocritical would it be of me not to accept him, and all that comes with him? Being a victim to public scrutiny is no different than being a victim to stress induced public fear.

I'm not blind. I can see the gorgeous woman in one of the pictures may look like a more appropriate match for him, but it's clearly not what he wants right now. Who am I to question that?

"How's he doing?" Jordy asks, when I carry him back into the nursery, where she is rocking in the chair.

"He's good. Aren't you, little bruiser?" His tiny body stirs in my hands at the sound of his mother's voice, and I make quick work of getting him dressed and in her arms.

"And how are you?"

My gaze lifts from where Ole is greedily latching on, to Jordy's concerned eyes.

"I'm okay," I tell her with a shrug. "A bit shaken up, I'm not gonna lie, but I'll be okay."

"This is the part he's always hated, you know?" Jordy says softly, lowering her eyes to her son. "Living in a fishbowl, every move you make seen, noted, and recorded. These last months here, he has been so much more relaxed than I can ever remember him being since his career took off. I've certainly never seen him look at anyone else the way he looks at you. It's killing him, that this has touched you."

"I know," I assure her.

"He's going to pull back. I know he is," she says with tears in her voice. "Men are so stupid. He'll tell himself it's the logical thing to do; push you away so this kind of thing won't affect you." I keep the chuckle I feel bubbling up inside. I tried doing that with him and failed miserably. And so will he.

"I won't let him." My voice is firm as I lean over and give her arm a squeeze.

Then I get up and walk out of the room, down the hall, and right through to the kitchen where Jared is standing at the sink. He turns when he hears me and barely has a chance to open his arms before I walk straight into them.

TWENTY-ONE

Jared

Damn, she's stubborn.

I tried hard to give her some distance. Some room to pull back. This situation can't be easy for her, for someone who needs their solitude to feel safe and at least until it's all sorted, it's better to cool things down.

Most of yesterday I stayed in my office, on the phone with Brian and legal, occasionally giving LeBlanc updates. I'd walked up to the new gate to check in with the security guy and took Griffin for a long hike, all in an effort to stay out of her way.

The responsibility is weighing on me. This kind of scrutiny by the press was just annoying before, but now that I have not only my sister and nephew to worry about, but also Mia, it's damn near overwhelming.

Last night I even urged her to get some rest, virtually shoved her into the spare room, but ten minutes later my bedroom door opened, and she crawled right under the covers with me, without saying a word. Every time I create some space between us, she's right there, making it impossible for me stay away.

I woke up early this morning, carefully untangled myself from her limbs and snuck out. Taking a coffee out on the deck to watch the sun come up. It's peaceful.

Griffin, who followed me out, is occasionally visible as he forages along the shore. He's the first to notice, as I watch his head come up from where it was stuck in the underbrush, and with his ears sharp looks in the direction of the house. Then I hear the sliding door shut and the soft fall of footsteps coming toward me.

Stubborn.

"We need to talk," Mia says before I have a chance to turn around. She walks into my field of vision, carrying a coffee of her own, and pulls the second lounger closer.

"Okay," I say carefully, half convinced this is where she's going to let me down easy, so I brace.

"I need to go into town today," she announces instead, her gaze focused on the water.

"What? No way," I blurt out immediately. She turns her head and with a small smile on her lips, pulls one eyebrow high.

"I can't miss my appointment with Rueben, my therapist," she reminds me. "There's a lot to cover with him."

Right. Of course there is. Mia's life has been rocked on its moorings and pretty much all of it's been my doing.

I drop my head in my hands and stare at the dock between my feet.

"I'm sorry…" A sharp sting on the back of my head, where Mia cuffs me, has me choke down the rest of my words and when I look at her, she looks angry.

"I wish you would stop that," she says sternly, before softening. "I know what you're doing, and I get it, but I'm not going to let you. Look…" She leans forward and takes one of my hands between hers. "Tell me honestly; has that article changed anything for you? When it comes to me, I mean?"

"Fuck no," I immediately answer, lifting my other hand to her face. "No." She smiles and leans her face into my palm.

"Have you ever let public opinion or gossip dictate to you?"

"Absolutely not," I inform her honestly.

"Then why are you now? Why, between yesterday when you left me satisfied in bed, and now, have you worked so hard at pushing me away?" I can hear the vulnerability in her voice and I hate that I put it there.

"I'm trying to protect you," I tell her, realizing how feeble that sounds. "I never cared enough," I explain. "But I care now."

"Just so you know," she says with a smile. "I appreciate you wanting to protect me. But what exactly are you protecting me from? Nothing in that article is technically untrue, and now that it's already out there, what's left to worry about? Unless it changes things for you, of course."

My answer to that is to pull her from her chair on my lap, letting her know with my kiss how I feel.

"You're amazing," I rumble in her hair when we finally pull apart.

"I'm really not," she says pensively. "I'm no more or no less than what you know of me." She barks out a laugh. "Or anyone who read that article," she adds with a grin before turning serious again. "I'm a mess. I'm struggling, but I've never felt such a strong urge to get better. You see…" She turns in my lap, straddles me and slips her arms around my neck. "I never cared enough either, but like you, I do now. Which is exactly why I can't skip seeing Rueben. I've let fear keep me frozen for too long, and I can't go back to that. Not after feeling the warmth of the sun on my skin again."

-

"Perfect," Jordy says later, when I tell her I'm driving Mia to town. It was my only stipulation and one she gratefully accepted. "I can pop into clinic at the hospital with Ole. It's about time for our six week check in."

"Sounds good to me," Mia says with a smile. "I'm curious to see how much that hungry little monster has grown. He's already up a size from his newborn clothes."

"I know, right?" Jordy pipes back, the two of them disappearing in a baby discussion I have no interest in.

"Come on, Ole," I tell my nephew, as I take him from his mother's hands. "Let the girls talk, us men have better things to do." I ignore the grunts of protest from my sister and wink at Mia as I take the baby outside. Time to do some bonding.

Thirty minutes later, the little guy is asleep in his baby seat beside me, under the cover of the large umbrella, and I toss my bobber back in the water with a fresh worm.

"You're missing all the fun," I say softly, rocking his seat with my foot when he starts to fuss a little. "We've caught a few nice sized rock bass, but you're sleeping through it."

"Don't you get worm guts on my baby!" Jordy calls out, as she hurries down the dock to where the boy and I are fishing. "What are you thinking?" She immediately fusses over Ole, wiping his face and hands furiously with the wet wipes she carried out. Poor Ole starts crying immediately. "See what you did?" she accuses me, snatches up the baby, and marches back inside. I'm left gaping after her.

"What I did?" I finally yell back indignantly, but only Mia, who just managed to step out of Jordy's way, hears me. The slight by my sister is instantly forgotten when Mia throws her head back and the sound of her laughter bounces like a warm melody off the water around me.

"You took your nephew fishing?"

It's a rhetorical question, and I don't bother answering as I watch her walk closer, a smile still on her face. I drop my rod on the deck and reach for her hand, which she quickly pulls back.

"Are you getting worm guts on me?" she teases, a glint in her eyes. I manage to snag her fingers and tangle them with mine.

"It's a rite of passage," I explain.

"Worm guts?"

"No, fishing with the boy. I remember Dad taking me fishing. Those are some of my best memories."

I lean back when Mia steps between my knees, her free hand running through my hair, before she leans down and presses a sweet kiss on my mouth.

"That's sweet," she mumbles against my lips and then straightens up. "You do realize Ole is much too young to remember, right?"

"Of course," I answer matter-of-factly. "But I'm not—I'll remember."

-

"I'm sorry," Jordy says beside me. "I thought it was just going to be a quick in and out. I had no idea it would be this busy.

I look around me at the waiting room. Every chair is taken, and had been for most of the hour we've been here. The girl at the desk had apologized a while ago, explaining that Dr. Winters was called away for an emergency. I've been trying to avoid making eye contact after the first few curious glances our way. Mostly the men, who may have recognized me.

"You had no way of knowing," I reassure her. "But I am a little concerned about Mia. She said her session would be about an hour, so she should be done by now."

I'd dropped Mia off at Rueben's office before taking Jordy and Ole to the clinic at the hospital, expecting to be done there soon enough to pick Mia back up. Jake, the guard at our new gate, told us he'd turned back a few cars earlier, and I'd kept my eyes peeled the entire way into town. Even though I never saw anyone, doesn't mean they weren't there. Which is why I'm getting a little restless hanging around the hospital when Mia could be out there alone.

234

"Go," Jordy says. "I don't know how long it'll be, but since I'm already here, I might as well get this over with. Go find Mia, grab a bite with her, and don't forget to bring me something back. I'll be fine. It's her you should be worried about."

"Love you," I tell her, something I don't do enough, and bend down to kiss her head. She knows I'm feeling torn. "Look after my boy," I add, giving Ole a kiss for good measure and earning a snort from Jordy. "Won't be long."

I step around one guy, who came in with a pregnant woman earlier, and has been ogling us the entire time from his perch against the doorway.

"Hey, are you Kesla?" he calls after me, and I turn around, debating whether to lie or be straight. May as well work it in my favour.

"Yeah," I answer casually. "I'd love to chat, but I've gotta run an errand. Do me a favour? While you're here, keep an eye on my family?" I watch as his eyes slide over to where Jordy is sitting, before looking back at me, his chest puffing up noticeably.

"Sure thing."

"Great, thanks, man, I won't be long."

Mia

"Well now," Rueben says on a grin, when I finish telling him all that's happened in the past few weeks. "When you decide to step outside of your walls, you *really* step out, don't you?"

I wince at his amused reference to the revealing exposé in The Sun. He notices and immediately straightens his face.

"Wasn't exactly how I wanted to be reintroduced to the world."

"I'm sure," he commiserates more appropriately. "Still, you appear to be unexpectedly composed, considering," he observes.

"I wasn't. At first," I add quickly. "But Jared's done everything he can to keep our sanctuary just that—a sanctuary. And he is working on a plan to divert press interest to other aspects of his life." It doesn't feel appropriate to discuss the details of Jared's plans, even with Rueben, although I have no doubt he would respect the confidentiality. It's just not mine to tell.

"You being one of those 'other aspects' you speak of?" I'm not sure whether that's a question or a conclusion, so I choose just to lift my shoulders. "I also note you talk about 'our' sanctuary instead of yours. Things have changed," he notes. "Your perception of the world is changing."

"Maybe it is," I concur. "These past weeks, and especially the past few days, it's like the blinders I was wearing have fallen off. I'm learning there are more ways the blackout and the aftermath have affected not just me, but others as well. Did I mention his parents died August fourteenth as a direct result?" Rueben nods his

236

acknowledgement. "It shamed me, to be honest, to see how well he and his sister have evolved from that point, and how little headway I've made." Rueben opens his mouth but I silence him with my hand. "I know the experience was not the same, but both were traumatic, and yet they never stopped moving forward, however I've allowed myself to become lodged there. I'm tired of it. I'm terrified, but I don't want those blinders back. Everything was the same colour while I was wearing them and now—shit, now everything is so much more vivid. Unpredictable, clearly, but I'm finding out there's an odd purpose to everything that happens, a beautiful release when you allow yourself to react, process, and move on. I don't think I got that before," I admit.

"I never doubted you'd find your way back to the living eventually," Rueben says. "But still I'm surprised how dramatic the change in you is. I wouldn't be doing my job if I didn't caution you, though," he adds in a more serious tone. "This is not a switch you throw—it's a long road that will include setbacks and relapses, and you need to be prepared for those."

Only minutes later, when I walk out of his office and onto the parking lot where I expect Jared's car to be waiting, I discover how true his words are.

"Ms. Thompson...Mia? Hold up?"

I watch a man rush toward me with a camera stuck to his face. I barely have time to register he looks a lot like the guy in the van, when I see a flash from the corner of my eye. Jared's giant frame moves faster than I would've thought possible, as he rips the camera from the guy's face, and hurls it across the parking lot, where it breaks

237

apart on landing. Loud yelling ensues and I can feel my hands tingle as my lungs seem to tighten. Everything around me disappears until there is just me, and the paralyzing fear I recognize all too well.

Next thing I know I'm lying on the couch in Rueben's office, listening to another argument, this one less threatening since it takes place in harsh whispers. Jared is attempting to gain access to the room, and Rueben, all of his stooped five foot seven inches, is throwing himself up as some kind of sentry. If I weren't so confused and shaken, it would be laughable. But I want Jared. I want to feel the comfort of his hands on me. I know he can make the shaking stop and my heart return to normal just by being near.

"Please," I try to get Rueben's attention, but it's Jared who hears and his eyes immediately land on me.

"Hey, Beautiful," his voice instantly gentles.

Rueben turns around and takes a step toward me, a move that gives Jared the opening he needs to squeeze in the door and beat Rueben to my side. His hand is on my face and I surge up to wrap my arms around his neck. He wraps an arm around me and twists us so he is sitting on the couch, with me cradled against his chest. My breathing instantly slows down, and I let out a deep sigh, barely hearing the words he mumbles in my hair, but finding comfort in his soothing rumble.

"Better?" he says a little louder.

"Much." I give him the truth, opening my eyes to see the worry in his.

"Christ, I'm sorry. The clinic was busy and the doctor was…"

238

I put my fingers over his mouth and cut off his words.

"You really have to stop apologizing," I gently insist. Before I can say anything else, Rueben clears his throat, drawing our attention.

"Maybe it's time you properly introduce us," he directs at me, but his bemused gaze is firmly fixed on Jared.

TWENTY-TWO

Jared

Holy fuck.

If LeBlanc's patrol car hadn't happened by, just as I went after that Taylor fucking Torrence in the parking lot, I might've killed the guy. As it was, John had to put in some muscle to stop me from pounding his face to a pulp. I can't remember a time, not even on the ice, where all I saw was red.

"Easy, man," John's voice had sounded by my ear, as his arms banded around me, pinning mine to my side. I was impressed. Even though I initially struggled to get free, his steel hold never let up. "Think, brother. Think. Don't make it any worse than it already is."

"I'm gonna sue you," the motherfucker lisped through his busted lips. "Officer, I wanna file charges."

"Shut the fuck up," John snapped at him, surprising both of us. "I'll deal with you in a minute."

When I turned my head to find Mia, she'd disappeared, but a woman standing in the door of the clinic motioned inside.

"Let me go," I growled at the man still holding me pinned.

241

"Are you gonna behave?" I almost lost it at his sardonic question, but the urge to see Mia was greater.

"Yes, man, let me go. I need to see to Mia." Without further argument, he released me and I made a straight beeline for the door.

I hadn't counted on the damn doctor to block my way to her. I probably would've nailed him too if he was younger and fitter than the seventy or eighty years he looks to be. God she looked so small, curled up into herself with her face chalk white, and the moment I saw my opening I had her up and in my arms.

She was still there, mostly because I was reluctant to let go. Even as the doc, Rueben, sat down after introductions, and pointedly ignoring me after, started softly talking with Mia. In fact, I was so keen on keeping her close, I didn't even object when LeBlanc walked in and announced he would pick Jordy up. He said he'd bring her home since he needed to ask me some questions. That's when reality hit home; I might be in some serious shit.

Mia sits quietly beside me in the car as Jake swings open the gate to let us through. The OPP cruiser is already parked in the driveway.

"Are you in trouble?" she asks timidly, spotting the cruiser.

"Nothing I can't handle," I respond with more bluster than I feel. The truth is, I may have just created a whole new reason for the press to hound me, and on top of that, cost myself any chance on a position with the Colts. They don't take kindly to coaches who can't keep their cool. Wonderful. I'd better get on the phone with Brian, see what damage control he can do. But first I have to make nice with our local law enforcement, who happens to have his eye on my sister. I swallow hard.

I have to swallow even harder when we walk in and he's sitting casual as you like, across from my sister who is feeding Ole. Mia's slight squeeze to my hand holds me back from walking up and shutting his eyes for him. Probably wouldn't be a great idea to beat up a member of the press, and a police officer, all in one day. Instead, I let go of Mia's hand, who rushes to my sister's side, and jerk my head sharply in the direction of the kitchen when I catch LeBlanc's eye. I don't wait, assuming he'll follow, as I dive into the fridge for a beer.

"A little early for that?" he says, grabbing a stool at the island and eyeing the bottle in my hand.

"Not after the fucking morning I've had," I snap back.

"Good point," he concedes. "Maybe I'll take one, too." I give him a long stare before grabbing another beer from the fridge, slamming it down in front of him.

"Isn't there a rule you're not allowed drink on the job?" I snipe, watching him take a long tug from his bottle before he sets it down.

"Probably," he shrugs, "good thing my shift ended an hour ago. I was on my way home when I saw you charging through the parking lot."

Christ knows I don't want to like the fucking guy, but damn he doesn't make it easy. I drain half of my beer before pulling a stool to the other side of the counter so I'm facing him.

243

"Okay," I sigh, looking over his shoulder to where the girls are sitting, talking softly. "Tell me how fucked I am." One side of John's mouth tilts up in amusement when I glance back at him.

"Mr. Torrence is pissed."

"Tell me something I don't know," I snap. "But not nearly as pissed as I am. He's messing with my family. Mia, she…" I stop when John lifts his hand.

"I get it," he quickly interjects. "If you'd just tossed the damn camera and got in his face it would've been one thing, but Jesus you did a number on him. He's dead set on pressing charges, it didn't seem to matter much what I said. I managed to hold him off till tomorrow. Told him to get some ice on his face and come into the Bracebridge Detachment in the morning to file his complaint. Give you a chance to get your damn ducks in a row before this charge becomes official. As it is, my ass is dangling on the line."

I run both hands through my hair and drop my head, clasping them behind my neck. What a mess. What a goddamn mess.

"I appreciate it, man," I finally manage, lifting my eyes.

"Good," he says, grinning from ear to ear. "Then maybe you won't cut off my balls and shove them down my throat when I ask your sister out." I glare at him, grinding my teeth, but he just keeps on grinning. Finally he straightens his face and leans forward. "Although, you should know that wouldn't have stopped me anyway."

I look over his shoulder and catch Jordy eyeing his back, a little smile tugging at her lips before she notices

244

me watching, and ducks her head, her face blushing red. Mia, sitting next to her, looks me straight in the eye, smiling big. I just shake my head and turn back to John, who's smiling again, his eyebrow raised.

"Whatever," I mumble, giving in. I guess she could do worse. "But you hurt her...? I don't care if you're the law around here, I will mow you down."

"So noted." Is the only response I get before he gets up, walks casual as you like over to the girls, says something I can't quite hear, which has Mia smiling and Jordy blushing, and with a light touch to the baby's head, he walks to the door. "I'll be in touch," he throws over his shoulder before pulling the door shut behind him.

I'd better go call Brian.

Mia

The moment the bedroom door opens, I'm awake.

Jordy had gone to lie down for a bit with Ole, and exhausted from this morning's events, I'd followed suit. I'd walked up to Jared, who was still sitting at the kitchen counter, and pressed myself against him. His arms automatically came up to hold me there.

"Going to lie down for a bit," I told him, to which he nodded in response.

"I have some calls to make."

245

"I'm sorry," I whispered. Not so much an apology as it was an expression of regret for what happened. He silenced me with his mouth, before he let me go, his eyes dark with worry.

Part of me wanted to stay in support, but I knew he likely needed some time and space to deal with the aftermath. So I dragged myself down the hall and fell facedown on the spare bed, exhaustion rendering me asleep in mere seconds.

"Hey," Jared rumbles, leaning against the doorpost, looking at me with a slight lift of his eyebrows. I push myself up so my back rests against the headboard.

"Hey back."

"Was hoping I'd find you in my bed," he says suggestively, moving to sit on the edge of the bed. I shrug in response.

"It was tempting," I admit. "But I'm trying not to overstep my boundaries."

"There are no boundaries for you to overstep," he drawls, lying down with his head on my stomach. My hand immediately finds its way into his hair, my fingers lazily massaging his skull underneath. He groans in appreciation, sending a ripple of awareness through my body.

"What did Brian say?" I probe carefully. He presses his face into the swell of my belly, groaning louder.

"Read me the riot act," he mumbles, before lifting his head and facing me. "How are you?" I let my hand trail down the side of his face and still against his jaw.

"Other than that I'm worried about you, I'm fine. The nap helped."

"Good," he says, effectively evading my concern.

He crawls up the bed and shifts until he's propped against the headboard, tucking me against him. I snuggle in gratefully, with my head on his chest and my arm draped over his stomach. We sit like that for a while, lost in our own thoughts, when the ring of a phone cuts through the silence.

"Let me grab that," Jared volunteers, and with a light peck on my lips, leaves the bed. I follow suit, but aim the bathroom instead.

When I walk out minutes later, I find Jared standing in the kitchen, his back toward me. My purse is open on the counter, and he has my phone to his ear.

"I'm taking care of it," I hear him say to, who I assume must be, Steffie. Hardly anyone else knows my number, let alone calls. "I know," he says, clearly pained. "I'm not that guy anymore. You're just going to have to trust me on that."

Okay. That's enough. It's clear from just his side of the conversation that my bestie is giving Jared a hard time, something he doesn't need after the day he's had. I walk up behind him and steal my phone from his hand.

"….one complaint, and I'll make your life a living hell. And one more thing…"

"Steffie!"

"Mia?"

"Yes it is and where do you get off tearing into Jared?" I'm angry and not afraid to let her know.

247

"Doug showed me this article. Said someone at work showed him. Jesus, Mia! I was worried sick. What has that man gotten you into?" I feel guilty I didn't call her to give her a head's up, but my hair stands on end when she tries to blame Jared.

"He didn't *get* me into anything! He's done everything in his power to shield me, literally has gone to bat for me. But you know what? I guess it was easier to jump to conclusions based on what you think you know from newspaper gossip, than to just ask." With that I end the call, unfamiliar anger coursing through me.

"Whoa," Jared's deep voice sounds in my ear, as he wraps his arms around me from behind. "I love that you want to defend my honour, baby, but that's your best friend you hung up on. She's just worried about you. Needs to look out for you. I understand that."

I turn in his arms and lift my face to him.

"But you don't deserve that." He shows a wry grin.

"I think we both know I deserve every bit of doubt she has. She's clearly aware I have a reputation. One I created myself." He shrugs a little sheepishly. "I may not be that guy anymore, but you can't blame her for being protective. A guy who has a name for being a bit of a partier, drags her best friend, who happens to value her privacy, onto the gossip pages of the newspaper? I'd be pissed, too." I feel a little sick to my stomach when he's done talking.

"Oh," I manage, ashamed I lost all sense of perspective with my own need to protect.

Jared bends his head and gently brushes his lips over mine.

"We make quite a pair," he says when he pulls back. His eyes boring into mine. "The way we jump into battle for each other, you'd think—"

"You're in love?" Jordy cuts him off as she walks in with Ole on her arm. "Yeah, that's not exactly news," she adds, as she moves past, heading toward the fridge. "What's for dinner?"

My eyes are still locked on Jared's, I'm sure mine are wide in shock, but his are warm and mildly amused.

"*I think she's right,*" he mouths silently, causing my heart to skip a beat before settling into a faster beat. Before I can change my mind, I respond on a whisper.

"That's quite possible."

"We'll have to address that later," he says with a wink. "But first let me get some food into my sister. She gets cranky when she has to go without."

"Hey!" Jordy lifts her head from the fridge. "I resemble that statement!"

I snicker and shake my head as the two of them start their now familiar sibling bicker fest. Stepping from Jared's hold, I walk over to Jordy and take a bright-eyed Ole from her hands.

During a quickly pulled together dinner, Jared explains what he and Brian discussed this afternoon. Brian feels it may be possible to nip this in the bud before official charges are laid, if Torrence is presented with a onetime offer. He also suggested Marie Blumberg, the local lawyer, should be pulled in, given that Jordy's ex is at the root of this issue. Jared had called her earlier, filled her in, and she'd wanted in on whatever was being put

249

together. She apparently contacted Brian, brainstormed, and a proposal was being drafted up right away.

It's clear Jared isn't happy with what will be on offer; an exclusive interview with photo op, here at his house, not to mention exposing Jordy and Ole to the cameras—Marie's idea—but Brian apparently feels it might kill two birds with one stone. By taking away the mystery, he hopes it will kill the attraction.

It's not until much later, after we watched the latest Jason Bourne movie, during which Jordy fell asleep on the couch, and we'd all retreated to bed—Jared making it clear I was to share his—that Jordy's earlier words resurface.

I carefully lower myself on Jared's hard length after working him with my mouth, making him not only slick and ready, but myself as well. He's sitting with his back to the headboard and his head tilted back a little. My hands are braced on either side of his head, using the frame for balance as I slowly, but deliberately move up and down on his glorious cock. My eyes are fused to his, and my mouth falls open as his hands on my hips force me down hard, while grinding himself against my core. I love seeing the dark red flush on his cheekbones and his pupils widen with need. It's powerful—heady—to see how I affect him.

Other than the puff of our breaths, the grinding of our bodies, there is no other sound. I focus instead on the sensations he creates inside me, and feel myself building toward orgasm. When his hips buck up underneath me, signalling his own pending release, I let myself fly.

That's when those words slip from his mouth.

"Jordy may have a point," he whispers, still gasping for breath.

I freeze just as I drape myself on top of him, a little thrown at the reference to his sister at this moment in time. But the next words he mumbles, his face buried in my hair, reduce me into a puddle.

"Thirty-nine years old, and I can honestly say I have never, in my almost forty years, felt what I'm feeling for you. I've tried rationalizing it, tried compartmentalizing it, but I can't. It's big, it scares the shit out of me, and I clearly have no choice in the matter."

I need a moment to let the full impact of his words wash over me. Then I lift my head and look him straight in the eye.

"I'm scared, too. And confused, and plenty torn, but I also feel more secure than I've felt in a long time. Even under these circumstances." I lift my mouth to his and allow myself to get lost in his kiss, before I gently pull back.

"And I feel alive—you make me feel alive."

TWENTY-THREE

Jared

"So what's the verdict?"

The proposal my lawyers drew up had been delivered yesterday, first thing in the morning. Turns out Mr. Torrence had already lawyered up, which was to be expected, and the past twenty-four hours I've heard little but that negotiations are underway.

John LeBlanc called yesterday, around noon, to let me know he never showed up to file an official complaint, which let me know he was at least considering the offer.

I'd suggested to throw some money at him too, to sweeten the pot, but Brian advised against it. Said if I started down that road, people would purposely throw themselves in front of my car to cash in.

Hard to believe there was actually a time I enjoyed all the attention—the recognition. As a young kid up in Sault Ste Marie, I'd basked in the glory. People there were rabid about their Greyhounds. Here in Canada, being a hockey player is akin to being a rock star at times. The last ten years playing in the U.S., I'd almost forgotten that. The hockey hype is not quite as big there. I could walk the streets and no one would be the wiser. I have trouble doing that anywhere here.

So Brian may have a point, but I've been worried perhaps offering an exclusive won't be enough.

"I need you in Toronto tomorrow afternoon," Brian answers. "To sign off on the agreement."

"He's taking the deal?" I let out a big breath of relief, the threat of an assault charge weighing heavier on me than I'd realized. I'd always been good at going with the flow, taking life on the chin, but that was when I'd only had myself to worry about. That is no longer the case. Now I can't wait for things to settle down, get the shit with Jordy's ex and Ole's custody sorted, get the damn press off my back for good.

I'm craving calmer waters.

"Looks like, but he wants you there. Says he wants to see you sign off on his final stipulation personally."

"Final stipulation? What the fuck?" The relief I felt earlier was short lived. "What is he talking about?" I heard Brian's deep sigh over the phone and guess I probably won't like what's coming next.

"He wants Mia there for the interview."

"Over my dead body," I bite off instantly, blood roaring in my ears. "He leaves Mia alone or no deal."

"Buddy, I get it," Brian tries to appease me, but it only heats me up more. "But keep in mind that this agreement could solve a lot of your problems, in one fell swoop. He's willing to sign an affidavit outlining how Nick Quarles approached him to make your sister's life miserable after what happened at your place. The man apparently is hard up for money—gambling debts—and was hoping to get to your bank account through Jordy and the baby. He admitted as much to Torrence. Fuck, Jared, the guy has that entire conversation on tape. Says it's the journalist in him. The moment he heard Quarles say your name, every word was recorded." Brian pauses before he hammers home his point. "Marie says with that tape she can make any claim for custody disappear. Permanently. Mia for Ole, my friend."

"Son of a bitch!" I roar, hurling the mug I was holding against the fireplace, shattering it against the stone. Griffin jumps up from his spot by the coffee table and starts whimpering, and I can hear Ole cry out in his room. *Fucking brilliant.*

I sit down on the couch, dropping my head in my hand, as my sister comes tearing into the room, Mia right behind her holding a crying Ole.

"Jesus, Jared—What the hell?"

I lift my head and watch as Jordy takes in the scene and takes a few steps toward me, but Mia shoots out a hand to stop her.

"Here," she says, calmly. "You take the baby in the nursery and feed him, while I clean this up." She enforces her words by shoving the baby in Jordy's arms and resolutely turning her in the right direction. Surprisingly she goes without argument. When Mia turns to me, there is concern on her face as she looks at the phone still clutched in my hand.

"I've gotta call you back," I tell Brian, my voice flat, and end the call. I watch while Mia moves to let the dog out, gently talking to him, before returning to bend down in front of the fireplace, picking up the shards of my coffee mug.

"Leave it. I'll do it," I tell her, but she ignores me, swiftly removing the evidence of my outburst, save for the dark coffee stain on the exposed stone.

This is the second time I've lost control in front of her. Because of her. She has every remaining Neanderthal gene raring to life. I used to laugh at guys who'd talk about *their* woman. Could never understand that whole possessive he-man thing. Not until Mia.

I stay put as she carries the pieces into the kitchen and dumps them in the trash, before she washes her hands. My eyes follow every move and watch as she finally turns and walks toward me. I fight the urge to rub my head against her as she reaches out and runs her fingers through my hair, before she takes a seat beside me.

"Talk to me."

Her touch, her voice, her presence; it calms me.

"Taylor Torrence wants you to be there for the interview. That's not gonna happen. I won't agree to it," I quickly add, the moment I feel her body go rigid.

"Why?" she asks, her voice quiet.

"Because I won't subject you to that."

"No. I mean why would he want me there?"

Good question, one I hadn't really considered until now. But I have a good guess.

"He knows it's a sure way to get under my skin," I explain, vaguely recalling what I yelled at him while I was rearranging his face just two days ago. "Told him I'd never allow him to even breathe the same air as you. Guess this is him, letting me know who's in control.

Fuck!" I move to stand up, but Mia's hold on my arm stops me.

"I'll do it."

I can barely hear her through the chaos in my head, as I turn to face her.

"What?"

"I said, I'll do it," she repeats, looking me straight in the eye.

"No way," I tell her adamantly. "That won't happen. We'll find another way to nail Nick."

"Nick? Wait…what aren't you telling me?"

"Not your concern," I bluntly state, and I can visibly see her retreat before her eyes turn to slits and she tilts her head.

"He's got something on Nick, doesn't he?" I don't respond either way, but I can see the wheels turning. "Something he'll only give to you, if you let him have his way."

"Can't put you through that, Beautiful."

"Not your choice, Jared," she fires right back, scrambling to her feet and turning on me with her hands on her hips and her face in mine. "I was going to do it when I thought it was only about you getting off the hook. If you think you're gonna stop me now that I know it could help get rid of Ole's sperm donor at the same time, you've got another thing coming. Not. Your. Choice." With that she swings around, and with her shoulders square and her head high, she marches down the hall to the spare bedroom.

I hold back from rushing after her.

257

Instead, I consider her words and clue in I'm not the only one with a protective streak a mile wide when it comes to loved ones. Probably without realizing it, Mia has just shown me in no uncertain terms how invested she is. Enough to go toe-to-toe with me.

I can't stop the smile teasing the corners of my mouth as I dial Brian back. I'm still pissed to have been forced in this position, but I'm seriously relieved Mia effectively took the choice out of my hands. Never mind that she took my balls in the process.

My ego is sustaining some serious bruising.

Mia

I can't believe I was that stupid.

I'd fallen asleep last night, still attached with Jared in every sense of the word, after letting go of all my fears and allowing my carefully guarded heart to bubble over. It was easier than I expected, once he'd opened up to me. But the warm and fuzzy blanket of emotions took a pretty drastic turn this morning when I woke up alone in bed, with the sticky evidence of careless behaviour on the tender skin of my thighs.

I haven't used the pill since I had my miscarriage. Even then, it had only been for a short time until Blair and I wanted to try again. When that never happened, I never bothered again. Just because I don't think pregnancy is really a concern, there are other things that are.

In a relatively short timespan, I've all but moved in here. Even if the reasons were protection and safety, and the move is only temporary, I can't deny that I could easily get used to this. The reality is, that not that long ago, I watched as Jared fucked another woman right out there on the dock. And I'm pretty sure he wasn't wearing a condom then.

It's not really fair to feel resentment over something that happened before I came along, and yet it eats at my gut. More so this morning than anytime before, I have to admit. Maybe this is all moving too fast. I feel like I've become caught up in a windstorm and I'm desperately trying to grab onto something solid. It's not that I don't believe he loves me. He's really done nothing to make me doubt the validity of his feeling. Nor do I doubt my own. It's just that instead of feeling like a changing tide, as Rueben so eloquently described it, this feels more like a tsunami. And having unprotected sex is only an invitation to more chaos.

I was set to talk to him, as soon as I could get some time with him alone this afternoon, but then the next wave hit with that damn interview. Oh, I put on a good front, but for all my bluster, I'm shaking inside. The stress of everything is closing in on me.

I find myself standing in front of the window, looking out over the water at my own cottage. My little sanctuary that has served me well for many years. I think of my garden that has been ignored for days at a time and my nightly paddles on the lake. The soothing comfort of steady routines. Part of me realizes that I can't go back there, not now, not after I've had a taste of all I've been missing. It comes with complications, though. Life is messy, and unless you want to live alone on an island, completely cut off from the world, the mess will find you.

Just then the door behind me opens. I already know it's Jared before his arms slip around my front, and I feel the press of his lips against my neck.

"Penny for your thoughts," he rumbles, and I can't hold back the snort.

"Believe me," I assure him. "You don't want in my head right now."

"You would be wrong," he says, turning me in his arms. I tilt back so I can look at him. "I very much want in there. I want in your head, I want under your skin, and I really want in your body," he finishes, lowering his head to brush his lips over mine. He gives me the opening right there and I take it.

"You already are. In fact you were so much inside my body last night, I could still feel you on me this morning," I tell him, watching his face go from smug to concerned.

"Shit," he whispers when realization hits.

"Yeah…shit is about right," I acknowledge. "Look, I hate to bring this up, but remember I saw you with her. On the dock," I clarify when he looks a little lost. It helps, because his face immediately turns remorseful. Before he can form the apology I know is coming, I lift up on my toes and get a little closer to his face. "You were not wearing a condom then, either."

"Shit," he repeats, this time dropping his arms from around me and running a hand through his hair. I feel the distance immediately.

"Right," I soldier on. "So I'm not on anything, but I'm not too worried about pregnancy. It would constitute a miracle for me to get pregnant."

"Why?" His reaction is instant and a little bit startling.

"Because other than one miscarriage almost fifteen years ago, I was never able to get pregnant again," I explain clinically, and I pretend not to see the flinch passing over his face. "I'm more concerned about disease." This time there's no ignoring the expression on his features.

"I'm clean," he says, barely able to disguise a hurt I couldn't quite place. "I was checked not long after…after that incident. I would never have come near you, covered or uncovered without making sure of that." He barks out a harsh laugh. "Amazing, how one minute you make me feel ten feet tall and the next like pond scum."

There it is, the reason for the pain on his face. Trust. Or rather the lack thereof—from me. I can justify my right to be concerned, but the truth of it is, I slapped him with a past he can't undo, even though he has done nothing since to give me reason to doubt him. Emotion chokes the words of apology that want to escape, when he opens the door and is about to step through.

"And for the record?" he says, turning in the doorway. "I wasn't concerned about any of it. Not disease and certainly not pregnancy. Because I never even considered the first to be an issue, and wouldn't have been able to see the last as anything but a blessing."

When the door slams behind him, I sit down on the edge of the bed and let the tears fall.

-

I never came out of the room after that.

Hours I spent listening to the boats on the water, ignoring Jordy's occasional soft knocks on my door, my mind in turmoil. Until the sun started going down and I finally stripped off my clothes, and in just a tank top and my underwear, I slipped under to covers and cried myself to sleep.

I'm not sure what time it is, when I feel a pair of strong arms slip around me and cradle me close.

"I told you I'm no good at this." Jared's voice sounds thick with emotion and immediately my tears well up again. "I overreacted. Turns out, I don't just have a temper I didn't know I had, but I also can hold a mean grudge."

I can't believe he's here apologizing when that should be me. The shame I felt earlier is back in full force and then some.

"Please don't," I sob, turning around and immediately burying my face in his neck. "I'm so sorry. I didn't mean…"

"Shhh," he hushes me, using his hand to hold my head even closer. "I know you didn't, Beautiful. So much is going on—I feel so fucking much, I don't know which way is up. It's making me stupid. Life gets crazy, and it's all I can do to hang on, but as long as I can hold on to you, I'm grounded. Don't let me go."

I wrap my limbs around him so there's not a lick of air that can get between us.

"Will it always be like this?" I finally ask when my crying jag runs its course.

"Sure as fuck hope not. Not if I have any say in it," he mumbles, tilting my head back, kissing the wet from my face before he softly presses his lips to mine. His eyes look heavy with fatigue but genuine and warm, and I finally close mine, letting sleep take me.

TWENTY-FOUR

Jared

My sister is already rummaging in the kitchen when I untangle myself from Mia and leave her sleeping a bit longer.

"Did you fix it?"

First thing in the morning and she's already throwing attitude. Granted, she's the one who threatened physical harm last night, if I didn't get my *dumb, knuckle-dragging ass* in there to make things right, but wait for the damn coffee before chirping at me. Instead of going on the defensive, I crowd her against the counter and wrap her in a hug.

"Morning to you too, sunshine. Got coffee?"

"Well, did you?" she repeats, pushing away. At least this time she fills my mug with my morning essential. Living with my sister isn't always easy, when she has a tendency to be all up in my face about stuff, but she knows how to set me straight and does a damn good cup of coffee.

"We're fine."

"That's it? That's all I'm gonna get?" she sputters.

"All I'm gonna give you. We talked, we slept, we're fine." I hide my smile behind the rim of my coffee mug. I know damn well she'd like a blow-by-blow, so she can chew on and analyze every word that was exchanged, but it's frankly none of her business. She opens her mouth to protest, but Ole chooses that moment to announce he's awake, so all I get is a glare. I quickly kiss the top of her head as I pass her on my way out of the sliding doors to have my coffee in peace.

That's where Mia finds me a little later.

"Need fresh?" she asks when she reaches me, indicating my empty cup.

"Maybe in a bit. Need a kiss though." I tilt my head back and wrap my arm around the back of her knees, when she bends down to make good on my request. "Morning," I mumble against her lips, while stroking the back of her leg.

"Morning." I like the soft smile on her face when she echoes me. "I need to work in my garden today," she says, sitting down beside me and glancing over to her place. "I think I'm going to have to do some canning or else a lot of my crop will go to waste." I reach over and put my hand on her knee.

"I can help," I offer. "I need to be in Toronto for the three o'clock meeting, but I have time this morning." I have no damn idea about gardening—or canning for that matter—but I have a feeling it might be a dirty job, which requires getting clean after. My mind has no problem seeing us doing either or both of those. Plus, we'll be all alone.

266

"What are you grinning about?" she asks, tilting her head as she watches me with a half-smile of her own.

"Nothing," I lie, putting on an innocent face. "Look forward to getting dirty."

"Riiight," she drawls, a twinkle in her eyes.

-

I'm not having so much fun about two hours later when the fun of watching Mia bend over, sticking her ass in the air, has worn off a little. Weeding seriously sucks. She'd tried me on the tomatoes, but after I squeezed a few too hard when picking them, she reassigned me to weed duty, which is killing my back and making my knee throb. Never figured gardening to be physically challenging. I straighten up and stretch my lower back, glancing over at the two bushel baskets filled to the top with vegetables.

"Want those inside?" Mia lifts her head from where she had it buried in the pepper plants.

"If you don't mind."

I'm at her sink, scrubbing the dirt from under my nails, when she walks in and closes the door behind her. When I look up she's leaning her back against it, a little smirk on her face.

"This is dirty work," I observe, wiping my hands on the towel.

"I know, isn't it fun?" The smirk spreads to a genuine smile as she tries to blow a curl sticking to her forehead.

"Up for debate, but I'm pretty sure the getting clean part can be fun," I point out, stalking toward her. She ducks under my arms and snickers, skipping down the hall to her bedroom. Baby wants to play.

I'm just in time to see a glimpse of her disappear into the adjoining bathroom. The pile of dirty clothes on the floor tells me she's not wearing much and I hurry to dump mine on top as I hear the shower turn on. The simple plastic curtain is drawn when I follow her into the bathroom, but I can see the outline of her body and stop to admire her for a minute. Mia is not tall, she just reaches my chin, but she fits there perfectly. Instead of the tall, lean, and tight bodies I used to be drawn to, hers is much different.

Curved, soft in all the right places, and wholesome in a way that makes me want to bury myself in her and plant my babies. I can say with conviction that thought never entered my mind with anyone but Mia. She's not some fantasy—she's a real flesh and blood woman I can't see myself ever tiring of.

"Are you coming in or are you just gonna stare?"

Pulling back the curtain, I step under the stream of lukewarm water and immediately wrap myself around her slick, wet body.

"You're beautiful."

Her face lifts up and she treats me with a brilliant smile.

"Hardly," she says. "But I'm happy that's what you see."

"It's all I see," I admit, bending to kiss her deeply.

The feeling of skin sliding against skin, her fingers tangling in the hair at the nape of my neck, and the rub of my dick—already hard in anticipation—pressed against her soft belly, has me moan against her mouth. My hands

268

slide down and each grabs a handful of her ass cheeks, and I can't help squeezing the soft flesh. It elicits a responding moan from her, muffled by our kiss. I let myself sink to my knees, pulling Mia down with me, and with one hand in the small of her back and the other coming up to cup her head, I lay her down on the shower floor.

"Jared…" she mumbles when I lift my body away from hers.

"Shhh…" I soothe, one hand, fingers spread wide, stroking her front from the base of her neck, down her chest and belly to the soft hair of her patch. I lazily caress my fingers through her folds, already slick with want. The flush high on her cheeks, and the slight purse of her parted lips, evidence of her need. But it's the deep green of her eyes that betrays her heart. Trust is all I see there as she lies back with the water streaming down on her, completely open to my hands and eyes.

I watch those eyes widen slightly as I reach for the handheld showerhead. A twist of the dial, and the water flow changes to the pulsing stream I was hoping for. I can hear her sharp intake of breath when I spread her pussy lips with the fingers of one hand, and with my other, aim the stream of water for her mons. She moans and lifts her hips into the pulse of the shower, moving so it hits at the top of her slit. Everything she feels is laid out plain as day on her face, and I can't drag my eyes away. I struggle to keep my hands still as I watch her get herself off with just the slightest of shifts against the water and my hands.

"Fuck, baby…you take my breath away," I groan, feeling her body wind up for release.

An urgent need to be inside her has me toss the shower to the side, and drop down between her legs. Already she has her hips tilted for me, and in one move I bury myself to the root. I fight for control but lose, as her core clenches around my cock. I can't do anything to stop the surge of my hips, mindlessly chasing my own release as Mia falls apart around me, my name from her lips bouncing off the tiles.

I can still hear the echo when I feel the hot stream of my seed pump into her.

"Mia? Are you here?"

Mia

"Shit!"

I'm frozen until I hear Jared's hissed curse and try to scramble out from under him, but his body continues to pin me down.

"Jared!" I hiss back, only to feel his body start shaking with laughter on top of me.

"Give us a minute," he yells, humour lacing his voice, while I close my eyes and die of embarrassment.

"I'll just be on the porch!" Steffie hollers back, clearly amused as well, and I listen for her footsteps to disappear down the hall.

270

"I'm not going out there," I whisper, as Jared gently pulls me to my feet. I drop my head to hide my burning face, but he won't let me. He lifts my chin with his fingertips and leans his forehead against mine. Our noses are almost touching.

"Oh yes, you are," he insists. "We're both going out there. We both have some fences to mend with your friend. Right after we get cleaned up." He gives me a quick brush of the lips and then quickly puts the shower back in order so we can rinse off.

"We did it again," I point out, as he hands me the bar of soap, much calmer than yesterday.

"I know," Jared declares with a grin, which only grows bigger when I glare at him. "Look," he adds, a little more serious as he cups my face. "You said the likelihood of pregnancy is very remote, and I like the thought that every time I'm inside you, we allow destiny to take its course. I've got to admit, I get a kick out of even just the possibility we might be creating something beautiful beyond that moment."

Damn him for making my knees buckle with his words, when my friend is pacing a hole in the floor of my porch.

"Jared…" I start a feeble protest, but I don't get far. His index finger firmly presses against my lips.

"Just go with the flow," he whispers, right before he steps out of the shower, grabbing a towel off the rack and disappears into my bedroom.

Right.

By the time I'm dry and dressed, I can already hear the sound of their voices coming from outside. I pause for a moment, listening for any tension between them, but all I hear are Jared's low chuckle and Steffie's excited chatter. Griffin snorts softly in greeting when I walk past his bed, giving him a distracted scratch behind the ears, on my way to the sliding door.

"There she is," Steffie greets me, a massive smile splitting her face before I disappear in her embrace. "And I've gotta say, getting some looks good on you." I roll my eyes to the ceiling at her lack of filter, but per usual she ignores me as Jared tries hard to hide his shit-eating grin. "And you've gotta forgive me," Steffie plunders on. "But getting told off by my best friend, whom I've never even heard raise her voice, was a shock to the system. No way I wasn't going to come check things out for myself."

I groan and drop down on the couch where Jared tugs me close and kisses the side of my head.

"On that note, I'd better check in with Jordy and get changed before I head out," he says standing up and facing Steffie. "Will you be staying?"

"Oh, hell no," Steffie answers, waving her hand dismissively. "I'm driving back after dinner. I've got a six a.m. induction and I'd like to try and get some sleep. Tomorrow's gonna be a long day."

"Well in that case, you might be gone before I get back," he says, nodding at Steffie. "Nice putting a face to the name."

My friend beams before blurting, "Nice putting a body to yours." I snort when I see Jared's eyebrows shoot in his hairline and a faint blush stain his cheeks. Steffie is her own brand of forward. "My Doug's gonna shit himself when I tell him I caught *The Enforcer* with his pants down."

With a quick distracted peck to my forehead, Jared makes tracks out the door, leaving Steffie and me in tears of hilarity.

"I like him," she says, unapologetically watching him make his way around the inlet, all the way into his house.

"Yeah, I like him, too," I admit when she turns to face me.

"You love him. You'd never have gone off on me like that if you didn't." She points her index finger at me and I swat it away.

"I might," is all I'll give up, but the smile on my face is too obvious.

Just like that, whatever wrinkle popped up in our friendship, is ironed out again.

-

"I made some fresh pasta sauce, do you want me to bring some over?"

Steffie helped me process this morning's harvest and a few very gratifying rows of jars of salsa, pickled beets, onion relish, and chutney filled my counter. With the remainders I'd been able to put together a thick tomato based sauce, most of which is in containers in the freezer, except for one large pot on my stove. I just got off the phone with Jared, who said things went well, but that he'd likely be late since Brian had something else lined up for him. I promised him I'd check in on his sister.

We didn't discuss this morning. Doesn't mean it isn't on my mind. Things are moving fast and it feels like I'm being swept along, but then I'm not exactly doing much to put the brakes on either. It's terrifying, and liberating at the same time.

"You don't have to. There's plenty of food here," Jordy answers, a little distracted.

"Well, I can give you a little break from Ole," I offer, struggling to get my mind back on the conversation.

"Actually, someone's already offered to bring me dinner," she admits. "I think we're good."

I don't have to guess at who that someone might be, I can hear it clear in her voice.

"In that case, say hello to John for me and I'm right here should you need me." The soft giggle on the other side makes me smile. "Want me to shoot Jared a message to come here instead of there?"

"God no! John has a shift starting at ten. This'll be breakfast for him."

I'm still smiling when she ends the call.

"Busy place," Steffie concludes, tilting her head in the direction of the other house, where the now familiar black and white SUV rolls to a stop in the driveway. We both watch the tall, uniformed man get out, holding a few brown paper bags and a pretty bouquet of flowers. I pull Steffie away from the screen and usher her inside, when we see Jordy opening the door.

After dinner, and helping me store away the jars for winter, Steffie gathers her things.

274

"Promise me you won't hang up on me again," she says, folding me in a bear hug. "I understand why, but it freaked me out."

"Promise," I mumble, my head buried against her shoulder where she is holding it. "And bring Doug and the kids next time. Maybe on Labour Day weekend?" I finally manage to untangle myself from her hold.

"I don't think he'll need much persuading," she says, already moving down the steps. "Call me, I want to stay up to date." She nudges her head in the direction of the OPP vehicle, still parked in the driveway on the other side of the water.

I watch until her taillights disappear behind the trees before calling Griffin inside and closing the door.

Steffie's last words have me emotional. In all the years I've lived here, it was always me who asked her to keep me up to date on her life. I simply didn't have enough of one to have anything new to report. But I have a life now.

The sound of a sliding door closing draws my eyes to Jared's house. Backlit by the indoor lights, I see Jordy's shape make its way to the end of the dock where John is rising from his seat. Almost seamlessly she slips in his arms and tilts her head back as his bends low.

I immediately turn and go inside.

Their first kiss should be theirs alone.

TWENTY-FIVE

Jared

"We need to move up the interview."

I'm surprised to find Brian on my doorstep and that's the first thing he says. From the look on his face, it's clear between last night, when I left the meeting with the Barrie Colts he'd managed to organize on short notice, and this morning, something happened.

"I thought we agreed we would wait until next week to give the Colts a chance to write up a proposal," I question him, as he steps past me into the house and heads straight for the kitchen.

I'd come in close to two this morning. After doing a quick check of my house, finding Jordy and Ole sleeping but no Mia, I made the trek to Mia's cottage. She'd been asleep too, and I wasted no time crawling in bed with her, exhausted from the long day.

Right now she's in the bathroom with my sister, giving Ole his bath. The two have been whispering since breakfast, their conversation stalling every time I come near.

"Things have changed," Brian says, shaking the coffee thermos to see if any is left before he grabs a mug from the cupboard. "Have you heard of E!Online?"

"E? I thought that was a TV gossip show?"

"Same difference. This is their online site. My secretary called me first thing this morning, I asked her to keep an eye on any reports that might pop up in the media. Apparently something did overnight."

I rush to my office and snatch up my laptop, carrying it into the kitchen and set it on the counter between us. Brian does the honours of calling up the website.

"What the hell? I thought we had this covered?" flies from my mouth, when I see the images on the screen. A picture of my car, my head visible behind the wheel and Jordy beside me. You can see the outline of Mia who was sitting in the backseat. The next shot is of her getting out of the car at her therapist's office, and a third shows me carrying the baby seat, my arm around my sister as we walk into the clinic. *It's Complicated?* Is the heading with a promise for more exclusive photos on the next page. I brush Brian's hands aside, twist the screen so it faces me, and click on 'next.'

Former NHL heartthrob and Calder Trophy recipient, Jared Kesla, appears to be enjoying his recent retirement from hockey. He has been spotted around the small town of Bracebridge, Ontario, where local sources claim Kesla seems to have

settled in—along with two women and
a baby?

Below the paragraph of text are two further images.
Both are clearly taken from the water. One with the
morning sun coming up, showing me sitting at the end of
the dock, with my head tilted back and Mia's riot of curls
bending over me from behind, kissing me. The next one is
also my dock but this time at night, a grainy shot of
another kiss. This time the woman is not Mia, and I'm
pretty damn sure that man is not me.

"Jordy!"

My sister rushes into the kitchen, putting on the
brakes when she sees Brian.

"What's the matter?" she wants to know, sounding a
bit breathless.

"Who's this?" I turn the laptop to her. She leans in
for a closer look, before cursing under her breath and
straightening up. I know that defiant tilt of her chin well.

"You know damn well who that is, Jared," she bites
off impatiently.

"Fine. Then maybe you'd like to enlighten me how
long this has been going on?" I'm not sure why I'm pissed
at her, except that she's an easy focus for my anger.

"Oh give it up, Mr. High and Mighty, I'm not fifteen.
That shot was taken last night, if you must know. Your
picture is right next to it, you know," she points out.

"They're implying it's me in both shots."

"So what?" Jordy retorts. "You know it's not, I know it's not—who the hell cares what the idiots who read this trash think?"

"All right, children." Brian raises his hands. "This is not productive. I didn't drive all the way up here at the butt crack of dawn to listen to you two go at it." He turns to Jordy, a soft look on his face. "You're right this isn't a big deal, at least it wouldn't be if we weren't in the middle of negotiations with the Colts. Impressions like this getting out there, just as you're trying to get a position teaching and mentoring kids, may not work out in your favour. It won't even matter if it's true or not." Swiveling around to me, his expression is not nearly as kind as it was for her. "And you—lay off your sister, she's in her fucking thirties and doesn't need you to defend her honour. They're quoting local sources, so you might want to worry about your own romantic entanglements; you're in enough shit as it is." He's barely said the words and Mia walks up, handing Jordy the baby, without taking her eyes off Brian.

"Are you referring to me?" she challenges my agent, one hand on her hip and the other grabbing on to the counter. Her hand is squeezing so tight it's forcing the blood from her knuckles. She doesn't bow under though, as she sticks her nose up and her chin out. She is sexy as shit, looking at Brian like he's a piece of crap she just scraped off her flip-flops. It's clearly impressing Brian as well as he flinches at her words.

"Not exactly," he says, visibly withering under her gaze as he offers her his hand, which she pointedly ignores. "I'm Jared's agent, Brian."

"I know who you are," she interrupts, and I decide it may be better for all involved, if I take over the introductions from here.

"Mia, this is Brian, my agent. Brian, meet my girlfriend, Mia." I don't know who of the two looks more surprised at that declaration. Although I think it has less to do with the accuracy of my statement and more with the fact I actually said that out loud.

I spend the next few minutes explaining to Mia what is floating around the Internet, trying to be cautious, but she surprises me.

"They're idiots," she spits out. "Just out for a cheap thrill, and people who actually read that garbage are idiots, too." I almost burst out laughing when she clearly directs that last accusation at Brian.

"My secretary," he scrambles to explain. "She was keeping an eye out. I'm just here to try and do damage control." Mia's eyebrow shoots up.

"Damage control? That seems simple enough; contact that creep for The Sun and tell him he can have his exclusive a little early."

I have my mouth open a few times to intervene, but it appears that's not necessary. Mia clearly has things well in hand, even though she's starting to wear on Brian, who puffs up his chest.

"That's exactly what the plan is," he says.

"Perfect, I'll leave you guys to it then, keep me in the loop. I've got more vegetables that need canning." With a smile for Jordy, a peck on the cheek for me, and a toss of her curls I'm sure is for Brian's benefit, she walks straight out the front door, Griffin scrambling to keep up.

"You're in the dog house, Brian," Jordy pipes up from the couch, where she's feeding the baby, a grin on her face. "You called her *shit*."

"I did no such thing!" Exasperated, he throws his hands up. "Why do I even bother explaining myself when my words get twisted anyway."

"I heard you call her *shit* quite clearly," I poke at him a little more, making Jordy snort out loud. Laughing is a welcome way to break the high tension in the room. At least it is for Jordy and me, because Brian doesn't appear amused at all.

"You're both assholes," he declares as he gets up off the stool. "When you're ready to act like grownups again, I'll be in your office, making phone calls to try and fix your mess."

When he's out of earshot, I turn to my sister. "I'm gonna quickly check on Mia. Be right back." Her answer is to wave me toward the door.

I catch up with Mia and Griffin, just as they make the bottom of the front steps of her cottage. She must've heard me come up behind her and turns to face me. The sight of her wet eyes shocks me to the core.

Mia

"What the heck?"

I'd been able to hold it together long enough to get halfway down the pathway, before I gave in. They'd clearly not heard me come in, and I was a little thrown by the tension in the room. I clued in quickly to what was going on when I picked up on the conversation, but when that man started talking, I could hear the unspoken implication in his words. *Local sources.* He's an idiot if he thinks I would ever talk to the press, or anyone else for that matter.

"Mia? What's going on?" When I don't immediately answer, Jared grabs me by the shoulders and shakes me lightly.

"He doesn't like me much," I finally manage, to which Jared throws a brief glance toward his house before turning back to me.

"Brian? Why would you say that?" He looks genuinely surprised.

"Were you not listening? He was all but accusing me." He doesn't stop me when I head inside.

I'm rummaging around the kitchen, putting away the dishes that were drying in the sink, when he walks up, reaches around me, and stills my hands. The tears I'd successfully forced down, instantly start flowing again.

"Talk to me?" His breath plays through my hair as he rests his cheek against the side of my head. "Brian can be an ass, especially when he's in protective mode, but there's no way he thinks you're in any way responsible for any of this. What's going through your head?"

I find myself leaning back into him, instinctively searching for stability, and I curse my body for it.

"It's too much," I blurt out, forcing myself away from him. "Too much, too fast, too overwhelming. I tried…I did, but I can't catch my breath. It feels like barrelling down a steep hill without brakes, and you seem to like it that way, but every day my simple, peaceful existence is further out of reach. What if I can't find it back? Everything is changing around me and it terrifies me."

Jared reaches out but I take a step back. My breath shortens, my heart is racing, my scalp feels tight, and I want to pull my head between my shoulders like a turtle.

He doesn't get closer, soothing me with only the sound of his voice, although I'm beyond understanding the words. My knees give out and I sink down on the floor, my back against the cupboard. I vaguely register Griffin's wet nose nudging my bare leg. Dark floods my vision, slowly forcing out any light.

"Just go." I'm not sure if I yelled or whispered, but right before everything goes black, I hear Jared's response clearly.

"Not a chance in hell."

-

I wake up to the smell of my own sheets. For a moment, I think he's done what I asked. I'm alone, with only Griff's big body curled against my back for company—but then I hear the porch floorboards creak. Squinting carefully, I can just make out it's still light out, although the sun is low. My head throbs, my throat is parched, and I have to pee like a racehorse. Griffin immediately jumps off the bed when I move. He knows damn well he's not supposed to be on here, but we have a system that works for both of us. I let him pretend he's getting away with murder and he doesn't rub his disobedience in my face. Besides, I like the weight of his big body against my back.

I pad into the bathroom and avoid looking in the mirror, since I have a pretty good idea of the kind of devastation that would stare back at me, and take care of business. When I walk out, I'm startled to find Jordy standing beside my bed—I'd expected Jared.

"He's over at the house with Brian," she says when she notes my surprise. "They're on the phone, trying to sort through this mess. Been at it for hours."

"Where's Ole?"

"Sleeping on the porch in his car seat. Jared told me you weren't feeling well and he asked me to stay with you. I made some tea, you should come have a cup," she said, walking out without waiting for an answer. I duck back into the bathroom to splash some water on my face and sort my thoughts before I follow behind.

"Look," I start when Jordy puts down a cup of tea on the table in front of me. I struggle with the temptation to pick the baby up for a snuggle, but instead leave him sleeping and sit down in my chair beside his seat. Jordy sits down on the couch and contemplates me over the rim of her cup. "Thanks for coming over, but—"

The slam of her cup on the table startles me and wakes Ole, who starts crying immediately. Before I have a chance to pick him up, she's already out of her chair and grabs him from his seat. Bouncing him on her arm, she starts pacing back and forth.

"No buts," she snaps, clearly agitated. "Don't you dare tell me to go like you did Jared. I know this situation is not easy on you. Jesus, Mia, it's not easy on any of us, but it passes. Jared and I went through this right after my parents died; Jared was still the new kid on the block, but the drama was too good to resist for some of the gossip rags. He did what he had to do, to protect me and eventually they went away. Off to the next victim." She stops right in front of me. "Don't break his heart, Mia. Please. Give him a chance to set this right." I watch as her eyes fill up.

"I just need a chance to catch up," I implore. "A chance to get my life back on track." Jordy snorts at that, taking a seat on the couch and pulling up her shirt to feed a squirming Ole.

"Really, back on track? You mean another decade in hiding, sitting on your porch, and watching life pass right by you is more like it." My eyes shoot up at her. I never told her the details of what happened to me and am wondering whether Jared shared. "All he told me that something happened to you the same night our parents died, Mia," she says, reading my mind. "So you should know by now that life has no track. It just bounces you around. But if you want to enjoy the good stuff, you have to take the bumps that come along with it. You can't control it—that's an illusion—because the moment you're in control, you're no longer living—you're merely existing."

Jared

To say I'm taken aback when I see Mia follow my sister in the door is an understatement.

All afternoon, I've agonized over the defeated tone of her voice when she asked me to go. I thought it had been a simple misunderstanding I needed to clear up when I went after her, but it had been so much more than that. I'd held her, trying to talk her through her panic attack, but it was clear she didn't hear me. I'd put her to bed and called Jordy over, determined to give her the space she wanted. It killed to leave her like that.

I watch, almost detached, as Brian stands up and walks over to Mia, his hands loosely on her shoulders as he softly speaks to her. I'd talked to him earlier, asked him straight out whether there was anything to what she'd told me, and he'd been mortified. The reference he made was to my indiscretions before Mia came along—he was concerned for her, not worried about her.

Mia's head nods lightly as she takes in what he's saying, until finally her eyes find me and a ball of anxiety threatens to choke me. For some reason, it's important she come to me, but it's almost impossible to stay seated on the stool. As she starts moving toward me, I want to rush and meet her halfway, but I don't.

The last few feet she runs, and I barely have time to open my arms and legs before she presses herself against

287

me. Brian and Jordy discreetly disappear through the sliding door, leaving us alone. I bury my face in her curls and wait for her to speak. She doesn't keep me waiting long.

"I panicked," she whispers.

"I know." I stroke my hand up and down the length of her spine. "We'll work it out," I promise her.

"I want that," she says, burrowing a little deeper into my arms, before she adds, "just give me a little time to work a few things out for myself."

TWENTY-SIX

Jared

The last three days have been hard.

What the hell, the last few weeks have been challenging. Especially for someone who normally likes having his socks and shirts organized by colour. It seems that since I chose the more relaxed lifestyle of rural living, chaos wasn't too far behind.

When Mia told me she needed time, the balloon of hope that had started filling my chest, just as quickly deflated. If not for Jordy being a voice of reason, cautioning me that by putting too much pressure on her, I'd only chase her further away, I might've gone after her again. Instead I did the next best thing, I watched her walk away, while I called Jake and asked him to get a couple more guys out to make sure her cottage would be covered from all sides. At least I could make sure nobody else would be able to spook her either.

Brian stayed the night Saturday because Sunday morning we were expected in the Colts' offices for ten o'clock. A little unusual, but I've gotten used to the fact that there are no weekends in this industry. Contracts are negotiated any day of the week. They'd made it clear they had something to discuss, so that was positive. Of course when we arrived at their offices, we soon found out that they'd gotten wind of the press buzzing. I swear I ground my teeth down to the bone to stay composed when they dove right into my personal life. Brian had prepared me for this, but it still felt like being called into the principal's office. They seemed satisfied with my explanation of things, indicated they would be happy to finalize our negotiations, but only after I'd made sure the threat of an assault charge was completely eliminated. That made the fact when Taylor Torrence notified us through his lawyers he wouldn't be able to do the interview until Wednesday, even more frustrating. The prick is dragging us all along and enjoying every sick second of it.

Jordy stayed in touch with Mia, who had asked to be kept up to speed. That, and the knowledge that she'd be here on Wednesday, helped. A little.

"Are you sure you'll be okay with Ole? I have two bottles pumped in the door of the fridge, but you should be fine with only one," Jordy says, coming from the nursery where she's just put her son down for a nap.

"Sure you don't want me to drive?" I try again, even though I already know the answer. Jordy smiles as she grabs her purse and walks over to kiss my cheek.

"Don't lose it now, honey. She had Steffie there all day Sunday—and let me just say, that woman is *so* in your fan club—and she had a good day yesterday. Today is therapy; her regular appointment and then my kind of therapy—the spa."

"I don't know if this is a good time to go out in public." I can tell from the dramatic roll of her eyes, my weak protest is falling on deaf ears.

"Bullshit," she calls me out. "And you know it. No one will bother us—we've got police escort."

Exactly.

I glare out the window where LeBlanc's cruiser is just rolling to a stop in the driveway. Damn cop's been by twice already this weekend. Granted, I called him first. Tore him a new one for putting his hands on my sister, and then asked him what he was planning to do to stop other idiots from coming in over the water and invading our privacy. Twenty minutes later he was knocking on our door, his eyes immediately searching out Jordy, and without a word to me, he went straight for her. At least he had the good sense not to kiss her in front of me.

I watch as he gets out of the vehicle and with sure strides walks up to the front door.

"Be nice," Jordy says, as she goes up on tiptoes and kisses my cheek. "I'll be back in a few hours."

My hands are balled into fists in my pockets, as she pulls open the door and smiles at the man on the other side. Fucking guy doesn't even notice me, his damn eyes are glued to my sister when he reaches out, lifts her chin, and plants a kiss on her. I turn away. It's either that, or assault on a police officer, and I really don't need that on top of everything else.

"I'll keep 'em safe," I hear him say from behind me.

"You fucking better," I growl, and I don't turn around until I hear the door close.

Like an idiot, I watch him help my sister into the SUV, kissing her a-*fucking*-gain, before getting in himself. I lose sight of them at the top of the hill, and wait for them to appear at the top of Mia's drive, where I know they're headed.

I watch the bounce of her curls as she comes out the door and down the steps where she stops. Her eyes turn this way and I swear she's looking right at me. Back up the steps she goes, opens the door and lets Griffin out. I can't hear what she's saying to the dog, but she's pointing in this direction, and he obediently comes trotting down the trail as she gets in the back of the cruiser and they drive off.

-

"He's gonna be there at ten tomorrow morning. I'll try and get there a little early, but if for some reason I get stuck in traffic, try not to put your hands on him."

"He'd do well to be on his best behaviour then," I snort. "One wrong word on his part and I can't guarantee he'll be walking by the time you get here." Brian audibly sighs at my admission, making me feel a little guilty.

"Maybe we should ask LeBlanc to play referee until I get there?" he suggests. Although my instinct is to blow that idea off, it might have some merit. From what little I know of him, I'm pretty sure John won't take too kindly to anyone even hinting anything negative toward my sister. The cop appears to be quite invested. Maybe it wouldn't be so bad to have some added pressure to keep Torrence in line.

"Maybe we should," I repeat back to him, rendering him speechless.

"Well, I'll be…I thought you didn't like the guy?"

"He had his mouth on my sister; of course I don't like him. But it won't hurt to have another set of eyes looking out for her," I grumble, to Brian's hilarity.

"I'll talk to him," I cut him off, mid-snicker, before ending the call.

I adjust my grip on Ole's little butt. Instead of putting him back in his crib, when he fell asleep on my shoulder after his bottle, I've kept him with me on the couch while watching some asinine daytime show. Between the white noise from the TV, Griffin's snores from where he's lying at my feet, and Ole's little breaths and whimpers in my neck, I was dozing off when Brian called.

A quick glance at the clock tells me I missed lunch. Griffin's droopy head lifts briefly when I get up. When I put Ole down in his crib, his face scrunches up, and for a second it looks like he'll protest, but then his little face evens out again and he's fast asleep.

I'm just putting the finishing touches on my sandwich when Griffin lifts his head and lets out a soft woof. I look outside, just as LeBlanc's cruiser stops in front of Mia's cottage. I try to ignore the pang of disappointment as I watch Mia get out, and with only a glance in this direction, make her way inside. It certainly sticks in my craw to see officer LeBlanc carry a few bags of groceries up to her door.

The dog is already by the sliding door. When I open it for him, he shoots out and with long, loping strides he rushes around the bay.

Dejectedly, I take a bite from my sandwich and wait for my sister to get home.

Mia

"So what is your plan now?"

I've just finished an exhausting session with Rueben. He didn't accept any evasion on my part. Drilled me on my reactions, expectations, and hopes; and had me verbalize any and all hesitations, fears, and emotions. At the end of my hour, I'd finished his box of tissues and felt wrung out, but my head was clear.

I wiggle my toes in the warm water as I contemplate how to answer Jordy, who had the massage chair next to me. It had been her idea to book us in for pedicures after my appointment, and at this moment, I can't remember the last time I've felt this relaxed. The spa is quiet on a Tuesday and I haven't felt even a hint of panic yet.

"I don't have a plan, per se. More like a list of things I'd like to explore," I try to explain.

"Does your list include my brother?" I look up, shocked at the sharp edge to that question, but then I see the emotion on her face.

"Top of my list, honey," I reassure her, earning a big watery smile.

"Thank God, I'm so relieved. If I have to put up with his mopey ass one more day, I might throw myself off the dock," Jordy shares with a touch of drama.

"The water's only about five feet deep there. You could probably stand, or else your cop could—'cause you know he'd jump in right after you," I point out chuckling.

"Did you pick your colour?" she asks, completely changing the subject.

She'd told me a little about their dinner Friday night. John had been attentive both with her and the baby and they'd talked for hours. He'd kissed her, which I already knew, and apparently left right after. And she hadn't seen him since. When he'd finally called last night to see if she wanted to grab lunch, she told him she already had plans, which had led to him driving us today. Something she made sure she let him know this morning, she wasn't too happy about. When he'd come to pick us up, she'd given him the cold shoulder, and I had to stifle my grin at his attempts to get her to talk.

"Yes, I did," I tell her, waving the bottle with dark grey polish in her face. Something a little rebellious. "But don't think I haven't noticed your determination not to talk about what's going on with you and John. What did he do? Saturday morning you were clearly taken with the man, almost giddy, and now?" I look at her but she turns away, her teeth chewing at her lips.

"He didn't call," she says in a soft voice.

"He *did* call," I correct her. "Did you not hear him explain he was tied up with that horrible crash on Highway 11 all weekend?" Her shoulders slump and her head drops down. "What's really going on?" I push when she still doesn't say anything.

"I don't know," she admits with a deep sigh. "I was thinking all weekend this might not be such a good idea. I mean, I just had a baby, I have a possible custody battle coming up with a man, who I couldn't even keep around long enough to see his child born. I barely have my feet under me, and now I'm getting involved with another guy, who might not want to stick around once he gets a good taste of the mess my life is in."

"Awww, Jordy," I soothe her, rubbing my hand on her back. "John doesn't look like a runner, doll. He appears to have his eyes wide open and knows exactly what he's walking into. Besides, your life is not a mess. Look at you—you're a wonderful mother to a beautiful little boy, you walked away from a job and the city, just so he can grow up in God's country, surrounded by the love of family. What's messed up about that? You're gorgeous, you're funny, and you're a wonderful friend. I'm lucky to have in my life. Even if you don't see all of that, I can guarantee you John does," I encourage her, handing over a box of tissues so she can dry her tears.

"Damn right he does." Neither of us had heard him come in, but John clearly heard at least the last part of our conversation. He ignores the two girls bent over our feet and moves straight to Jordy's chair. He leans down, bracing himself on her armrests. I can't help the smile when I turn away to give them whatever privacy I can, but I still hear his deep rumble.

"I see my attempt to slowly let you get used to me left you with enough time to get some cockamamie ideas in your head." I almost snort out loud at the audibly offended gasp from Jordy and struggle not to have a look at her face. "It's apparently not working," he continues. "And just so we're clear, you *are* gorgeous, you *are* funny, you *are* a great mother, and there is no way you'll see me running from all that. I'm sticking around." It would appear he heard enough of our conversation.

I turn just in time to watch the big man in uniform press a hard kiss to her mouth. He straightens up and walks away, only to sit down in the waiting area, grab a copy of *Cosmopolitan* from the table, and with jerky movements, starts flipping through. I look at Jordy, whose face looks like mine feels, eyes wide, mouth half-open. Then both of us look at the ladies at our feet to find them much in the same state.

That's when I burst out laughing.

-

"Are you coming over?" Jordy asks, when John stops in my driveway.

She'd wanted to stop off for a few things at the grocery store, and I felt brave enough to go in to pick up a few things of my own. John insisted on coming in. We must've looked funny, the big cop following right behind us, but I barely noticed, because Jordy was chattering the entire time. When to start the baby on solids, what's a good age to wean, did I have a preference for diapers. I didn't get a chance to panic. She was firing off questions left and right. Only after we'd loaded everything in John's SUV, and we'd climbed in, she fell quiet and turned to me with a smirk on her face. She'd known exactly what she was doing.

"Nope. I'm gonna put this stuff away, and then I'm going to do a bit of research."

"About what?" she wants to know.

"Your brother. I don't want to look like a moron if that asshole starts asking specific questions. I know nothing of hockey and had no idea who Jared was until Steffie told me. I just want to be prepared for tomorrow."

"You already know everything that's important about him," she counters, and I smile at her as I get out of the vehicle.

"You know that, and I know that, but he doesn't," I clarify, leaning back in to grab my bag. "I'm anxious enough about the whole thing, it'll help me settle down."

"Fine, just don't believe everything you read online."

A couple of hours later, I remind myself of those words.

It's almost like there are two different people, the Jared I know and the one everyone else sees. I'm actually glad that I opted not to Google him when Steffie first told me he was someone famous. It would probably have unfairly skewed my opinion of him. But now I'm glad I did, because there was enough material there for Mr. Torrence to completely blindside me if he wanted to. Not so much the hockey background, but the numerous pictures of him in the company of one or another beautiful woman. Given the spirit of his earlier article, I have no doubt Torrence would find great pleasure in trying to embarrass me again. I won't let him.

After a quick salad for dinner, I grab a towel and head outside. I've missed my kayak. Griffin launches into his usual complaint of pitiful whimpers when he sees me head to the dock with my towel. For a while, when I first got him, he would jump in and swim after me, but I quickly cured him of that. I occasionally go out in the canoe so he can come, something he loves to do, but I generally prefer the kayak. It's great exercise, and I can actually go fast enough to feel the wind in my hair. Tonight I could really use some fresh air to clear my head.

I sneak a quick glance at Jared's place, but don't see any movement outside, and push off quickly. It's been harder than I though to stay away the past few days, but it's been helpful. Whenever I'm around him, I can't seem to think straight. It becomes difficult to identify what is what. The lines between want and need, lust and love—it all becomes blurred—and I really felt I needed the time to pick through it all in my head, without my body taking the lead.

When I paddle back and round the corner into our bay, I immediately spot Jared sitting on the edge of his dock. His feet are dangling in the water and my dog, the traitor, is sitting next to him. Both are keenly watching my approach.

I nudge the kayak right up to his dock and Jared reaches out to grab the rope I left curled on the bow. He pulls until the kayak is parallel with the dock and I reach out to give my dog a little attention, and at the same time avoid looking at Jared.

"I miss you," he says, his voice soft and low. My eyes come up and his hand reaches out to brush the curls out of my face.

"Me, too," I admit.

We silently stare at each other for a moment before I take his hand and press a kiss in his palm.

"This was never about trusting you. It was about trusting myself. Believing the truth of my feelings. I needed some time without peripheral noise."

"Did you find the answer?" he asks, and I can feel the barely suppressed tension in that question.

"I did." I smile and shove away from the dock hard. Jared jumps to his feet and watches me drift off with his hands on his hips.

"And?" he calls after me, and I throw a glance over my shoulder.

"I'll be there tomorrow," is my non-answer.

"Mia…" I don't know how he manages to make my name sound like a threat, but he does. I smile, pulling myself out of the water at my own dock, before I put him out of his misery.

"I love you."

The words aren't loud—I all but whisper them—but they bounce over the water until I see their impact written all over Jared's face. Then I grab my towel and hurry inside.

TWENTY-SEVEN

Jared

I don't like the smirk on the face of that asshole when Brian opens the door for him.

At least he's on time, I'll give him that. Ten o'clock, on the dot, he walks up to my door, loaded down with camera equipment and a messenger bag. *Douche*.

"Morning," he says, way too cheerfully, and I force a curt nod, which is about all I can manage. His sneaky eyes scan the inside of my house and land on Jordy, who just walks into the kitchen. "Are we missing someone?"

"Ms. Thompson will be joining us soon," Brian says quickly, hearing the low growl coming from me.

Had it been up to me, she'd be far away. Especially after last night.

-

I heard her clearly, but the words had been so unexpected, I stood there frozen, only moving when she snatched up her stuff and beelined it inside. The moment the door closed behind her, I became unstuck and hurried up the dock to get around to her place, but Jordy stood right outside the house.

"Let her come to you," she said, putting a hand on my arm.

"You don't understand." I shook her off and continued toward the trail, when her next words stopped me in my tracks.

"It's important, Jared. She's building up her strength, don't take that away from her by storming over there. You'll only minimize the courage it took for her to put herself out there. She said those words as much for you, as she did for herself." I swing around to face my sister.

"You heard," I concluded.

"I did," she said, a smile on her face. "And I know you're dying to tell her you feel the same way, but what she just did was huge. Let her have that moment without taking it over with a grand gesture of your own."

I hated that she made sense, but I let her guide me inside the house anyway. I couldn't let Mia's statement go entirely unanswered though, so the moment I hit my bed, I pulled out my phone and sent her a message.

Sweetest words I ever tasted.

I didn't hear anything back, but I closed my eyes smiling. The Enforcer has officially retired.

-

"Before we start," Brian addresses him. "I'd like to make sure you brought the tape we'd discussed as part of the agreement?" Torrence glances at Jordy, who slides a coffee in front of him, before digging through his bag and coming up with a USB key.

302

"I saved it on here. Feel free to check." Brian takes the key from him and disappears into the office, probably to spare Jordy from having to hear the voice of her ex.

In the awkward silence that follows, my eyes are drawn to the sliding doors and Mia's cottage on the other side. I catch a glimpse of something moving into the tree line, but it's so brief, I can't be sure if it's human or animal. Not wanting to draw attention to the fact I'm feeling a bit anxious that Mia still hasn't shown, I turn to Torrence and force myself to speak.

"When will this go to print?"

"Friday edition," he responds just as curtly. I'm just thinking this interview will be a riveting event, when Brian walks back in.

"Sent the files to Mary," he informs me as he sidles up to the island, picking up his abandoned coffee cup. "It's all there, so let's get this show on the road," he directs at Torrence.

"Still waiting for Ms. Thompson," the asshole says again, although I'm still at a loss what his hard-on over her being there is.

"She'll be here," Jordy jumps in before I can question his motivations. I face her and lift my eyebrows in question. Her light nod is all I need to know she's probably spoken with Mia already this morning. "Let's take a seat in the living room." She grabs her tea, and moves in that direction, without waiting for an answer, fully expecting us to follow.

Torrence is the last one to take a seat when there's a knock. Jordy's already on her feet to get the door, showing

303

Mia followed closely by LeBlanc. I have no idea what he's doing here, but it's clearly not a surprise to my sister. Remembering Jordy's caution, I remain seated, but my gaze is firmly locked on Mia, who hugs my sister back, before her eyes dart through the room and finally land on me. She seems a little lost when Jordy gives her attention to LeBlanc next. He leans down and has the good sense to kiss only her cheek, while Mia hesitates in the doorway. I give her a little encouraging nod and that appears to be enough to get her moving—straight for me. I figure I've been patient enough and meet her halfway, pulling her in my arms. I smile in her hair when hers slip around my waist right away.

"We'll talk after," I whisper for her ears only. She seems to understand instinctively, pulling away from me and plastering a smile on as she faces first Brian and next Torrence. He seems unhappy to see LeBlanc here, which fucking thrills me, even though I may not have been excited about it myself at first. I give Mia the chair and sit down on the armrest myself.

"Good to see you again, Mia," Brian says.

"You, too." She smiles a little shyly and I realize the last time they were in the same room they weren't exactly seeing eye to eye. Another wrinkle that needs to be ironed out, but not now.

Brian encourages Torrence to ask his questions, once Jordy and John sit down, saving Mia the need to acknowledge the guy. At first the questions are as expected. How do I feel about Gunnarson, the guy whose hit caused my final injury? Do I hold him responsible for the end of my career?

Then he moves to my retirement, plans for the future, and I'm able to let him know there are some job leads I'm looking into. Brian cuts off that line of questioning quickly, letting him know in no uncertain terms that there is no more he'll get on that subject for now.

His next question throws me off.

"I did a little research; your parents died tragically your first full year in the NHL, how did that affect your career?" I don't trust the quick glance he shoots at Jordy, and I notice LeBlanc catching that as well. He drapes his arm around my sister and tucks her closer.

"They did, and if there was any effect on my career, it would've been that I worked even harder after," I recover quickly and think I'm back in control, but then he turns to Jordy.

"Must be tough, raising a baby as a single mom," he suddenly shifts gears again with his focus on my sister.

"Hey," Brian interjects before anyone else can. "Is there any purpose to this?"

"Just getting a feel for the family," he says with a shrug and a look of fake innocence. "You've got to admit, it looks like there've been some dramatic changes since Jared got injured. I think the public would be interested. The whole familial, domestic scene is a far cry from the hard playing, hard partying Enforcer we know."

"Shows you how little that is," Jordy snaps, taking the bait. "My brother has always been much more than what the press chose to focus on. The only difference is that our family of two has expanded."

And like a well-seasoned fisherman, Torrence sets the hook.

"It certainly has," he says, a smug grin on his face as he takes in not only LeBlanc, but shifts his eyes to Mia. "I can tell you've settled in nicely with the locals. Although, you're a transplant yourself, aren't you, Ms. Thompson?"

Mia

Jared's arm tightens around my shoulders when the man's focus falls on me. I'd been waiting for it, knowing he probably had a reason for demanding I'd be here for the interview as well, but I still had to suppress the urge to go hide in the nursery. Instead I square my shoulders and look him straight in the eyes.

"I moved here five years ago."

"You must've thought the gods were smiling on you when you saw who your new neighbour was," he says suggestively. I snort at his implications.

"Not quite," I inform him. "First of all, I know nothing about hockey, so I had not the faintest idea who Jared was. If anything, I was upset when I discovered my wonderful, quiet neighbours had sold to someone with a speedboat."

"Right, but you don't seem too upset now."

"I'm not quite sure what point you're trying to make, but I know there is one, otherwise, you wouldn't have demanded I be here." I could feel Jared shifting after Torrence's last remark, but I put my hand on his knee to hold him back. I don't want to be rescued, he's done enough of that.

"There is." The smirk is back on his face, like he can't wait to pounce on me. "I think it makes a fascinating story that a woman whose mental instability lost her everything—her clinic, her career, her house, her marriage—managed to snag herself one of hockey's most eligible, rich bachelors."

The room immediately fills with indignant shouts from Jordy and Brian, and I have to hang on to Jared, or he'd have the guy decked out on the ground. Even Ole joins in the fray, his loud cries piercing the heated exchanges. I am remarkably unaffected. Cool as a cucumber as I watch a grumbling Jordy take off to the nursery. But that doesn't last long.

"You've done your homework," I say, loud enough to be heard over the din, as I stand up. One by one, all eyes come to me and suddenly I'm not so cool anymore, but I forge ahead. "Too bad you didn't do it well and only bothered to take what fits your story. Otherwise, you might've known someone diagnosed with PTSD and resulting agoraphobia, would not voluntarily put themselves in the public eye for anything. Trust me, I fought hard not to fall for a man most of whose adult life has been lived in the limelight. I never expected anything but to live my nice, quiet existence out on this lake. But we don't always get what we hope for—If we're lucky, we get what we need."

Having said all I plan to, I follow Jordy down the hall and close the nursery door behind me, leaning my back and head against the door.

"How the hell did you stay so calm?" Jordy wants to know. She's rocking back and forth in the glider, feeding Ole.

"Not that calm, trust me. Right now my heart is wanting to pound out of my chest, and I feel like I'm going to black out," I admit.

"Do you want to sit down?" I slide my back down the door until my ass hits the carpet. "I meant the chair," Jordy says, chuckling.

"I'm good here," I mumble with my eyes closed, concentrating on breathing in and out.

The quiet of the nursery, with only the occasional little noise coming from Ole, does wonders to settle me. By the time a knock sounds on the door, my heart rate is back to normal, and I open my eyes to find Jordy observing me.

"Better?" she asks.

"Much," I tell her, scrambling to my feet to open the door.

I'm expecting Jared and am surprised to find Brian standing outside.

"I left your cop out there to make sure Jared doesn't wipe the floor with Torrence," he directs at Jordy, who has the baby on her shoulder, rubbing his back. "Came to check if you ladies are up for a few pictures. It looks like we won't get rid of the guy until he has those."

"Fine," Jordy answers for both of us. "But no pictures of Ole."

"Of course," Brian acknowledges. "I believe that's been made very clear already, by both your men."

-

Forty-five minutes later, we all let go a collective sigh when the journalist's van disappears over the hill.

John had taken Ole from Jordy, and seemed quite at ease with the little guy, keeping him occupied and eventually rocking him to sleep. Torrence had us all over the living room and kitchen, as well as out on the dock and even in the boat for his shots. My jaw hurt from smiling so much. It certainly isn't something I'd want to do again anytime soon, the close scrutiny with the camera a bit too invasive for my taste. Jared was clearly an old pro at this and looked at ease in front of the camera, despite the frustration I knew was bubbling right under the surface.

Brian had walked the man to his vehicle to, as Jared explained, remind him of the stipulations of their agreement. This was supposed to be a one time exclusive, and he was to steer clear of our personal lives from here on out

"Come out on the boat with me?" Jared asks, as he turns me in his arms. We're the last ones out on the dock. Jordy followed John in the house to put the baby down and Brian had to take a call. Jared had gone to let the dog out, who'd been cooped up in the cottage and came running when he saw me out here.

"Sure." I look to the house. "Should we let them know?"

"They'll figure it out," he says, leading me to the edge of the dock and helping me in. Griffin isn't about to be left behind and makes his own way into the boat.

He finds his way onto the bench in the stern and has his face stuck in the air, his eyes almost squeezed shut against the wind, as soon as Jared hits the throttle. All the tension of the day disappears as I do the same, stick my face into the wind that whips my curls around my head. I let myself sink into the moment, feeling the weight of the past few days slip off my shoulders as we speed across the water. I'll never give up the leisurely pace of my kayak, but I have to admit, I have a new appreciation for speed.

When I hear the engine slow, I open my eyes to find Jared looking at me, his eyes warm. I look around to find us coasting toward a familiar spot. I spot the moose standing knee-high in the water the moment Griffin does too, and I quickly put my hand on his back when he emits a soft growl. Jared cuts the engine completely and carefully moves from the pilot's seat to wedge himself behind me on the bench, both his arms coming around me to pull my back into his chest.

"Wait for it," he says softly in my curls, and as we watch, a calf steps out from behind its mother.

"Oh, he's so beautiful." I keep my voice low as well, knowing how rare a sight this is, especially when the sun is still fairly high in the sky. Dawn and dusk are the times to spot wildlife. During the heat of the day in summer, they prefer to stay under the canopy of the trees, where it's much cooler.

"First time I saw her with her calf was the day Ole was born," Jared tells me. "He was much smaller then. It was right here, at this spot, where you came to our rescue and everything changed." I tilt back to get a look at his face. His eyes are set on the moose and her young, but his focus is on me. I can feel it in his touch. "Since Mom and Dad died, I'd done a pretty good job of avoiding feeling anything too deep or too profound. Lived my life on the surface. But that day there was no avoiding it. Not with Ole's birth impacting me the way it did—and most definitely not with you appearing out of nowhere, and being the calm in the raging storm of my emotions. I may have fallen for you right then." Now he drops his eyes to my face, the moose and her baby all but forgotten as he seems to take in my features.

"Jared…"

"You did it again today, Beautiful. I know you were probably shaking inside yourself, but still managed to instantly calm the hothead in me." His hand curves around my jaw, lifting my face as he covers my mouth with his in a sweet, lazy kiss before releasing me. "Not sure what I've done to deserve you in my life, but I'm keeping you here. I love you, Mia."

TWENTY-EIGHT

Mia

His words are still ringing in my ears, long after I hear his breathing deepen with sleep beside me.

By the time we'd docked, John had left and Brian was helping Jordy put dinner together in the kitchen. I'd no idea we'd been out that long, the afternoon had somehow slipped away. If there was any question as to where I'd be staying the night, Griffin answered that the moment he curled up in front of Jared's couch, once Brian headed home after dinner.

My first impression of him had been all wrong. Something he proved quickly with his whispered apology for giving the wrong impression a few days ago. He managed to catch me at the sink tonight, assuring me once again he'd never seen Jared more relaxed than he is around me. From someone who's known him for years, it felt good to hear I have the same impact on him as he appears to have on me.

Jordy ducked into her room shortly after Brian left, which left Jared and me, the dog at our feet.

"What do you want to watch?" he'd asked, remote in hand.

"I'm not really in the mood for anything." Jared's arm tightened around me.

"Not in the mood?" His voice dipped low against my ear.

"For TV," I clarified, and stifled my giggle when he lifted me clear off the couch, earning an annoyed grunt from Griffin, and carried me straight to his bedroom. There he showed me exactly what he was in the mood for.

The weight of his sleeping body, half-draped over mine, is welcome. I came hard after Jared used that body to worship mine. There'd been no words needed as he showed me with his hands and mouth, as well as other parts, what he conveyed earlier on the boat. He loves me. The language of his touch a much stronger impact even than his voiced thoughts. It's like he needed to impress his feelings on my skin, so there'd no longer be room for any doubt. And there wasn't.

I love you.

I still hear the words as I let them settle in my heart and succumb to sleep myself.

-

I've only been back to my place to pick up some dog food, clean clothes, and some groceries that would otherwise spoil. It didn't take much to convince me to hang out at Jared's. There was still security necessary at the gate. Apparently curiosity kept interest from the press high and likely would until the Friday newspapers hit the stands. So anticipation had been high for the article in *The Sun* to come out.

I'm up early Friday morning, letting Griffin out, and enjoying my coffee and book on the dock, when the sliding doors open and Jordy sticks her head outside.

"It's up!" she calls out, and I don't need to ask what she's talking about.

Grabbing my empty cup and my Kindle, I rush inside after her.

Jared

"Did you read it?"

I walk into the kitchen to find Mia, a scowl on her face.

I just finished showering after waking up and finding her gone from bed. I figured if I didn't hit the bathroom right away, I might not get a chance to today. That proves to have been a good call, judging by Mia's reaction.

"Not yet," I calmly reply, walking into her space and giving her a good morning kiss. Satisfied I managed to momentarily distract her with my mouth, I use the brief pause following to my advantage, and quickly pour myself a coffee. "Show me." I nudge her, as I sit down at the counter beside her.

"Where did he get this nonsense?" she says, poking her finger at the screen of the opened laptop. I lean in and immediately note the headline.

315

Domestic Bliss for Kesla
The Enforcer shackled and chained

"Is there a problem?" I turn to her, more than a little confused. The headline is nothing other than what I'd expect from *The Sun*, designed to hook the reader in. A quick scan through the photo spread and accompanying article, shows nothing really offensive.

"He makes it sound like we're all living together in some kind of commune," she pouts, clearly not happy.

"What's so bad about that?" I probe, and it earns me a fierce glare. "Look," I try to appease. "I get that this is new to you, this kind of public exposure, but it's old hat for me. Reporters like adding a little innuendo to get people's imaginations going. People love reading that shit. I've learned not to worry too much about it, unless what is printed is blatantly untrue or damaging. This is surprisingly tame, as far as articles go. It doesn't really state untruths, it's just suggestive."

"Well, it suggests I've ditched my *little hovel* in favour of your *dream home*," Mia points out, clicking to the next page where two images are set side by side, one of her cottage, and the other of my place. My house looks like a mansion in the manipulated image, whereas Mia's cottage is made to look rather desolate and dark. I have to bite my lip not to laugh when I see Mia's crestfallen face.

"I happen to love your little hovel," I try to tease a smile out of her.

"Yeah, well, he may not have said it in so many words, but the implication I'm a gold digger is out there," she says wistfully. "And I still live there."

I slide a hand up her back and around her neck, gently turning her face toward mine. "A technicality," I point out, my nose almost touching hers.

"Jared…" she starts, but I don't let her finish. I cover her mouth with mine, and stop the protest I know was forming on her lips. By the time my tongue tastes her, I've forgotten what we were talking about myself.

"It's one thing to know stuff is going on behind closed doors," Jordy says, as she comes in through the sliding doors. "But watching you two chew each other's face before I've had a chance to get something solid in my stomach? That's just not right." With a healthy dose of drama, she covers her eyes, and stumbles down the hall to the nursery, making Mia giggle.

-

"Absolutely. Yes, I can be there at nine."

I smile as I watch Mia try and help Jordy into her canoe. My sister had made us laugh when she announced she wanted to be more 'outdoorsy,' but Mia had been quick to offer her help. The girls had decided mastering the canoe would be the first requirement.

Brian's call had come in just as they'd headed across to Mia's dock, leaving me in charge of a sleeping Ole. He'd been in touch with the management at the Colts' office and they were ready to firm up their offer now.

Tomorrow is the first day of the Colts' training camp and, apparently, they want me there. I don't mind being

317

thrown to the wolves right off the bat. There's no better way to prove myself than during two days of scrimmages and instruction. Training camp generally starts with a large contingent of hopefuls but is whittled down to a viable team by the end of the weekend. After that, training starts for the upcoming season. Funny, even though I'm no longer a player, the prospect of being part of a team again is just as exciting.

I watch the girls push away from the dock, and ease onto the lake, rocking the canoe in the process. In true big brother fashion, I'm half-waiting for the damn thing to tip over so I can have a good laugh, despite a bit of wobbling, they stay afloat.

Grabbing the baby monitor off the counter, I head outside to the garage, where I'm hoping to find my skates. It's been a while since I've been on them, but skating is as instinctive as walking, after spending most of my life on the ice. A large metal shelving unit against the far wall looks to hold all my sporting equipment, as well as a bunch of boxes.

Curious, I lift one down. On the flap it says: *Memorabilia.* I pull the flap loose and open the box up. On top of what looks like a pile of newspapers is a puck wrapped in hockey tape. On the side a date is written. My first goal. I haven't seen it since I proudly handed it over to my father after that game. I put it aside and pull out the newspapers, all featuring a different milestone in my career; that first NHL goal, selection to the Olympic team, trades, trophies. Underneath are ribbons and medals from my junior hockey and rep days. An album with every team

318

and individual picture from the time I was six and joined my first team.

That's when it dawns on me that these boxes came from my parents' house. Brian had taken charge of packing up most of their belongings after they died. I hadn't been in any shape to tackle that task. I'd been too busy trying to stay upright for my sister's sake. These must've been in storage with a lot of my other stuff. I'd taken to storing things I didn't need in my everyday life, to make it easier to pick up and go. I'd lived in a number of different apartments, in different cities, over the years. Always with a minimum of clutter. I used to tell myself it was more convenient that way, but I realize now it was more than that. Unpacking my baggage would mean setting down roots, and I wasn't ready for that.

By the time Ole's little whimpers sound through the monitor, I'm sitting on the floor of the garage, every last box pulled down from the shelves and the contents spread around me. My life spread out on the cool concrete. As I get up to see to my nephew, I wonder if maybe I'm ready now.

"Hey, little man," I murmur in his downy hair when I lift him from the bed. He's not crying, just complaining and I soon discover it's because of a soaking wet diaper. Poor kid's romper is drenched. "Let me clean you up, buddy. I've got something to show you."

Mia

"That was fun, but I'm sure my arms will be sore tomorrow," Jordy says, as we pull the canoe up on the dock.

"Mine will be, too," I admit, feeling the slight pull in my muscles. "Only a few weeks without my daily exercise and it feels like it was my first time."

We paddled straight to Jared's dock. Jordy wanted to get home, since it was close to Ole's next feeding. I follow her inside the house and turn to the kitchen while she continues to the nursery. I down a glass of water, while checking the fridge for something to make for dinner. I wonder if Jared is in his office, it's awfully quiet in here.

"Where the heck are they?" Jordy comes out of the back hallway, confusion on her face as she turns down the other hallway, leading to Jared's office and bedroom.

"Nothing?" I ask when she reappears seconds later.

"I don't get it." She moves to the front door and I follow behind. Jared's car is still parked in the drive, as is Jordy's, so they can't have gone far.

"Hey," Jared's voice rings out. He's in the garage, the door is halfway up, and he's sitting amid a big mess on the floor, Ole in his lap.

"What are you doing?" Jordy wants to know, walking ahead of me.

"Looking through some stuff I didn't even realize was in here," he says, handing Ole to his mom. He started squirming the moment he heard Jordy's voice. My attention is drawn to an opened album, showing a picture of a young boy with a toothless smile.

"Is that you?" I ask, as I lean down to pick it up to study it more closely. Undeniably Jared, with the same clear eyes and mischievous smile, minus a couple of front teeth, and no older than maybe seven.

"He was cute then," Jordy says looking over my shoulder. "I'm gonna feed this boy. You guys figure out dinner?"

"Sure," I mumble, a little absentminded, as I flip to the next page. It's not until I no longer hear her footsteps that I realize how easily that slipped out. The assumption I'd be here for dinner, as if I belonged here. My eyes find Jared, who is looking up at me from his perch on the floor. "You were cute," I say a bit uneasily. I'm not quite sure how to place the look he is giving me.

"Were?"

"Cute is not a word I'd associate with you now," I point out.

"Thank fuck for that," he groans, but does it smiling. "Come sit." He clears a spot on the floor beside him and I sink down, clutching the album in my lap.

"What is all this?"

"Stuff I haven't seen in years. Not since my parents died. My entire career up to that point is in these boxes. They kept everything." Despite the smile on his face, I hear the pain of loss in his voice and scoot a little closer.

"They were proud of you," I gently suggest, rubbing my hand along his spine.

321

"That they were. Of both of us," he says, pointing out another few boxes left on the shelf. "Those are Jordy's. I doubt she's ever seen them."

"So how did they end up here?"

"Brian shipped it all from storage when I moved in." I watch him idly flip a puck between his large fingers like a coin, a sad smile on his mouth. I put my head on his shoulder and flip a page of the album.

"Tell me about this one…" I point to a picture of Jared, lying sprawled on the ice, in front of a team of grinning boys, a large trophy in the middle. I can feel the low chuckle vibrate in his body, as he drapes an arm around my shoulders and pulls me closer.

"The OMHA championship trophy."

I listen to the rumble in his chest as he recounts his first real taste of success, and every one after. It becomes clear to me how much he's lost. After the death of his parents, his career was what kept him grounded, and now that is over, what does he have left?

"I have my sister, and Ole, and more than I'd hoped for in you," he says softly, correctly guessing at my thoughts as he wipes a pesky tear from my cheek.

TWENTY-NINE

Mia

"Where are you going?"

I turn around from the open door to find Jared behind me, a scowl on his face.

He'd been in Barrie the whole weekend and had just come home, just as I was cleaning up our dinner dishes. I'd offered to stay with Jordy, when he told us he had to head out Saturday morning and would likely be gone until Sunday night. In hindsight, Jordy would've been fine on her own, since John showed up midday on Saturday. He left only when Jordy started dozing off on the couch, close to midnight, and was back again first thing this morning, with coffee and pastries from a bakery in town. I tried not to look when he said goodbye to her this afternoon, his arms tight around her waist, and hers wrapped around his neck as they spoke softly with their foreheads touching. He was scheduled for afternoon shifts the next few weeks and wouldn't be able to see her as much as he'd like.

"Home."

"Why?" he asks, genuine confusion marring his face. I drop my bag and close the distance between us. I lift my hand and stroke the scruff on his jaw.

"Because I live there," I tell him gently. "Things have calmed down since the article came out. Jake says things have been quiet at the gate, and I think I need to go home." I know I'm not explaining myself well when his expression turns back to a scowl.

"I thought you liked it here." His words are forced out between clenched teeth, and my other hand comes up, soothing the other side of his face. Pushing up on tiptoes, I press my lips to his chin.

"I love it here. I love being here, but this is not my home. I can't just walk away from what has been my life and slip into yours. I'm only a short walk away." I open my mouth to say more, but decide against it. I could tell him that staying with him would feel more like a convenience and not a wish or a need. That living together with him, his sister, and a baby would have to be a choice we all consciously make. I could say that despite the size of the place, it would likely get crowded, especially now that Jordy has John in her life as well. I might point out, all three of us are trying to find our feet again, find our own worth, and we might need some time to ourselves to do that. But somehow I don't think Jared's open to hearing all my reasons. It's not that I don't want to be with him, it's just that I need for him to ask for all the right reasons. He's used to getting what he wants, and I want him to work for what he needs.

"I'll see you tomorrow," I mumble into his neck, as I hug him to me. A hug he isn't returning. "Come on, Griffy," I call out to the dog, who reluctantly gets up and lumbers out the door behind me.

"My door is open, Jared."

-

It's harder than I thought, leaving him standing in the doorway, knowing he's following me with his eyes. Dusk is setting in, making it dark in the shadow of the trees. Part of me wants to turn around, but I know that won't help anyone in the long run. All that's happened this summer forced us together at high speed. Extreme circumstances can't be a solid basis to build a life on, right? I can't deny my feelings—heck, I know down to my core that Jared loves me as he says he does—but that doesn't mean I shouldn't listen to my gut, and my gut says this is the right thing to do. For now.

Griffin is dragging his ass, clearly unhappy about leaving his cushy spot in front of Jared's fireplace, but when we emerge from the path onto my driveway, he takes off running.

"Griff!"

I'm not surprised he doesn't listen. He's been cooped up in Jared's house most of the weekend and didn't venture too far whenever I let him out. He probably needs to reestablish his territory, and I leave him to it, walking up my steps and pushing open the door.

Even though the days are no longer stifling hot, the air inside my house is pretty rank. Dropping my bag, I rush around to open all the windows, in an attempt to blow out the smell. It's only been a couple of days since I was here to pick up a few things, and I swear it didn't smell then. When I get to the bedroom, the smell is worse. Much, much worse, and it's buzzing with flies. I flip on the light switch and am almost gagging in my rush to the window, only to find it already open, the screen on it torn. *What the hell?*

I don't see it until I turn to the bathroom. The still shape of what looks to be a bobcat, is covered with flies, the dark stain underneath its body evidence its death was a violent one. Although normally quite a bit larger than a domestic cat, this one is abnormally swollen as a result of decomposition. Not only that, there is dried blood on the walls, on my bed, all over the carpet. It looks a bloodbath in here. Desperate for some fresh air, I rush past it and straight outside, taking in deep breaths, and struggling to fight down the bile.

In my years living here, I've found the odd dead mouse or chipmunk inside, but never an animal quite this size. Or encountered a smell quite this pungent. I longingly look across the water at Jared's house, where the air is at worst tainted with a hint of Ole's diaper, but nothing like what's festering inside my cottage. Only one way to get rid of it, and that is get rid of the body.

Armed with a flashlight, I find a shovel in the shed behind my RAV and grab a large bucket. When I walk out, I spot my compost bin open, the lid hanging off to one side. Damn bear must've come back. Instead of heading back inside, I round the side of the house to have a look at the outside of my window, which appears to have been how the cat got in. I find Griffin pacing underneath, his nose sniffing alternately up in the air or on the ground below. I shine my light and see a smear of blood on the outside sill, along with a few, long claw grooves marking the logs just below. They look too big to have been made by the cat. I'm guessing there was a pretty pissed off bear, who may not have been too happy finding a bobcat digging through his next meal. Clearly the cat thought escaping inside my house for shelter was a good idea, but not before the bear got him good.

Satisfied to have solved that mystery, I grudgingly head back inside, keeping Griffin outside for now. God knows I don't want him rolling around in dead bobcat.

It's already pitch black when I roll the last big rock on the bobcat's grave, a fair distance from the cottage in the trees. I could've tossed the carcass in the underbrush somewhere, but Griffin seemed much too interested, and I was afraid he'd drag it back to the house. So instead I dug a hole, only to realize that wouldn't be a deterrent for my dog. The rocks covering the shallow grave would have to do. I grab the flashlight and head back, allowing myself that hint of doubt that's been nagging me all night long. *Did I make the right decision coming back here?* And that is immediately followed by the next: *Will Jared understand?*

I don't hear anyone approach, so when a large body suddenly appears in the beam of my light, my heart almost stops.

"Everything okay?" Jake's deep voice is a bit of a disappointment. I guess I'd hoped it might be Jared.

"Other than the heart attack you just gave me? Yes, I'm fine." The rumble of his chuckle is pleasant enough, but his voice sounds stern.

"Sorry, but when I saw a light in the trees, I had to investigate. Make sure you're safe. Jared called earlier, letting me know to keep a close eye on your place."

I'm not sure what to make of that. Not sure how I feel about that. I wanted to make sure I'm a choice and not a convenience for him, but maybe I'm neither? *Ugh!* I'm driving myself insane with self-doubt. Jake is staring at me intently, and I realize he's waiting for some kind of explanation.

"Oh, uhh…found a dead bobcat inside," I explain, waving at my house. "I had to get rid of it."

"That happen a lot?" he wants to know, his gaze turning to the cottage. I shrug my shoulders, even though he can't see, and my eyes follow where his are fixed.

"My first bobcat," I mumble, as I step around him and walk back to my house.

The stench is a little less overwhelming when I get inside, thanks to the open windows and the bottle of bleach I scrubbed into the floor, but my bedroom is still not habitable for now. Instead I take a quick shower to get the stench off me and pull both the bathroom and bedroom doors closed. I grab a quilt from the living room, I open the sliding doors and settle in on the couch in my screened-in porch.

With the soft lull of the water lapping at the shore, and the fresh scent of pine and lake in my nose, it doesn't take me long to drift off. My last thought is how much I already miss those strong arms.

Jared

"You're an idiot."

328

It doesn't surprise me Jordy feels it necessary to repeat that thought once again. She's only told me the same thing at least ten times tonight. Starting when I stood there watching Mia walk away. Having my sister tell me I'm an idiot for the tenth time doesn't make it any clearer than when she told me that first time. I'm still lost as to why I'm the idiot.

All I did was come home from training camp and chill out with my family. I'm not sure what happened this weekend that had Mia pack her bag and head for the hills, and little of what she said in explanation made sense to me. Was she done with me? I'd left her in bed early Saturday morning, still limp and drowsy from the orgasm I gave her with my mouth. I'd withheld my own, thinking it might give me a sharper edge during camp, and had every intention of claiming my own release tonight. Then she walked out that door and my need turned to anger.

Fuck.

I'd all but bared my soul, right into her lap, when all she'd done is whisper a few words into the dark. Maybe she hadn't even been talking to me.

"God, Jared. Get your head out of your ass," Jordy hisses, squeezing herself between me and the sliding door I was peering out of. My gaze slides down to meet her exasperated expression. "You're acting like she's left you."

"She has," I counter immediately.

"You're blind *and* you're an idiot," she huffs, shoving lightly against my chest. "It's not that complicated, but you can't seem to get it through your big head. And for the record, it's not just your head that's big.

329

Your ego could stand to take it down a notch or two as well. Let me see if I can dumb it down for you. Everything is a struggle for Mia. Nothing comes easy for her. She's had to adapt and adjust, and she's had to fight to do it. You, on the other hand, are so used to simply expecting to get what you want, you don't even know what it means to struggle." Her hand comes up to stop me when I want to protest. "I know things haven't always been easy. Especially not after Mom and Dad died, but you've always had people around you working to smooth things out. You know I'm right," she adds when she sees me raise my eyebrows. "Even with Mia. She's done nothing but adapt, since we basically forced ourselves into her life. We forced ourselves, but we never had to adjust to her being there. Not ever. That was all on her. Even your reaction now; you're pissed and standing here all self-righteous, glaring at her cottage from the safety of your house. Why? Because you didn't get what you expected? Because she chose for herself? Think about that, Jared, think about it hard," she says, accompanying her words with a solid punch to my shoulder. "I'm going to bed. I want to get a few hours in before my little bottomless pit wakes up again."

I don't say a word as she moves away. I barely notice her disappearing down the hall to her room. My eyes are focused, once again, on the dark cottage across the inlet. I take my sister's advice; I think hard.

-

When the sky starts lighting up again around six the next morning, my eyes are gritty, and no longer angry, as they continue to stare across the water. I may have dozed

330

off a time or two since I flipped a chair around to face the glass doors and sat my weary ass down, but every time they'd open, Mia's cottage was front and centre. And I thought…I thought so damn hard all night, my head's throbbing with it.

Jordy spouted some stuff last night that wasn't easy to listen to. Brutal even, but also the truth. As a result, I'm feeling less than stellar about myself this morning. I tried hard to disprove the picture she painted last night, the one where I've not had to fight for much, but I couldn't. Other than my parents' death, life has been pretty damn accommodating for me. And I've done little but sit back and have all good things come to me. Even my grand gesture of taking in my pregnant sister, was more selfish than it was selfless. I wanted her near—my family near—and didn't have to fight for it either.

Everything I've done this summer was to satisfy *my* needs.

"Did you even go to bed?" Jordy's voice has me twist my head around. She walks up to me, her hair piled messily on her head, clearly straight out of bed, with Ole happily snuggled under her chin. She lets him go when I reach out for him, and lay him on my chest, kissing his warm head.

"No," I softly admit.

"Mmmm." I feel her fingers run through my hair, and I grab her wrist before she can pull away.

"I'm an idiot," I whisper, pressing her hand against my face. Her lips ghost over my other cheek with a soft peck.

331

"I love you," she gently says as she pulls away. "And you need a haircut."

"Not the beard, though." I smile at the easy transition from the heavy to the mundane, as only my sister can manage.

"I'll leave the beard, but the hair's gotta go. Next thing you know, you'll be donning a man bun. I don't think I'd be able to live with that." She shudders dramatically as she comes back to the chair, toting scissors.

"Actually, buzz it?"

"What? The hair? That short?"

"Yeah," I confirm with a smile. "Clippers are in the vanity in my bathroom. I don't want bald, but as close to it as you can get."

"You sure? You only used to do that at the beginning of a new season." I can hear the hesitation in her voice, but I'm determined.

I've had my head up my ass, thinking a new start in life meant all I had to do was change my circumstances. But if I truly want a new beginning—a total change in tide—I have to start with me.

"That's what I want. Mark the start of an entirely new season."

THIRTY

Mia

A knock at my door has me scramble to my feet, almost tripping over the quilt tangled around my legs.

-

I haven't slept well. Not last night and not the night before. The porch couch might be good for a nap, here or there, but spending entire nights on there has my body aching. It doesn't help that I missed Jared yesterday. I haven't seen him at all. When I went over yesterday, Jordy and Ole had been outside. Apparently Jared had left early to sign the contract with the Colts.

Brian had stayed in Barrie Sunday night, but Jared had wanted to come home according to Jordy. Well, if that didn't make me feel all kinds of guilty. He drove all the way home, knowing he had to be back there in the morning anyway, and I basically walked right out of the door when he got there.

When John popped over in the early afternoon, I came back here and spent the rest of the day stripping my bedroom. Pulled down the curtains, took off my bedding and stuffed it all in garbage bags. Too big to wash by hand, so I'd either have to take them to the laundromat, or see if I could wash them at Jared's. If those rust coloured stains could even be washed out. Maybe throwing them out would be the best option. I managed to wash down the walls, and any blood I could see on the furniture, but the carpet had been beyond salvaging. So I started pulling that up.

A fucking mess. I spent four hours last night cursing the idiot who thought it was a good idea to glue carpet straight to the floorboards. And not just in a few places, every-damn-where. I was barely able to get one corner up, resorting to cutting away at it strip by strip, with an old box cutter I found in the kitchen drawer. The metal spatula I'd tried to use to scrape the glue off the boards was still laying in the bathroom where I'd tossed it. In two pieces.

That's when I'd given up. Frustrated I'd plopped down on the couch, only to see Jared's car parked in his driveway. No idea how long he'd been home, I tried not to feel hurt he hadn't shown himself.

-

I manage to wrap the quilt around me and shuffle to the front door, where Griffin is already waiting at attention. Despite my efforts not to get too hopeful, I can't help the nugget of hope that Jared might be on the other side, but when I pull open the door it's clearly not him. An older man, maybe late fifties, shuffles his feet a little as he clamps his baseball cap in his hands.

"Morning?"

"Yes, morning, Ms. Thompson?"

"That's me," I prompt the man, who looks to be a little nervous. I peek over his shoulder to check if he's alone, but all I see is an old beat up pickup truck with *Contractor* painted on the side. "Can I help you?"

"Ah…I'm here to fix window?" This time it's his turn to check behind him.

"Oh." I must look as puzzled as I feel, because he hurries to explain.

"Mr. Kesla not here? He call."

"He did? I'm sorry, I'm afraid I don't understand. Mr. Kesla is my neighbour. Perhaps you took the wrong turn?" As soon as the words leave my mouth I realize this man knew my name, so maybe he *is* in the right place. Pulling the quilt a little tighter around me, I probe a little. "Why don't you tell me what brought you here?"

He straightens his shoulders visibly before he answers. "I was at daughter house yesterday. I miss the call. Check message this morning, Mr. Kesla say window need fixing at Thompson cottage, first thing. So I come right after breakfast. My name is Joe Manusco. I not live far; down road in Gravenhurst. The wife and me move here when daughter leave home. That's where I was last night. Julia, my daughter, she and husband have house in Orillia." I bite down a chuckle at his tendency to over-share in his thickly accented English. When he notices he suddenly snaps his mouth shut.

"Well, Joe," I jump ahead. "I wasn't aware a call had been made, but let me show you the problem. And it's not the window, it's actually the screen." I step aside to let him in as Griffin cautiously sniffs.

"Holy sh…oot!" Joe says grabbing for his nose when we walk down the hall to the bedroom. Right. I probably should've warned him about the smell. "What died?"

"Bobcat." I explain the state I found my place in, while he pokes around my bedroom, hissing disapprovingly when he sees my handiwork on the floor.

"Need tools," he grumbles, squeezing past me, and leaving me standing in the middle of the stinky room.

I look longingly in the direction of the bathroom, where I'd hoped to have a shower at some point, but it looks like that might have to wait. I'm not getting naked with a strange man in the house. I snatch some clean clothes, and still wrapped in the quilt, shuffle back to my spot on the porch, where I quickly get dressed underneath the cover.

-

"How did he know?"

I finally called Jordy, after spending the better part of my morning trying to get a hold of Jared. He either has his phone off, or is ignoring my calls, because I ended up in voicemail every time.

I'm due at Rueben's for my weekly appointment in an hour and would like some reassurances before I leave Joe alone in my house. The screen is fixed, but last time I checked, he was chipping glue off my floor boards. I have a feeling he won't leave until my carpet is up.

"Jake told him about the bobcat, and I may have mentioned you were busy trying to clean the place," she says carefully.

"He asked about me?" *Crap*. Now I sound, and don't just feel, like a teenage girl gagging for attention. Jordy's chuckle proves my self-assessment is right on the money.

336

"Chill, chicklet," she teases. "He may have been a bit pissy at first, but it's not like you broke up with him. He gets that, and I promise he's not purposely ignoring you, he's just busy in all-day meetings, putting together the team for the coming season."

Don't I feel like a fool? Of course he's busy in his new job, which makes taking the time to contact a contractor for me a pretty sweet gesture. I'm starting to wonder if it wouldn't have just been easier to stay over there.

"Okay, but do you know anything about this guy he sent over? I have to go into town."

"Ms. Thompson?" The guy in question pokes his head outside. I hope I didn't say anything offensive, but he just smiles when I pull the phone away.

"Yes?"

"Sorry for interruption. I have to go. I'll come back tomorrow. Eight o'clock."

Before I even have a chance to open my mouth, he's disappeared back inside, and a few seconds later I hear the front door slam behind him.

"Problem solved," I announce to Jordy sheepishly.

"I heard. Look, I've gotta run; my boy is demanding attention." I can hear Ole exercise his lungs in the background.

"Talk to you later. And, Jordy? Thanks." There is a lot said with that single syllable, but somehow I think she hears every last bit of it.

A quick glance at the clock shows I'm going to have to hustle to make my appointment in time. The temperature's dropped a little the last few days, so I shrug on a zippered hoodie and grab my purse.

"You stay here," I say to Griffin. "I won't be long." Pulling the door shut, I make my way over to my RAV, my fingers crossed it'll start without a problem.

I'm halfway there when I see it; a slip of paper wedged under my windshield wiper. Immediately, I scan my surroundings. Jared kept Jake on, at the gate, for a bit longer, until he is sure the press has lost interest, but maybe someone slipped by. I'm a little jittery when I snatch the folded note from the windshield and can't hold back blowing out a deep breath when I open it.

> *Beautiful,*
>
> *Hope you have a good day. Joe is a solid guy, let him do his thing.*
>
> *Drive safe!*
>
> *Jared*
>
> *PS. Waking up without you SUCKS.*

I don't bother hiding the smile as I slip behind the wheel and start up the car. And the smile stays, all the way into town.

Jared

"Home opening game, September twenty-first, folks. Two more weeks to go. We've got a good group of boys, some new blood on the bench as well as behind it." The Colts' head coach gives a nod in my direction, before addressing the team again. I let his words flow over me as I look down at the phone in my hand.

You made me forget what alone feels like.

That was probably too sappy. I'd had this grand idea of sending her little messages, but I'm clearly running out of material.

Yesterday, Joe started at her place. When I first heard what happened, I'd been halfway out the door before Jordy stopped me.

"Let her," she said. Those two simple words enough to stop me in my tracks. *Let her.* Jake had just chuckled and walked past me out the door, and I was tempted to wipe the smirk off his face. I was pissed that everyone seemed to understand Mia better than me. Even the fucking security guy. It had taken everything out of me to turn around, head into my office, and get in touch with the contractor who'd built my deck. My ability to let her handle things only went so far.

Practice and meetings kept me busy well into the evening yesterday, and I ended up spending the night in Barrie. An empty bed is just that, wherever it's located. Tonight I have plans, which is why I've been sending her texts, every now and then, after leaving that note on her windshield yesterday morning on my way out.

She hasn't responded to any of them.

"Alright people," coach says, breaking into my thoughts. "As promised, an early day today, a day off tomorrow, but I expect everyone back here Friday morning, bright and early. Three hour practice to start, and then we hop on the bus to Sudbury. Our first pre-season game against the Wolves." Cheers and whistles go up from the team. These kids are hungry to get on the ice. Coach claps me on the shoulder when he passes me. "Nice haircut, Kesla."

I follow the crowd outside, where my car is in its assigned slot. The only sedan here, everyone else drives utility vehicles. I guess the rugged SUVs are more suited to living in the snowbelt. On a whim, I drive straight to the Toyota dealership by the highway. What can I say, sometimes money is handy. It gets things done.

When an hour later, I'm about to drive a decked out floor model 4Runner off the lot, a text notification dings on my phone.

I miss you too. xox

-

"Can I drive it?" Jordy is pushing every damn button and opening all the compartments in the new Toyota. She had the passenger door already open, before I'd even turned the engine off.

"Fuck no," I react. "Get your own new car."

340

"Maybe I will," she says, sticking her tongue out. Suddenly I feel sixteen again, when I came home with my driver's license, and Jordy pestered me until I took her to the Dairy Freeze in the old pickup Dad saved for me. It makes me smile and I turn around in my seat.

"How about when the season gets underway, before winter hits, we go see what else they've got at the dealer's? That cookie tin you're driving probably won't make it up the hill after the first snowfall."

"Red," she blurts out.

"Sorry?"

"It's gotta be red. I don't care what it is, as long as it's red."

"I was thinking along the lines of all-wheel drive to get you up the hill. Something with a little higher wheel base, so you wouldn't get stuck in the snow that easily, and you're worried about the colour?" I throw her an incredulous look as she shrugs her shoulders at me.

"Those things are fine…as long as it come in red." The big grin on her face is contagious as she slips from the passenger side.

I hadn't noticed what she's wearing, but with her hair curling down her back and the skirt of the pretty, floral dress bouncing around her legs, it's clear she's dressed to go out. I track behind her inside.

"Where are you off to?" I want to know as she starts moving toward the nursery, not stopping as she answers.

"John is picking us up soon." I follow her into Ole's room, where she's just picking him up from the crib. "Will you grab his diaper bag for me?"

"Us? You're taking Ole out?" I can hear myself and I wince at the whine in my questions. She turns to me with a little smile teasing her lips.

"We're not going out," she says, burying her face in the baby's neck. "He's cooking me dinner at his house." She walks into her bedroom, the baby on her arm, and snatches an overnight bag from the bed. "He's dropping us off before his shift tomorrow. Today's his only day off."

She's fucking staying the night. There are so many things I want to say right now, but I bite my lip when I see the plea in her eyes. Swallowing down the bile crawling up my throat at the thought of my sister getting it on with the cop, I turn back into the nursery to grab Ole's bag.

"Be happy for me?" she asks softly, when I join her in the living room where she's strapping Ole in his car seat. "He's a good man, Jared. And he doesn't care I'm a used-up single mom." Her voice wavers and I realize how low her self-confidence has fallen at the hands of that cocksucker, Nick. When she straightens up, I'm there to wrap her in my arms. She presses her face in my shirt.

"Far from used-up, Pipsqueak. Any man's lucky to have you. I just worry," I mumble in her hair.

There's a light knock, right before the door opens, and the man in question steps inside. I'm about to say something about him barging into my house, when I notice the concern on his face when he spots Jordy clinging to me.

"What did you do?" is the first thing from his mouth, as he takes two long strides and plucks my sister away from me, pressing her face into his own chest. "What's

342

going on?" This time his eyes burn when he looks at me, one of his large hands soothing over Jordy's hair.

"It's okay." Her voice is muffled and she pushes back a little, looking up in his face. "Jared was being nice." LeBlanc's face softens instantly as his gaze drops down to her.

"Okay," he says simply, and I can feel some of my reservations slide. There's no denying he's gone over my sister if he's willing to take me on in her defense, and then at her urging just as quickly lets it go. He listens to her. "I've got her," he says to me before turning to Jordy. "Are you ready?" She nods, freeing herself from his hold, and lifting up on tiptoes in front of me.

"Love you," she says, before she presses a kiss to my cheek.

"Love you more," I tell my sister before turning to Leblanc. "And you, keep in mind she just had a baby."

"Jared!" Jordy yells, shocked, as she lands a well-aimed punch on my shoulder.

"What? Did you forget I had a front row seat on that one?" I wince at the memory of seeing more than I was comfortable seeing of my sister.

The guy just chuckles, and I try not to scowl, when he tosses both bags over his shoulder, grabs Ole's seat, and throws a proprietary arm around Jordy. As I watch them walk out the door, I can't help the sting of apprehension, but I believe him—he's got her.

THIRTY-ONE

Mia

It worries me when I get home and see a strange car parked outside the house, across the water. Jake had been at the top of the drive by the gate, but what if someone got by him? My phone is already in my hand and I'm dialling, as I shove open the door, letting out a very relieved Griffin.

My trip to town had taken a bit longer than I anticipated. My session with Rueben had run long, but in a good way, and I'd stopped for some groceries. This time without incident. No panic attacks, no blackouts, not even a tingle. That deserved a celebration, so I went to that nice little bakery on Main Street. That's where I ran into Dr. Winters, Jordy's OBGYN. I was surprised he even recognized me, from that brief time in the hospital, the night Ole was born. He invited me for a coffee and we had a nice chat.

"I don't mean to pry," I start when Jordy answers her phone. "But are you okay?"

"Mia? I'm fine. Did Jared call you to check on me?"

"No, he didn't. It's just that…"

"I'm with John," she says, cutting me off. "He called after I talked to you this morning. He's cooking for me."

345

I smile at the tone in her voice, excited and yet slightly apprehensive.

"That's great, honey. Then who is at the house looking after the baby?"

"Ole is with me. Jared's home, why?"

"Oh." Jordy's answer hits me for a loop but before my imagination has a chance to run away with me Jordy continues.

"Yeah, he got off early."

"Then whose car is in the driveway?" I finally get to the point and she starts laughing.

"Jared's idea of adjusting to his environment."

-

Nice wheels.

I shoot off the text, once I've put away the groceries and Griffin is fed. Jared doesn't take long to respond.

Wanna go for a drive?

The answer is so typically male, it makes me smile. I quickly type back.

Just got home. Have some stuff I want to do. Raincheck?

I almost drop my phone when it rings in my hand. Jared's name shows on my screen.

"Thank you for the note, and for Joe," I jump right in, the smile obvious in my voice.

"My pleasure," he rumbles. "What's the stuff you want to do?"

"Pull up some more carpet." I want to do what I can myself in the bedroom, to make it easier on Joe. He left some of his tools this morning, so I had a sturdy putty knife to scrape the glue.

"Need some help?" Jared wants to know, putting a grin on my face. "Not like I have something better to do, with Jordy and Ole gone. Maybe it'll keep me from thinking about what my sister might be up to with Dudley Do-Right," he adds, when he hears my hesitation.

"Isn't Dudley Do-Right a Royal Canadian Mountie?" I snicker.

"Same difference," he growls. "All I know he's probably got his hands on my sister right now."

"He's a good man, Jared. Jordy could do so much worse," I soothe, but it's met with a derisive snort.

"She just had a baby, for crying out loud." He's worried, I can tell by the tone of his voice.

"Just about two months ago, honey. She's fine. And besides, doesn't that tell you all you want to know about John? Takes a pretty decent guy to be able to see beyond the dirty diapers, the baby spit, and the fatigue straining her face, to the beautiful, big-hearted prize he wins in her."

"And Ole," Jared adds.

"And Ole," I quickly agree with a smile, realizing that was part of what was bugging him. Jared stands to

347

lose his spot as number one man in Ole's young life. I get that, but it takes a village to raise a child, and Ole will only be better off having two, strong male influences to guide him. Something I'm sure Jared understands rationally.

"So can I come over?" This time there's vulnerability in the question and I don't hesitate.

"Do you have a putty knife?"

"I'm sure I can dig one up. Be there in a bit." Before I get a chance to answer, he ends the call.

-

By the time I have a pot of tea and a few easy sandwiches made, his knock sounds at the door.

"Hey," he says gently when I open the door and step back for him to walk in. He waves a putty knife, that's seen better days, in my face as he passes and heads straight for the kitchen. "Found one."

I follow behind, perhaps a little disappointed that was all the greeting I would get, but then he puts the knife on the counter and turns around to face me.

"Need both hands to say hello. Missed you, Beautiful." His deep voice is like silk over my ruffled feathers. "Come here." Without hesitation I move straight into his arms. His hand comes up to tangle in my curls, tilting my head back. The sting of his hold instantly soothed by his mouth, soft on mine. The contrast is delicious, as he plunges his tongue deep between my lips. The kiss is forceful, demanding, but also tainted with need, and perhaps even a hint of desperation.

"Fuck, I missed you," he repeats, his lips still against mine, before he dives face first in my neck, holding on like it's been months since he's last seen me, not mere days. "Thought I'd fucked it all up," he mumbles.

I ease him back so I can look in his eyes. "You didn't do a thing," I reassure him. "I just need to find my balance. I want to make sure I don't get swept away by the tide, without having my feet pointed in the right direction. Make what comes next a conscious decision and not just a result of circumstance." He nods his understanding, his expression warm as his eyes trace my features. "For you as well," I add gently.

"So if, say, I was hoping you'd stay the night with me, so I can wake up with you in my arms tomorrow, on my day off, I should probably let you know beforehand?" he asks, with a teasing glint in his eyes.

"I could do a sleepover." I smile at the way his eyebrow shoots up.

"Thank Christ—I'd hate to see the one night I have the house to myself wasted."

"We don't want that," I react, rolling my eyes, before I slip from his hold and change the subject. "You hungry?"

"Starving," he says, eyeing me, but accepting the plate I hand him nonetheless.

"Your hair!" I blurt out when he takes off his ball cap and tosses it on the counter.

"Jordy buzzed it," he says, grinning sheepishly as he runs his hand over his nearly bald head. "It's something I used to do at the beginning of every season. A fresh start,

349

new options open, and the possibilities endless. Seemed appropriate in more than one way this time." I smile back, hearing the message clearly.

"I like it."

-

"Holy shit."

That's Jared's reaction when we get to my bedroom. I'm sure it's mostly the lingering smell he's reacting to. I've had the window open, with the new screen—thanks to Joe—firmly in place. I've even had a fan blowing to disperse the air, but as long as we have this carpet in here, we'll never be able to get rid of the odour.

"We're gonna have to repaint too," Jared says, running his fingers over some of the stains I tried washing off the walls.

"I know. I think I'll probably end up tossing everything in this room. The curtains seem to hold on to the smell, and I can even smell it on my towels and in my clothes.

"We can wash those. I'm sure a few cycles through my state-of-the art Maytag will get it out."

I chuckle at his description of his washer. As long as it has a motor of some kind, it's automatically a prized possession. *Guys.* "I'll take you up on that."

Two hours later, my hands are almost blistered and my knees feel like someone's shoving splinters in my joints. But what has me toss down my putty knife and clamber to my feet are the beads of sweat on Jared's forehead, and the way he winces with every move.

"Enough for today," I announce, feeling all kinds of guilty I didn't think about the state of his knee. He's been on the ice more than he has in a year, in just the past little while, and if my healthy knees feel like this after a couple of hours, I don't even want to think about his injured knee. "I'm getting you some ice," I announce, already turning to leave the room to give him a chance to get to his feet, without losing his pride. I'm pretty sure that's what held him back from opening his stubborn mouth.

I try not to notice his limp, when he finally walks in the kitchen, and try to be casual about handing him the bag of frozen corn. He sits down at the counter, and lifts his leg up on another stool to ice down his knee.

"I don't have beer, but I have some Scotch left?" I offer.

"I have beer, and Scotch, and any other damn alcoholic beverage you could want. We'll head over to mine."

"Sure. Let me clean up a little first. Joe will be here at eight so I'll have to be back here early."

"We'll leave him a note, or we can leave the key with the guard," Jared orders. "No one's getting out of bed before at least nine." I raise an eyebrow at that, but Jared holds my gaze firmly. "Why don't you do what you need to do, and maybe grab some stuff we can load in the washer. I'll go drop off a key for Joe at the gate." He tosses the frozen corn in the sink, walks up to me and tugs me close, an arm around the small of my back. "Don't make me wait too long," he whispers against my lips.

A spare key in hand, and Griffin at his heels, he walks out the door and I head into the bedroom, armed with a fresh stack of garbage bags.

It takes longer than I thought. I empty my dresser and closet, before hopping in the shower to rinse the lingering stench and sheen of sweat of my body. I don't want to get dressed in smelly clothes, but the night is too cool to walk around naked, so I sniff carefully to find the least offensive shirt and sweats I can find. Ready to head over, I look at the six full garbage bags, knowing there's no way I can carry those all over at once, but I can fit at least three in the canoe with me and paddle across. Locking up the house, I toss my keys in the little backpack I loaded up, and grab hold of the garbage bags I'm bringing. Half-carrying and half-dragging, I manage to get them around the house to the dock.

Flickering light, coming from the direction of Jared's place, draws my gaze and my breath catches in my throat when I see the source. His house is dark, but a few candles dot the outline of the upper deck. What grabs my attention are the bright flames, licking up from the portable fire pit placed on the end of the dock. In the their orange glow I can see the unmistakable outline of a familiar body.

Jared's waiting for me.

Jared

I have my phone out to find out what's keeping her when I see her appear at the water's edge. I'd hoped she might see the fire from inside and make her way over.

She stops when she spots me, and even at this distance, I can see the light of the flames play in the shine of her eyes. A slow smile spreads over her face as she resumes her path down the dock, toward her canoe. Clever girl, she tosses the garbage bags she was toting into the waiting canoe and climbs in after.

I left Griffin inside, he'd curled up in his favourite spot, while I took a quick shower and barely budged when I scrounged around to look for candles.

Watching as Mia starts slicing her paddle through the mirror surface of the water, I step off the blankets I spread out over the dock and pull off my shirt. Next are my shorts that I pulled on commando, knowing I probably wouldn't have them on long. The air is cold, but enough heat comes from the fire to keep me comfortable. Though even without, the hot flow of blood pounding through my veins is enough to warm me from the inside out. Knowing my girl gets turned on by watching is something I'm banking on tonight.

It could be my imagination, but I swear I can hear her sharp intake of breath when I walk around the fire pit, my rigid cock jutting out unashamed. I lower myself on the edge of the dock, my feet dangling in the surprisingly warm water, and wrap my fist around my erection, slowly moving from root to tip.

She sees what I'm doing. The light clatter of her paddle on the edge of her canoe makes that clear. Floating about halfway between her dock and mine, her hungry gaze follows every move of my hand. It's highly erotic, feeling her eyes burn me. The sheer heat ramps up the speed of my movements, when she suddenly starts paddling again, faster than before. Her tongue darts out, licking a trail across her bottom lip that glistens in the light bouncing off the water.

Just out of reach, she lays her paddle across the canoe, and lifts her arms, pulling her shirt up with it. Tossing her shirt in the back, she resumes paddling. Her breasts swaying with every move as she closes the distance. The tip of the canoe bounces against my legs, and she tosses the end of the rope to me. I quickly tie off on the dock cleat, before I wrap my hand around my dick again.

"Save some for me," her hoarse voice sounds almost breathless, as she pulls the canoe sideways, forcing me to lift my feet on its edge. She cleverly manoeuvers her body between my legs, holding onto me with her hands braced on my thighs. I groan as she leans in to lick at the bead of precum on the head of my cock, the tip of her tongue slicking along the small slit. My ass clenches at the rasp of her touch, and goosebumps rise all over my body. I almost lose it when she sheaths me in the warm, wet heat of her mouth, working the length with lips and tongue. I'm already primed, so when she hums in the back of her throat, I can feel the vibrations run all the way down from the crown to my balls, which draw tight in warning.

"Not like this," I rumble, as I reach down and pull her up and off my dick, straight out of the canoe. "Hang tight," I instruct her as I scoot us back far enough, so I can get my legs under me. Before I have a chance to try lifting us both, Mia's already on her feet, her hand reaching out to help me up. God knows I need it, because my knee is still throbbing like a son of a bitch.

I pull her toward the stack of blankets I piled up and lower myself on my back.

"Ride me," I bite off, barely able to form a coherent word, as I watch Mia tuck her thumbs in her waistband and slowly lower her sweats down her legs. She's beautiful, but in the soft light of the flames; she's absolutely breathtaking. The soft slope of her breasts, the gentle swell of her belly, and the generous curve of her hips, a picture of luscious temptation as old as time. "Please…"

She grabs the hand I reach out for her and lowers herself, one knee on either side of my hips, until I can feel her slick heat settle over my groin. She leans forward, her arms bracing her beside my head, and as she lowers her mouth to kiss me, I can feel the hard peaks of her nipples brush against my chest. A deep groan escapes me when her tongue slips inside my mouth, and she rolls her hips at the same time, catching the tip of my cock at her entrance.

I don't think I'm breathing at all while I let her kiss me, only loosely holding her hips, as she slowly takes me inside her body.

-

"Wake up."

I feel the light brush of lips against my own and it takes me a minute to get my bearings. The weight of Mia's body is solid against my own, both of us wrapped in the blankets I'd brought out. I must've fallen asleep. Mia exerted her power over my body in a slow and yet intense

355

connection, the likes of which I've never experienced. She dragged every last ounce out of me, until nothing was left but bone deep satisfaction and exhaustion.

I slowly blink my eyes, only to notice the fire has burned out in the pit. Mia's beaming face looms over me.

"Look up," she urges, dropping her head back down to my shoulder, and placing her hand in the middle of my chest.

It's the most awe-inspiring thing I've ever seen.

"My God," I manage, pulling Mia closer as if to ground me.

"So beautiful," she whispers, the wonder evident in her voice.

Streaks of hazy colour paint the sky, undulating like a sheet in the wind. Mist rippling from left to right across the dark expanse, like the changing of the tides, in hues from green to purple.

I'm transfixed in the ghostly glow touching my skin.

Aurora Borealis.

THIRTY-TWO

Jared

"Are you ready?"

Brian's question puts a smile on my face. I'm more than ready for the season opener tomorrow, but that's not all I'm ready for.

It's been almost two weeks since the first exhibition game, and the boys have made massive strides since that first loss. I was glad for the defeat, to be honest. A win might have made them too cocky, right off the bat, and it's hard to convince these competitive kids they need to be better, when they already think they're top dog. Nothing like a loss to make you hungry. And I loved feeding that hunger. I loved the promise of possibilities.

Ever since Mia woke me up on the dock to see the Northern Lights, a spectacle I never expected to see in my lifetime, I've had this sense of renewed purpose. No longer searching for my place, but knowing I've found it. On the team, in my home, with Mia, and even with my sister, who seems to have found her own stride. With LeBlanc.

Jordy had come back the morning after the midnight display, full of excitement. Apparently they'd seen them too, from John's back deck. I tried my best not to think about what she might have been doing in the middle of the night. I may have seen her give birth to a baby, but I still prefer to think of my sister as innocent and requiring my protection.

She assured me she'd take things one day at a time, for now, making it clear her main priority was her son, but that she was nevertheless falling for John. I could see that; not only in the way Jordy lit up whenever he'd call or come around, but I could see why. He was good to her with a gentle but strong hand. I couldn't deny he scored high the minute he picked up Ole without flinching, when the kid had just sharted all over his diaper and his sleeper, and took him in the bathroom to clean him up. Big points for baby shit.

So when I finally answer Brian's question, it's with more in mind than just the game.

"Absolutely."

"I'm planning to come up and Sandy wants to come. Maybe we can go out for dinner after? Celebrate your birthday?"

I hadn't really thought about my birthday much, although I've walked in on more than one suddenly stilted conversation between Mia and my sister. They may well be up to something.

"Not sure if Mia will make it. She's not good with crowds, and has offered to look after Ole so Jordy can come." It's not only the crowds in the arena, but the noise and the constant shuffle of bodies in tight quarters that would surely be too much for her. So I didn't ask, and she didn't offer, she was happy to look after the baby so my sister could be there. That's more than I can expect, even if I'd love to have her by my side.

"We'll figure it out," Brian says easily, not pushing the issue. "We'll meet you by the locker room after. Have a good game."

Mia

Jared left early this morning, but not without a little bit of a birthday celebration in the shower. I wasn't about to let him sneak off while I was asleep, as he does sometimes. Instead, I slipped into the bathroom, surprising him when I slid the door open and stepped under the water with him. He managed to show me he hadn't retained any permanent injuries from helping me pull up the carpet, when he fucked me up against the tile wall, under the hot spray. I was able to send him off with a satisfied smile on his face and a promise I'd be waiting for him when he got home after the game.

As he explained, his day would start with morning practice and then tactical meetings, which sounded painfully boring to me, but put a light of excitement in Jared's eyes. After those they'd have a light afternoon meal with the entire team, and then it would be time for them to dress for their warm-up.

He explained this to me, so I would understand how it would keep him busy the entire day, when I mentioned wanting to do something for his birthday. Instead we agreed to maybe do a little celebrating on the weekend, something I'd wanted him to believe. In the meantime, Jordy and I have been concocting our own plans.

I spend my morning making room in Jared's dresser and walk-in closet. After washing all of my clothes and linens over the past weeks, I kept them here, in the spare bedroom. Today I was going to move them into the master suite.

I'd made the decision the night of the Northern Lights. Life is too short to wait for circumstances to be perfect. As they say, if it stays in your mind, it's worth taking the risk—and I've not been able to think of anything else. Once I made the decision for myself, it was easy to talk to Jordy, and it had been ridiculously simple for the two of us to come up with the perfect solution. That's why Jordy is at the cottage, talking to Joe, and why I am here, fitting my underwear in a drawer.

By the time I have my clothes all tucked away, Joe's truck is rolling down the driveway, with Jordy riding shotgun. There'd been only a few things I'd wanted from the cottage and most of it I'd already put aside for them to bring over. Jordy comes in first, carrying my laptop and printer, and as if on cue, Ole's cries call out.

"Can you believe that kid? I swear he can smell me," she complains, dumping her load on the couch, before stomping down the hall to the nursery.

Joe follows in at a slower pace and carries in a box of my favourite kitchen stuff. I'd packed that, as well as a few of my favourite books, a couple of pictures and albums, some knick-knacks, and my mother's china. Those made up the most valuable of my possessions, and I needed them to put a mark on my new home.

"Just put them in the spare room over here, Joe," I direct him, leading the way down the hall. That had been Jordy's idea, to convert the spare bedroom into an office for me, so I'd have a place to put my stuff and do my graphic work.

"Just three more," he says, heading back outside.

"Did you fit everything?" Jordy asks, when I walk into the living room, finding her on the couch, nursing Ole under a towel—for Joe's sake, I'm sure.

"Yup. Your brother is less of a clothes horse than I expected, and what I have fits on five hangers and in one large drawer. It's pathetic."

"We'll go shopping sometime soon. It's been way too long since I've hit a good mall," she says, a big grin on her face. I can't hide my revulsion at that suggestion. "Or not," she adds, laughing out loud. "Maybe I'll just hook you up with my favourite online stores."

"Now that I can get onboard with," I sigh, relieved.

It doesn't take Joe long to carry the rest of my stuff in, and he takes off back around the bay to the cottage.

"How much does he have left to do?" I ask Jordy.

"Not much. He just needs to finish putting hardware up in the bathroom. The fans have been running all morning and you can barely tell we painted this morning. That new non-toxic paint really works."

It's already four o'clock when John walks in, and by now my stomach is in knots, despite the pep talk Rueben gave me over the phone earlier. John gives my shoulder a squeeze before walking over to Jordy, cupping her face and kissing her sweetly. It almost distracts me from my nervousness. Almost, but not quite. I was grateful he'd been willing and able to change his shift, all so he could look after Ole when he heard from Jordy what we were thinking about.

With Jared gone a good eight to ten hours every day, it hadn't been too difficult getting done what we needed to. Even Jake, our security guy, had been coerced into keeping mum about the increase in activity at the cottage.

I quietly followed Jordy out of the house after we said our goodbyes to Ole and John, and I stayed quiet during most of our drive. But seeing the sign for Barrie on the side of the road, I'm getting cold feet and sweaty palms.

"Don't," Jordy snaps when she sees me wring my hands. "Get out of your head, girlfriend. I know I promised you could back out at any time, but I lied. I'm not about to let you do that. I know you'd regret it."

Indignant anger surges over me, effectively chasing away the jitters. Just as fast as my temper flared, it's gone again.

"You're a manipulative little witch, aren't you?" I accuse her, only half-serious, and smiling widely. "Well played." She simply shrugs her shoulders and with a cocky smile, reminiscent of her brother's, she drives us to the arena.

As promised, with the first period over and the second underway, the crowds are already in their seats, and there is barely anyone in the parking lot. Jordy firmly holds my hand as she leads me past the Kingston Frontenacs' big tour bus, the Colts' opponents tonight, into the back entrance, where she stops and gives me a moment to adjust.

Aside from the guard, who checked our names upon entry, there is no one in this hallway, but the roar of the ongoing game is all around us. The cheering crowd and loud music, with the bass pounding, is almost deafening. My heart rate speeds up significantly, but the breathing exercises I've been practicing help me keep the blinding panic at bay.

Jordy squeezes my hand to get my attention, and points toward a short tunnel. At the end I can see the ice under the bright lights. Taking in a deep breath and letting it out, I nod sharply. We slowly start moving in that direction, the noise getting impossibly louder the closer we get to the ice.

I stop right where the tunnel opens up. I don't want to be visible, and I need that escape route at my back in case things get to be too much. The entire time, Jordy holds my clammy hand tight. It takes a while, but by the time the buzzer sounds to end the second period, I've started to get a feel for the rhythm of the game and am no longer as startled by cheering and sudden loud music. Even my heart rate has returned to an easier pace. But when I see a few members of the opposing team stepping into the tunnel, it picks up again.

"Let's get out of their way and hide out in the washrooms," Jordy says, quickly leading me back into the hallway that runs all the way around the arena. The washrooms already have a line up, so instead we slip past the security guard to wait outside.

There are a few more people out here, mostly folks having a smoke, but thankfully no one pays us much attention.

"Are you ready to try the home side, this time?" Jordy wants to know when people start filing in the doors again. She'd led me into the visitor's tunnel earlier, to minimize the chance of Jared spotting us. I was worried if he saw me, he wouldn't have his mind on his job, but I wanted to be there to greet him when he came off the bench after the game.

"Absolutely," I confirm with much more conviction than I'm feeling. Jordy knows it, which is why she laughs as she pulls me back inside. As earlier, there's hardly anyone left in the halls and this time we turn the opposite way. Just as we round a turn, we bump into the back of a Colts' player who, along with a his teammates, seems to be listening to someone talk. My first instinct is to turn back, until I hear Jared's voice.

"I want you to play hard but goddammit, play fair! No more dirty hits, no slew-footing, no spearing. You've wasted enough time in the box. I see that shit again and your ass is on the bench indefinitely!" A rumble of protests goes up, but quickly dies down as Jared continues at a more moderate volume. "The guys you face have signed up for battle, just like you. But they signed up for an honest fight, taking the risks that come with it. Can you imagine what it would feel like if you were responsible for badly injuring someone, ending their career, and you had to live the rest of your life with the knowledge it happened because YOU played dirty? I'm not even talking about the consequences you'd have to face at the hands of the league." He pauses, clearly for effect, before he raises his voice and his passion rings through. "Don't do it. I promise you the victory will be so much sweeter when you claim a fair win. With integrity. *That* is the sign of a superior player. Something I know each and every one of you have the capacity to grow into. Start NOW!"

Jordy and I jump back when amidst yells and cheers, the team turns as one and marches right by us, and into the tunnel.

I don't have time to panic, I'm still reeling from Jared's impassioned speech. I only know he was a great player because of what I'm told, but I've just heard firsthand proof of the amazing coach he is. Pride puts a big smile on my face, even as Jared's face goes slack with shock when he catches sight of us.

Jared

What?

The last thing I expect to see, right after tearing a strip off of the boys for trying to overpower the other team with force, rather than skill, are the beaming faces of Mia and my sister.

I'm standing there, slack-jawed and rendered dumb, when finally Jordy's giggle breaks me out of my stupor and prompts me to form words.

"What are you doing here?" I ask almost on a whisper, but Mia hears me, even over the whistle for the puck drop and the resulting cheers from the crowd.

"Happy birthday," she grins, and I can't believe she's actually smiling. The din of the game is ear-splitting but all I hear is her voice.

"Kesla!" The yell bounces around the walls of the tunnel, just as I step up to cup Mia's face.

"I love you," she whispers against my lips, closing over her mouth.

"Jesus fucking Christ—Kesla! Get your ass out here!"

"Go," Mia mumbles as she pulls back, long before I'm ready to let her go. "I'll see you after. Go look after your guys." I manage to tap my sister on her nose before I find myself pushed into the tunnel.

I rush to join my team on the bench, but not without throwing a last glance back at the two most important women in my life.

-

The girls are still there when I come out of the tunnel, following behind the excited shouts of victory from the guys.

I'd wondered a few times in the past forty-five minutes. The noise from the enthused home crowd had risen, along with the intensity of the game. We'd gone into the third leading by one, the equalizer came with eight minutes left, and that had been the only time the arena had gone almost silent. Those last minutes had been a wild frenzy, with the Frontenacs scrambling to keep the Colts

366

from scoring. Until the clock started ticking down the seconds, and in a volley of shots on the Kingston goal, the puck finally found its way to the back of the net. The roar of the crowd had been thunderous.

I keep my eyes locked on Mia's, who looks a lot less confident than she did earlier. This is costing her. I notice her hand holding on to my sister's like a lifeline, and trying to disappear in the shadows against the wall. Yet the moment I'm within reach she lets go, and throws herself in my arms.

"You won."

Not giving two shits about the hallway full of pumped up, sweaty kids, I haul her on tiptoes and take her mouth to loud whistles and catcalls. It doesn't matter. The moment she opens her lips to me, every sense in my body is focused on her. Her taste, her scent, the way her curls cling to my fingers when I plunge them in her hair, and the sound of her soft moan when my tongue says everything without forming a word.

I kiss her like my life depends on it. Maybe it does.

THIRTY-THREE

Mia

"He'll be here soon."

I turn to Brian's voice and nod in response. I'm barely hanging on and it seems everyone can read it right off me. It only makes me more on edge.

It had felt like a victory for me, too, when Jared swept me up in his arms and every nerve crawling like insects under my skin instantly disappeared. I no longer saw the flashes of the press cameras or heard the cacophony of sounds. His kiss left a mellow haze behind that lasted until Jordy drove us down the drive toward the house.

Brian's car had been parked at the end, along with John's. Although I'd briefly met Brian and his wife at the arena after the game, I was nervous walking into the house when they were already there. Jordy's enthusiasm, when she walked in ahead of me, helped and after a quick hello, I could escape into the kitchen to heat the food she and I had prepared earlier.

"Good," I answer with a smile. I guess my relief is obvious, because Brian chuckles softly as he drapes his arm around my shoulders.

"I'm happy for him," he says, surprising me. "Don't get me wrong, Jared's always been a good guy. A kind and decent man, who would turn into something else completely the moment he strapped on his skates. Outside of hockey, he rarely let anything touch him. He lived on the surface." I find myself turned sideways to face him, pulled in by the insight of Brian's words. Not just his agent, but clearly a good friend. "It was only on the ice he gave his heart," he continues. "That's where his passion showed. Where the world would disappear and he'd completely come alive." He shifts slightly, so both hands are resting on my shoulders, and his head dips down a little to look me in the eye. "I thought he'd lost that when his career ended. Thought I'd never see that pure emotion in him again—until you."

"I…He does the same for me," I manage to rasp out, more than just a little overwhelmed. Before either of us can say anything else, headlights cut through the window.

"He's here!" Jordy announces, almost bouncing on her feet.

Instantly, the fist squeezing my stomach unfurls and a feeling of excitement takes over.

Jared steps in the door and freezes on the spot. He takes one look around the room Jordy had taken great pleasure in decorating, with a ridiculous amount of balloons and garland, and zooms right in on his sister. Jordy giggles at the slight shake of his head and barely hidden grin on his face.

"Happy Birthday!" The loud cheer startles Ole, who is nestled in Sandy's arms, and he promptly bursts out crying. It gets everyone moving. Jordy is first, giving her brother a big hug and kiss before directing her attention to her son. It's a bit of chaos with everyone talking at once. There are hugs, handshakes, and shoulder claps; through it all I see Jared's eyes searching, until he finds me.

Half-hidden on the far side of the kitchen, leaning against the corner beside the fridge, I smile at the determination in his eyes as he untangles himself from the well-wishers and stalks in my direction. His hand reaches out and cups my jaw before it slides to the back of my neck, pulling me close. Both of my hands automatically come up to rest on his chest.

"Love you more," he says, resting his forehead against mine and letting me read the depth of his feelings in his eyes.

"Not possible," I whisper, while wrapping my arms around his neck and burying my face under his chin.

"I have everything I need right here," he rumbles in my hair, before continuing in a lighter tone. "Although, could've done without LeBlanc pawing my sister."

I bark out a laugh and slap his shoulder. "Behave."

"Okay, this kid is sucking the energy out of me," Jordy calls out, and I twist my head in her direction. "Can somebody please feed me before I waste away?"

-

Jared closes the door when the lights of Brian's car have disappeared over the hill.

"Best birthday ever," he says, turning to me with a smile.

"Trust me, brother," Jordy says as she walks up with John right behind her, carrying Ole in his seat. "It's gonna get even better."

"Where are you off to?" Jared wants to know.

"I'm going with John. I'll catch you guys tomorrow." She winks at me right before she pulls the door shut behind them.

That's my cue.

Jared

"Thank you."

Mia turns around from the sink with a smile.

The whole night—hell, the whole day—had been a great experience. The eager energy during practice, in the meetings, and during warm-up had been a charge in the air. One I thought I wouldn't feel again, but dammit if it didn't settle under my skin the moment the puck dropped. Those kids worked like beasts these past few days, and the payoff had been at least as sweet for me as it was for them.

But nothing tasted sweeter than Mia's mouth during second intermission.

I care little about my birthday. Haven't since I was maybe twelve years old, and Marina Yates told me happy birthday, just before she flashed her boobs at me behind

372

the gym during recess. That had stayed the highlight throughout high school and into my years in the OHL. Each year after that, I'd be so focused on the next season, there just wasn't time. Then my parents died and it never felt worth celebrating, no matter how hard my sister tried.

Mia's kiss at the arena blew Marina's boobs clear off the map. No match.

"Don't thank me, most of it was your sister's idea. The woman is a machine when she gets her sights on something," she says, wiping her hands on a towel before hanging it back up. She tries to move past me, out of the kitchen, when I snag her wrist in my hand.

"It was you who walked into that arena, facing what must've been every single possible trigger, and obliterating them." I pull her against me. "And you did it for me," I add, my voice hoarse. I want her to know what it meant to have her waiting for me.

These past few weeks, I've tried in different ways to show her how much she means, and it's humbled me to see how easy it was to please her. Just sending a text during a busy day, putting a travel mug of coffee by the bed, feeding the dog, or even squeezing toothpaste on her toothbrush and leaving it ready for her to use. Each little gesture was noticed and she showed me her appreciation every time. Yet, it all pales in comparison with what she did for me today.

"I did it for both of us," she says, slipping her arms around my waist, and tilting her head back to look up at me. "But I would never have even considered it, if it wasn't for you. So maybe I should thank you."

Christ. This woman.

373

She trails her fingers along my jaw and down my bobbing Adam's apple as I strangle down the lump in my throat.

"Ready for bed?" she asks with a teasing glint, and I can only imagine what other things she has planned for me tonight.

"Only if you'll be in it," I retort with a predatory grin.

She doesn't say anything, just turns toward the bedroom, pulling me along by the hand, flicking off lights as we go. I follow willingly, and despite being bone-tired, my cock hardens in anticipation. Clearly more alert than the rest of me.

The moment I step into the dark bedroom behind her, my senses heighten. I'm sure part of it is the way she walks up to the bed and slowly turns back the covers. But there's something else, a feeling something is off. Or maybe just different. I notice her hand shaking when she reaches over to flick on the bedside lamp on her side of the bed.

Is she nervous?

That's when I spot a picture frame at the base of the lamp in the soft glare. One that hadn't been there this morning. My eyes start traveling and I see more. Sheets I swear I've seen before—but on Mia's bed at the cottage. A pillow tossed casually on the club chair in the corner. A print over the fireplace that had previously hung over Mia's bed.

It's not until I see her threadbare robe, hanging on the bathroom door, that the significance of what I'm seeing registers.

Mia

I can tell the moment he realizes.

His back snaps straight and his mouth falls open as he slowly turns to face me. I have my fists clenched by my side. It is a ballsy move. Way out of my comfort zone, but Jordy had assured me he would be over the moon. I can't really tell from the shocked look he's sending me.

I startle when he swings around and yanks open the door to the walk-in closet, flicking on the light switch. Next he stomps to the single dresser in the room and starts yanking open the drawers. My nerves swirl to a pitch when he grabs a handful of my underwear before letting them fall back. His head drops low on his chest, and all I can see is the tension rippling over the muscles of his back.

"I...I'm..." I stammer, my voice sounds almost shrill against the thick silence shrouding the room.

"Don't," he growls in response, and I snap my mouth closed.

Fuck. Did I mess up? Was it too fast? A mistake? Maybe Jordy doesn't know her brother as well as she thinks she does.

The second and third thoughts are still bouncing around in my head when I find myself flying, landing on my back on the bed, with Jared's weight pinning me down, and his mouth hungrily attacking mine.

Ah. Not a mistake.

Not the way he is devouring my body with his hands and stealing my breath with his kiss. I finally have to tilt my head back to get some air.

"For real?" The question is muffled against the soft divot between my collarbones, where his mouth has travelled.

"Mmmm," is all I can manage as my shirt is tugged up and his big hands curve around my breasts, plumping them up. His mouth is close behind, closing over one and then the other, sucking my nipples deep into his mouth.

"Beautiful? You're here?" he asks, lifting his head slightly, waiting for an answer. His full, half-open mouth is wet, and his eyes—normally a clear steel blue—are now almost indigo, as they burn into mine. I take in a deep breath before I trust myself to answer.

"I am."

"*Fuck me.*" He does a face-plant in my cleavage and mumbles something intelligible. All I can hear is, "*...better than...* " and then what sounds like a girl's name, before he lifts his head up, and grins from ear to ear.

"Best—fucking—birthday—ever."

I don't even bother asking who Marina is.

376

THIRTY-FOUR

Two months later

Jared

It's really fucking cold out.

We've been spoiled with a gorgeous Indian summer. Temperatures that had me out in shirtsleeves until almost the middle of October. It wasn't my first time seeing the leaves change. I'm Canadian—I was raised on it. But driving through, or seeing it in pictures or on film does not compare, even a little, to living in the middle of the most vivid colours nature can produce.

The past months have been pretty damn amazing. Save for few panicked calls from Jordy, when our resident bear ventured a little too close to the cottage in its quest to fatten up for the winter. She lives there now; in the cottage. Another one of the girls' schemes.

The morning after my birthday, John had brought her and Ole home, only to help her pack the rest of her things. She needed some time to find her own feet, she'd said. I wasn't too excited, at first, at the prospect of not having her or Ole around. But then Mia pointed out she'd be just a short walk away, and that I'd be able to keep an eye on her from the damn window.

Not that she needed me to. Not anymore. Ole's sperm donor had signed off on his parental rights, just last week, and LeBlanc's truck is in her driveway more often than not. I'm pretty sure he won't waste too much time before he moves her into his place. Not going to like that much either, but I have to agree that it would be much easier once Ole is old enough for school. I guess LeBlanc is growing on me.

It's been a pretty damn good summer and fall. But with the season's first two feet of snow expected over the weekend, winter is here.

I yank my beanie down over my ears a little more before taking another sip of my coffee. Mia makes fun of me when I tell her winter doesn't scare me; that I'll continue to drink my morning coffee outside. And I do, albeit on the steps, a little closer to the house, but still overseeing our little corner of the lake. I glance over my shoulder to where I know she is enjoying hers, looking out the window from the comfort of our living room couch. Probably laughing her ass of at my blue lips.

The first flakes of snow drifting down and melting in my cup of coffee get me moving. Mia's soft laughter greets me as I pull the door closed behind me.

"Giving up already?"

I shrug out of my leather jacket and hang it on the hook by the door, yanking off my beanie and stuffing it in a pocket.

"Nope," I lie. "I need a refill."

"Liar," she grins, peering at me over the rim of her mug.

The closed off and painfully private woman has certainly come out of her shell, since I met her. She's taken to being almost as much of a smartass Jordy is. The smile looks good on her.

She's been a bit quiet this past week and I wonder if the occasional work she's taken on through Dr. Winters, Jordy's OBGYN, is proving to be too much for her. He'd asked her to provide some in-home support for some of his patients. Mostly women at risk for postpartum depression, something she tells me is more prevalent than most people know. Especially for women who live a little further off the grid and who lack social contact.

It had seemed like a good idea. Mia certainly was eager, and knowing how much she missed her lost career, I had been a strong supporter. She wouldn't have to go into town and risk running into crowds. Doc Winters sends the files via email and it's up to Mia to make contact with the patients.

The only near argument we had, was when I insisted we get her a new, more reliable vehicle, since her RAV was well beyond its expiration date. I only got my way because the damn thing had broken down one night, when she was on her way back from a patient in crisis.

She was stranded on an unlit dirt road, in the middle of nowhere, and could barely dial my number for help. By the time I found her, she was in the unrelenting hold of a massive panic attack. It took me half an hour to talk her down far enough so I could buckle her in my passenger seat and take her home.

I'd called for a tow the next morning and had them drag the car straight to the wrecking yard. We bought her a new RAV later that afternoon.

"What time is your appointment this afternoon?" I ask as I sink down in the couch beside her, putting my hand on her knee.

"Seeing Rueben at one first, but I might pop in on a patient afterwards. I'll probably be home around four?"

"Sounds good." I squeeze her leg, pleased to know she's seeing her therapist. I've asked a few times if she was okay, only to have her tell me she's fine. I lean over to kiss her neck. "I've gotta go, Beautiful. I may beat you home. Need me to pick anything up?"

"Don't think so. I'll get stew going in the crockpot before I go."

"Perfect for this cold-ass weather," I mutter, as I stand to bundle up again to go out there.

Mia's chuckles follow me all the way out the door.

Mia

"How is that even possible?"

The family doctor Rueben referred me to, in the same building, just chuckles as she washes her hands at the small sink.

"Do you really need me to explain it to you?"

I'm in shock.

I'm not an idiot. I've known something was up for over a week, but when you've known something to be outside of your possibilities for over a decade, it's hard to even consider it. Menopause seemed a more acceptable explanation than this.

I don't know what to make of it and I sure as hell don't how Jared will react. It changes everything. Doesn't it?

I can feel it crawling under my skin, as my breathing grows more rapid and my pulse starts pounding in my ears.

"Easy," the doctor says as she pulls a Doppler out of a drawer. She puts the earbuds attached in and glides the wand over my stomach. "Breathe in through your nose and out through your mouth. Nice and easy." Easier said than done, but I try anyway. "Ahhh, there it is," she says with a smile, as she pulls the earphones from the small device. A strong steady heartbeat fills the small examination room.

"Maybe you should," I tell her in a shaky voice. "Explain it to me, that is."

-

"How is that even possible?"

I wasn't ready to go home yet. I thought I'd been prepared, especially after voicing my suspicions out loud to Rueben for the first time. He'd just seemed happy and immediately called his colleague to see if she could slip me in.

381

Funny how I told Jared I'd probably not be home until four, giving myself the extra time I somehow knew I'd need, despite still being in full denial.

When I left the doctor's office, I drove right by the turnoff to Spence Lake, and I didn't stop until I got to Gravenhurst, where I pulled into the almost empty parking lot at the wharf. Not many folks here in the winter. During the summer and fall months, this place would be packed, and I'd avoid it like the plague. Now the Segwun, North America's oldest, working steamship, is docked for the winter.

Going on one of its dinner cruises during the fall is on my bucket list, and somehow it seemed fitting to come here. Who knows, with the way my life keeps throwing me these wildcards, I might just do this one day as well.

"Mia?" Steffie's voice drags me back to the conversation.

"I don't know," I finally answer, but my wobbly voice betrays me.

"Oh, honey," she coos. "Want me to come up? I can move my last appointment easily and be up there in a couple of hours."

Tempting. So very tempting, and only a few months ago, I would've probably taken her up on it, but that's not me anymore.

"I'm okay. I'm forty-two years old, I should damn well be okay with this. Even if it scares the shit out of me."

"Are you gonna be upset if I happy-squeal?" Steffie whispers, making me laugh, despite the tears coursing down my face.

"Not like I can stop you." My words are barely out when I have to hold my phone away from my ear. Steffie takes squealing seriously.

"Jared will be over the moon," she says when she finally settles down.

"God, I hope so." I'm not quite as confident as she seems.

"Bullocks. Nothing makes a man happier than to hear his swimmers went further than any man's have gone before."

-

Jared doesn't make it home before I do, so by the time his lights come down the driveway, I've been wringing my hands and doing my breathing exercises. Although admittedly, I'm not sure at this point if I'm trying to stave off a panic attack, a bout of manic hysteria, or just an everyday nervous breakdown. It's a toss up.

The moment he walks in, he knows.

Well, he doesn't *know*, know, but his eyes never leave mine, even as he toes off his boots and shrugs out of his coat. He doesn't say anything. Not until he makes his way over, sits down beside me, and pulls me straight onto his lap. Then he talks.

"Tell me."

He's scared, I can hear it in his voice, and realize in that moment that I should've talked about my concerns with him sooner. He's made it clear he's been worried.

"Nothing bad," I hurry to reassure him, twisting on his lap so I can cup his face, the scruff on his jaw rasping against my palms as he grinds his teeth.

"Tell me," he repeats.

"I'm pregnant."

My heart is pounding in my throat, and it's even harder saying it out loud to Jared than it was when I told Steffie. Other than the tightening of his grip on my hips, sure to leave a bruise or two, he hasn't reacted.

"Jared?"

"How?" he finally whispers. "How is that even possible?"

I almost laugh, wondering how many more will blurt out that question.

"I don't know." I start carefully. The truth is I don't. Not really. "I never lied to you. I was told years ago it wasn't in the cards for me, and I never had reason to question that. I tried to get pregnant again after I miscarried my first time, but never did. I—" Jared's sharp shake of the head has me swallow my ramblings.

"That's not what I mean," he bites off between clenched teeth, sounding like he's barely containing his anger. His eyes are turned down, but when he lifts them up to meet mine, it's clear anger is not the emotion he's trying to contain. "What I mean to say is; how is it possible that when I thought I already had everything— beyond anything I could ever have conjured up—there is more yet?"

When the first tear rolls down his cheek—my own well ahead of his—I wrap my arms around his head, pulling him to my shoulder. There is nothing to say, but so much to feel.

Griffin nudges my leg with his nose, no clue what to make of us, I'm sure, but eventually lies back down. I don't really know how long we sit like that, having lost all concept of time, when Jared suddenly lifts me up and off his lap.

Reaching in his pocket, he pulls out his phone, dials, and puts it to his ear.

"Hey, Pipsqueak. Guess what?"

Maybe I should be upset he dumps me so unceremoniously, before calling his sister, but I can't. Not with the brilliant smile he's wearing on his face.

"I'm gonna be a father." Jordy can be heard screaming, even from where I'm sitting, and I swear I can see his chest puff up.

"Of course it's Mia's." He looks irritated now and I choke back a snort. I know exactly what his sister asked. He touches his phone and suddenly I can hear Jordy's voice.

"…is that even possible? I thought she couldn't have kids?"

This time I don't hold back, I throw my head back and laugh. Jared turns to me with a cocky smile.

"I know," he says, winking at me. "But it's clear nothing can hold back the Enforcer's little soldiers."

EPILOGUE

Jared

It's hot already. Not even seven and already the sweat is beading on my forehead. It'll be a scorcher. I best finish that sprinkler system before Mia's vegetables shrivel up.

I'd cleared half an acre of trees from the back of the house, two years ago, to make room for a greenhouse. A place where she could start seeding before the frost cleared the ground, and a large raised garden where she could grow.

She had little time to water by hand this year, not with a new puppy to tend to, so I promised her to put an irrigation system in. After all, it was me who'd brought the little critter home. Poor Griffin will probably never forgive me; he's still not used to having the little bundle of energy around.

"Daddy, what do I do now?"

I turn to JT, who apparently has a fish on the line. Jon Thomas Kesla was born on a beautiful May morning, a little over four years ago. When I found him beside our bed at five this morning and asked why he was out of bed so early, he announced he wanted to catch a fish. It's his cousin, and best friend, Ole's birthday today and he's dead set on catching him a fish for his birthday. Ever since Ole caught his first meal-sized fish off my boat earlier in the spring, JT has been itching to catch his own.

"Come here, Buddy." I sit down behind him and scoot up, my legs either side of him and my arms bracketing him in. I carefully put my hands over his little ones and gently pull back on the rod. "Feels like a good one, kid."

"You do it," he says, trying to pull his hands out from under mine.

"No way. This is your fish, you're gonna have to bring him in. I'm just lending you my muscles until yours grow big enough."

"Ole's muscles are big enough," he says wistfully and I bite back a smile. Ole certainly inherited the Kesla male genes. Thank God for small favours. With Jordy the runt of the litter, and his sperm donor a tiny weasel, Ole is promising to be a bruiser. True to the nickname I gave him when he was just born.

"Ole is a year older, Buddy. You'll catch up with him yet, just you wait," I tell him as I take a firmer hold on the fishing rod. "You ready to bring this fish home?"

"'Kay." He doesn't sound too sure, but he spreads his short legs and braces for battle, like a good little sport.

By the time we finally pull the nice-sized bass onto the dock, JT's ant-sized attention span has already run its course.

"Mommy!" he yells, dropping the rod and running toward the house, his small feet slapping on the dock. I keep my eye on him, praying Punk, the new puppy, doesn't trip him up.

Mia has the sliding door open before JT has a chance to start pounding on it, something he's taken to doing despite our many warnings. She braces herself as both boy and dog barrel into her legs.

The soft smile, the one she only shares with her 'boys,' the two-legged and four-legged ones alike, lights her face.

Mia

I blow Jared a kiss, before turning my attention to the Energizer bunny hanging off my legs.

The only time I've seen my son relatively quiet is when he's out with his father. The same calming effect Jared has always had on me, seems to be working on JT as well. He keeps me on my toes, though. Something I'm actually quite grateful for.

Since he was born, I've not had a single panic attack. It's the weirdest thing, but even as a baby, he would demand my attention the moment I felt any of the early warning signs.

I'll never be one to enjoy going to the mall, a concert, or climb on a train or an airplane, but I'm much better with the more mundane things like grocery shopping. I don't go to every Colts' home game, but I try to go a few every season.

"Wanna come see my fish?" JT smiles up at me. He's still in his PJs, and it's clear his hair hasn't seen a brush yet, but his father is in much the same state, as am I. We're a pretty laid back bunch, and during the summer, often don't bother getting dressed at all, other than maybe in a bathing suit.

I ruffle my hand through his hair. "I'd love to see your fish. Are you gonna help Daddy clean it?" I ask, grabbing his hand and closing the door behind me.

"Yucky. It's smelly." The one thing my son and I are equal in. Normally it's catch and release here, so we're mostly spared the yucky cleaning, but this one is special.

"Morning." I smile at Jared, who leans his head back for a kiss, when I touch him on the shoulder.

"Morning, Beautiful. Did you by chance grab your phone? I left mine inside."

"Sure did." I pull my phone from the pocket of my kimono and open the camera app.

"Are you ready, Buddy?" Jared asks him, and both of us have to bite our lip not to burst out laughing at JT's scrunched up face.

Jared has to help him hold up the large fish while I snap a few pictures.

"Can we wrap it up now?" JT asks, wiping his fishy hands on his PJ's which elicits a groan from me. Jared on the other hand, throws his head back and his carefree laugh bounces across the bay.

"What's funny?!!" Jordy yells from her perch on the brand new dock across the water.

-

Last year, after living in Bracebridge with John, for a couple of years, my sister-in-law finally married the man. He'd actually come over one night and cleared his plans with Jared. It instantly dissolved any lingering doubts Jared may have had.

But a marriage proposal was not the only thing he'd come over to discuss. He also wanted to talk to me. He brought with him a rough, but very good drawing of the house he was hoping to build his bride. Right where my cottage stood.

It had been mostly empty since Jordy moved out, and the only time it was used was when Steffie, Doug, and the kids came up the odd weekend and a few weeks in the summer. But I still had to swallow hard, until I saw the look on Jared's face.

I transferred the property in a private sale, and although it was the second spring in the past five years that I'd waken up to the noise of heavy machinery, I was thrilled when the house was finally built.

True to the original cottage, this is a log home, at least on the outside. Unlike the original, this house is substantially bigger, with room for an expanding family. Something they were already working on by the time they moved in July of last year.

Jared and I got married in a quiet ceremony in Gravenhurst, right after our first Christmas together. No fuss, no muss—much as we live our day-to-day life.

It's not all been a smooth path, and I feel every bump, but with each one we hit and moved beyond, I feel stronger—more alive.

No longer hiding in fear.

THE END

ACKNOWLEDGEMENTS

I am always blessed with a contingent of fantastic people who help me bring a book to the point of publication.

There are names you will find in most every single book I've released thus far, simply because they share a common love of the written word, and they are as loyal to me as I am to them.

Thank you to my editor Karen Hrdlicka, my Alpha reader Natalie Weston, my proofreader Joanne Thompson and my fantastic Betas, who are always eager to pick over my latest manuscript.

Ahhh and you, my readers. I am so humbled by your ongoing, and in some cases new, appreciation for my books. I'm grateful for your word of mouth, which sends new readers in my direction with every subsequent release.

My gratitude always to my PA Natalie Weston who looks after me, and let me assure you that she works very hard to keep me on the straight and narrow.

To Ena Burnette and her team at Enticing Journeys, as well as the numerous bloggers, who have made sure that my past few releases have reached you, the readers.

As always a big loving thanks my family who suffer through my writing madness with me. They make sure I'm reminded there's an entire world outside of my imagination.

ABOUT THE AUTHOR

Freya Barker inspires with her stories about 'real' people, perhaps less than perfect, each struggling to find their own slice of happy. She is the author of the Cedar Tree Series and the Portland, ME, novels.

Freya currently has two complete series published, and is working on two new series; the Snapshot series, and Northern Lights. She continues to spin story after story with an endless supply of bruised and dented characters, vying for attention!

Stay in touch!

https://www.freyabarker.com
https://www.goodreads.com/FreyaBarker
https://www.facebook.com/FreyaBarkerWrites
https://twitter.com/freya_barker
or sign up for my newsletter:

http://bit.ly/1DmiBub

ALSO BY FREYA BARKER

CEDAR TREE Series

Book #1
SLIM TO NONE

Book #2
HUNDRED TO ONE

Book #3
AGAINST ME

Book #4
CLEAN LINES

Book #5
UPPER HAND

Book #6
LIKE ARROWS

Book #7
HEAD START

PORTLAND, ME, Novels

Book #1
FROM DUST

Book #2
CRUEL WATER

Book #3
THROUGH FIRE

Book #4
STILL WATER

SNAPSHOT Novels

Book #1
SHUTTER SPEED

Book #2
FREEZE FRAME

Made in the USA
Columbia, SC
26 April 2017